Praise for the books of

LEE NICHOLS

"A delightfully silly, vivacious debut.
This good-natured, irrepressible fairy tale
is better than a box of bonbons;
Shopaholic fans may have a new heroine."
—*Publishers Weekly* on *Tales of a Drama Queen*

"[A] funny, utterly winning story of family,
love and self-discovery."
—*Publishers Weekly* on *Hand-Me-Down*

"[A] delightful tale about a young woman coming
into her own and finding love in the process."
—*Booklist* on *Hand-Me-Down*

"This fast, entertaining novel has colorful characters
and clever plot twists....Readers will become
engaged by these quirky personalities, who are a
source of comic relief, and then become entranced
when situations morph from 'not what they seem'
to the completely unexpected."
—*Romantic Times BOOKreviews* on
Wednesday Night Witches

"Charming... Fans of the first book will be thrilled
to see zany Elle back in action."
—*Booklist* on *True Lies of a Drama Queen*

Also by
LEE NICHOLS

Wednesday Night Witches
True Lies of a Drama Queen
Hand-Me-Down
Tales of a Drama Queen

LEE NICHOLS
RECONSTRUCTING BRIGID

**RED
DRESS
INK** ™

RECONSTRUCTING BRIGID

A Red Dress Ink novel

ISBN-13: 978-0-373-89562-5
ISBN-10:   0-373-89562-3

www.RedDressInk.com

Printed in U.S.A.

Many thanks to Nancy Coffey, Margaret Marbury, Melissa Senate, Adam Wilson and all the unsung heroes at Red Dress Ink who've made the books such a success.

Aaron White was sipping hot cocoa on the balcony when the SWAT team exploded through the door.

He'd been pacing his room at the bed-and-breakfast, too distracted to watch TV. He noticed the Swiss Miss packet by the coffeemaker, and thought: *Swiss Miss, Mr. Coffee, Uncle Ben's, St. Pauli Girl...* Maybe Swiss Miss and Pauli Girl were related. Pauli would be the black sheep of the family, and Mrs. Butterworth and Aunt Jemima would suck their teeth and worry over the poor lost girl. Why couldn't she be more like her sister?

His mind had been doing that a lot lately. Since Jody disappeared. He'd made cocoa and sat on the balcony, listening to the quiet of the countryside. It was early September in Cumberland, Maine, ten miles north of Portland. The B and B was called The Copper Pot, located on a family farm with sheep and goats and a couple of alpacas. Aaron had spent the afternoon feeding apples to the alpacas, the two halves of their mouths probed and nibbled like gentle feelers around their sharp teeth.

He sipped the cocoa, trying to relax. Crickets chirped in the field and a distant car drove past. The moon was a hazy sliver behind clouds. Then the door burst open and there was a blur of motion— six or seven guys in dark uniforms with guns and intent eyes.

Aaron froze, the mug an inch from his lips. A long pause, and one of the guys spotted him on the balcony. The man shouted and pivoted—his gun a great black sucking hole.

Aaron said something, and a couple seconds later was no longer sitting, no longer sipping cocoa. Handcuffs were biting his wrists.

Aaron had slept with Jody Hulfinger two times before she disappeared.

The first was after she'd heard him laughing at Cate, her twin sister.

Cate was twenty-eight, blond, with perfect teeth and a horsey face that was enough like a model's to convince her she was beautiful. But she tried too hard to be hard—like a diamond, glittering and impenetrable. It was a pose, but there was something beneath it Aaron found appealing. He wanted them to move in together. Cate laughed every time he raised the subject.

"I'm serious," he told her. "It'll be great—like playing house."

"Wow, Aaron, that *does* sound serious."

"You like playing doctor well enough. We could rent a house in Cambridge."

Cate shook her head. "You know Bethany's husband, the chef?

He cooks all day and serves TV dinners at home." She smiled softly. "I'm eating fine as it is."

Actually, she was too skinny, but Aaron said: "How about L.A., then?"

Not L.A.

"Portland? Boulder? San Francisco?'

Cate said no, no and no, a little tightly. It was a conversation they'd had before. He knew he was annoying her, but couldn't stop.

"We could live abroad," he said.

"Don't be sexist," she snapped.

"What?" he said.

"Abroad. A broad."

He thought she was kidding. "Well, broadly speaking…"

"Not funny, Aaron. If you——" She stopped at a noise behind them.

Jody was framed in the doorway. She and Cate weren't identical twins. Not even close. Jody was short, dark and plump. She wore round glasses that mirrored the shape of her face, with square bangs and an uneven smile.

"Excuse my sister," Jody said. "Sometimes she's as thick as a broad."

Aaron couldn't help laughing, and Cate swept from the room.

Jody moved her head and her glasses caught the light and flashed. She sat next to Aaron on the sofa, her legs folded under. They talked. Then went for a stroll which ended in her bedroom. She was lively, quick and——Aaron couldn't help comparing her to Cate——softer. Afterward, she'd stood, naked but for her glasses, and had given the venetian blinds a quarter turn. Stripes of warm light had brushed her, making topographical patterns on her soft and rounded skin. At that moment, Aaron regretted that he'd ever taken up with Cate.

* * *

The second time Aaron slept with her, he'd been at the Hulfinger's summer camp—otherwise known as an estate—for almost two weeks. He'd been sitting on the back patio reading the "Best Places to Retire" issue of *Money* magazine when Jody opened one of the glass doors, walked the ten yards to the stone steps and sat. She picked at the moss poking through the cracks and stared at what they called the back lawn. It was five minutes before she noticed him. Maybe her eyeglasses didn't flash a greeting. Or maybe they did. He sat next to her.

"My father," she said. "Not good with shades of gray."

Aaron waited.

She took a breath. "It's his company…"

"Which company is that?"

"You don't know?"

"Cate said service industry. Hotels?"

Jody squinted though her glasses. Her eyes were dog-brown. Nothing special about them. "You really don't know what he does?"

Aaron smiled. "I really don't." He'd never been interested in the story of her father's wealth. "Small" was her father's nickname— he insisted you call him that, especially if it made you uncomfortable—and he seemed like the sort of man who was wealthy from nothing in particular.

"You don't want a job?" she asked. "A contact? Some venture capital?"

"I have enough money," he said.

Well, he had *almost* enough money, because a million dollars wasn't what it used to be, not when his income was zero. It wasn't penury, but he didn't qualify as idle rich. More like idle middle-class. But *idle* was the key, and spending a couple weeks with Cate at the Hulfinger "summer camp" was pleasure, not business. Sure, he was waiting for the next big thing, but Small wasn't the next big thing. If he were, his name wouldn't be Small.

Jody's smile went lopsided, and she flicked her fingernail against the stone step. "You interested in a rematch?"

Aaron tilted his head, not understanding.

"I should warn you," she said, "nothing's changed."

"Nothing's changed," he agreed, still with no idea.

She pushed her hair behind her ears. "I'm saying, Aaron, I'd like to take advantage of your good nature."

A synapse fired.

Jody touched his hand. "Would that be okay?"

She led him to her car, drove a couple miles to Fire Road 26, and they hiked five minutes to a clearing. She'd always wanted to bring someone here, she said, but was afraid what they'd think about being outdoors. For some reason—and she smiled when she said this, a coy and self-confident smile he'd never seen before—she figured it wouldn't bother him.

"Is it okay?" she asked again.

"Yeah," he said, stroking the nape of her neck with his fingertips. "It's okay."

It was more than okay. He could no longer pretend he had feelings for Cate.

Jody disappeared the next day.

It was two weeks before they found the body.

Two days ago

My name is Brigid Ashbury and mornings were the worst. I
dreaded all of it: the hike, the driveway, the sidewalk. The oil-black
asphalt with its ribbon of white—an imaginary barrier against a
sudden incendiary death. Mornings were the lingering scent of
exhaust, forever mingled in my mind with that explosive, violent
crash. Then the eerie quiet before the whimpering cries.

I closed the cabin's front door behind me. The *cabin*. It was a
trailer. I almost laughed. I lived in a trailer—not even a double-wide.
That's where life had led me. At least it was in the hills, a half mile
off the road, with a pleasant hike through Santa Barbara's low-slung
oaks and chaparral. The morning air smelled of desert and ocean
and of Highway 101, running like a scar up California's length.

No, I couldn't really smell 101. It wasn't a scar. It was just my too-vivid imagination—the double-edged blade of my imagination—and the only way to root it out was one step at a time. That's why I had my supplies delivered to the front house, my landlady's house. So I'd have to face the road every morning.

I gathered my hair into three hanks and wove them into a loose braid. Then pulled the lid off a bucket I kept by the front door and scattered a handful of seed for the finches and sparrows and dark-eyed juncos. The one-legged junco I called Teeter didn't show, the little ingrate. I gave him a couple minutes before I started walking.

It was getting easier. Last week I'd seen two SUVs hurtling toward each other around the curve on Calle del Sol. I'd watched the drivers' faces, both complacent that a five-inch strip of white paint protected them from an onrushing mass of steel and plastic.

The shakes had only lasted eight minutes. A month ago, I would've passed out. So it was getting easier. Dr. Kugelmeyer would be pleased. Of course, she would think it was the antidepressants I pretended to be taking.

I stepped off the path and onto my landlady's driveway and didn't let myself slow as I approached the sidewalk. Not until I heard the boy crying. My landlady's son, ten years old, standing at the foot of the driveway over a crumpled bicycle.

"She ran over my bike," he said.

"Who?"

"Mrs. Quinney." The next-door neighbor. "She was always saying that I ride it on her lawn, which wasn't me—and it was an accident anyway."

"Accidents happen," I said. There must've been something in my voice, because the kid stared. I looked down at the wrecked bike. "You jumped it a lot, huh?"

"Nah, my mom told me not to."

He was lying. "See where the front fork's bent? That's from jumping."

"Could be where it got run over."

"No, it's still symmetrical. That means there's no damage from the collision itself." I knelt by the ruined bicycle. "Does Mrs. Quinney ever pull her car into your driveway?"

"Our driveway?" He shook his head.

"She only has the one car?"

"Yeah, big old clunker."

"Cutlass Sierra, '94 or '95." A good car, one of the lower crash-death ratios.

"The bike was a Christmas present from my dad." The kid kicked a clump of dirt. "Mom says it serves me right for taking it."

"Well, there are three quick things," I said, to distract the kid, before he started crying again. "Strike point, paint transfer and scrape marks. See that?" I pointed to a crumpled spot on the frame. "That's the strike point. It tells you the bumper height of the impacting vehicle. Too high for Mrs. Quinney's car. We're looking for a pickup or SUV, something like that."

"Or a van, right?" The kid getting interested now.

"Exactly. Then there's paint transfer." I showed him a smudge of paint on the bike frame. "What color is that?"

"Black. Like Mrs. Quinney's car."

"Look closer. It's dark green. And third is—"

"My mom drives a green Explorer."

"—scrape marks. Here, on the drive. They show the direction of travel during impact. See?"

"They're coming from our driveway." The kid jerked the distorted back wheel of the bike, and it half turned before catching on the frame. He all of a sudden looked older than his years, and I realized what I'd just done.

I'd been so caught up in the puzzle, I hadn't considered the kid at all. For my next trick, I'd kick his dog. I tried to think of something to say, but he got there first.

"Don't tell my mom, okay? She probably didn't even feel it. It doesn't matter. Okay?"

"Sure."

I helped him drag the bike next to the trash cans and winced as a white Civic hatchback, 2002, zipped past, but my hands remained steady. See? Better all the time.

"I wanted a skateboard anyway," the kid said. "How come you don't have a car?"

"Same reason I don't have a rattlesnake."

He made a snorting half laugh. Kids were so easy. "You here for your stuff?"

"Yeah."

"There's a FedEx package for you and a letter from my mom. She's raising your rent."

On my *trailer?* It wasn't even an apartment over the garage. What kind of slumlord raises the rent on a trailer? Well, at least she could afford a new bike for the kid.

I loaded the deliveries into my pack. Usually I kept it simple;

rice and beans, veggies and pasta and toiletries. But yesterday, I'd splurged. There was Brie and fresh orange juice and a bottle of port. And Aveda rosemary-mint shampoo. I couldn't afford it; but I couldn't afford the hiking boots I'd bought last week, either. Too late to worry about it now. No one was going to let me return Brie.

Back at the cabin, I sat on the front steps and opened the letter from my landlady. My rent was going up three hundred dollars a month. "Sorry, but that's market value." Sadly, she was right. Since the housing boom, trailers were selling in the half-million range. I should just be grateful she wasn't kicking me out to sell it. And that I wasn't living in a trailer park.

But my two monthly envelopes—one from early retirement, a benefit of having been a federal employee, and the second an SSI check for disability—weren't gonna cover it. Not with the credit-card bills I'd run up.

I heard a flutter of wings and the juncos singing—sounded like a bank of telephones. I scattered a handful of feed. The birds swooped toward it and I picked out Teeter, the one-legged junco I could almost hand-feed.

"Three hundred dollars a month," I told him. He tossed a seed over his shoulder and hopped forward. "You can forget that pros-thetic leg."

I picked up the FedEx package. Didn't have to look at the return address to know it was from Ralph Nicencio—my ex-boss and mentor. And I didn't have to open it to know what it contained. Except for the details: the discovery of the vehicle, the condition of the deceased, the size of the check.

Ralph had called yesterday, first time in a year. I'd returned from my afternoon hike—the new boots gave me blisters—and had thought it was my mother on the line. I'd picked up anyway.

"Yeah," I said.

"Brigid Ashbury." He didn't introduce himself. I'd worked for him enough years he expected me to recognize his rough, nasal voice, despite the long silence between us. "You finish the manifesto yet?" Because I was living alone in the hills. This was Ralph's idea of a joke.

"Hi, Ralph."

"I've got something for you."

"If it's not from Nordstrom, I don't want it."

"Give me a minute, Brigid. That's all I ask."

I didn't say no.

"Good," he said. "And this doesn't count toward the minute—how are you?"

"I'm okay."

"C'mon, Ashbury."

I took a deep breath. "Getting better."

"Ever think about coming back to work?"

"Every morning."

He must've heard something in my tone, because his became professional. "Stanwood Hulfinger, you heard of him? Big money, big noise. Personal friend of everyone worth being a personal friend of. His daughter went missing almost three weeks ago."

"You do missing persons now?"

"They found the body three days ago, what was left of it. Submerged vehicle, critters got busy. Up in Maine, lobster territory. Girl didn't look like much—"

"What's her name?"

"Jody. Jody Hulfinger."

"How old?"

"Twenty-eight."

Two years younger than me, but still. "Not a girl."

"Get to be my age, Ashbury, your own mother's a girl. Scene was partially contaminated by the civilian who found the car. Then the Department of Evidence Destruction—" which is what Ralph called any law enforcement who got to the scene before his people "—and the dive team finished the job."

"Doesn't sound like an NTSB brief." The National Transportation Safety Board, of which Ralph was a directing board member.

"Locals called the state. State called the feds, due to Hulfinger's request. Feds wanted the OHS." The Office of Highway Safety, one of the three nonaviation sections of the NTSB—and the department I used to work for. "The car went off a causeway. The girl was young, healthy, good driving record, no drugs. They want to know why, when and how. Want a full-jacket reconstructionist."

"So why are you calling me?" Plenty of other reconstructionists in the OHS and FBI.

"You know why."

"Hulfinger got my name from the articles."

"He got your name when he asked Rosenblatt who's the best accident reconstructionist in the country."

That was at most half true, but I didn't bother with it. "How am I supposed to get on-scene?"

"As a party, seconded to the FBI," Ralph said, intentionally mis-
understanding the question.

The NTSB was such a small agency that they assigned outside
parties—consultants—to every investigation. For airline investi-
gations, they'd assign the FAA, airframe and engine manufactur-
ers, experts from the Bureau of Technology and someone from
Flight Standards or Air Traffic Control. Highway accidents were
lower priority, despite a far greater number of fatalities, but they
might assign the vehicle manufacturer or an expert from the Department of Transportation.

But not outside investigators. Definitely not ex-NTSB investigators. And it didn't answer my question: how would I get on-
scene?

I let it go, for now. "You put together a Go Team?"

"Too small. This is nothing major, Brigid, it's just you were
asked for by name."

"Who's the IIC?" The Investigator in Charge.

"Theresa."

Theresa Udall, the only other female lead investigator in the
OHS—the only one at all, now. A good investigator, we'd almost
become friends. It had been a relationship based on support and
respect and a lot of competition, which is why the *almost* came
before *friends*.

"Then let Theresa handle it."

"She's got that school bus in Pennsylvania that flipped the
median. Elementary school."

"How many?"

"Eleven, and three still critical. Plus the driver."

I pressed my hand to my eyes, willing myself not to picture it. Eleven schoolkids. Doing the vehicle-damage analysis, measuring the tissue smear, finding imprints of dead children's faces on the back of cold vinyl seats.

When I was sure my voice would be steady, I asked it again: "How am I supposed to get on-scene?"

"I'll assign a driver. Great guy, his name's Len Ganapi, you're gonna love him."

I didn't bother responding.

"We'll lease a Lincoln Navigator or an Expedition, Brigid. How about that? Or a Lexus RX300—safest SUV on the road. Your choice."

"It was real nice talking to you, Ralph," I'd said, and hung up.

"Ashbury." Ralph again, two minutes later. I'd picked up the phone despite myself. "I have a dead girl from a prominent—read, easily targeted—family and no indication why she went off the road."

"She was the driver?"

"She's got the complete DS profile." Meaning all the injuries commonly sustained by the driver. "No question she was behind the wheel."

"Of that car?"

"Whaddya mean, of that car? She wasn't found in any other car."

"You want a mystery, I'm giving you a mystery. Maybe she sustained the injuries in a different crash and they moved the body to the vehicle under investigation."

"They who?"

"Jesus, Ralph, I don't know. Am I getting paid for this? If I was a lawyer, you'd be in the hole three-hundred bucks by now." Which I only said because Ralph was a lawyer.

"You would've liked her. Jody Hulfinger. She was a firebrand."

A *firebrand?*

"Mousy-looking, chunky little thing, but passionate," he said, trying to make her sound pathetic to rope me in. "Majored in Women's Studies, got arrested protesting the war in Iraq. Donated a hundred percent of her income to charity and lived off her father, and then went to stockholder meetings and screamed at him. She had—what's that Jewish word? *Challah?*"

"That's the bread, Ralph. *Chutzpah.*" Which he almost certainly knew. He was trying to get me involved in the conversation, to give himself time to convince me.

"Chutzpah. She was a sweet girl with a big mouth. Like you."

"You're melting my heart, Ralph. You want some advice? Tell Len Ganapi to start mapping the skid marks. They're those long dark things you see on roads sometimes."

"You still shopping?"

I felt a pang. "I shop."

"Get it all mail order, huh? Must have quite a stack of catalogs."

"E-commerce, Ralph. It's the wave of the present."

"I can wrangle a generous consultant fee."

"I'm doing okay."

"Go look in your closet and tell me you don't need another pair of shoes. This fee'll keep you shod for a year."

Right, as if he didn't know to the penny how much debt I was carrying. Probably knew my rent had been raised, too. "I appreciate your concern, Ralph."

"You gotta get back on the horse, Brigid. You've got to——"

I'd hung up again.

I poured a handful of seed into my palm and extended my arm toward Teeter. He hopped backward and cocked his head. Picked a seed from the ground and flew ten feet away to eat it.

I sat motionless for five minutes, but he didn't come closer. Sometimes he'd stand three feet from me, making his telephone-chirps, until I dumped the seed on the ground, then would dart forward to eat right next to me.

Today, he wasn't so trusting.

I knew how he felt. Had Ralph asked my landlady to up the rent? The timing was too coincidental, but I couldn't see it. Ralph was pushy, but not Machiavellian.

I went inside, and put the Brie and OJ in the fridge—despite the fact I had a French ex who insisted the cheese should sit out until it wept. I sat in my only chair, a ruby-colored overstuffed armchair, and stared at my hands. The scars were faint, had been faint for years. The accident that caused them had put me in the hospital for three days, but didn't touch me at all.

No. It was the second crash that shattered me. Two dead, one walking wounded. Everything faded but memory.

I forced myself to smile. Memory and credit-card bills.

"Fine," I said. "Get back on the fucking horse."

I ripped open the FedEx package. The check would cover the rent increase for a year, and make a hefty dent in my Visa bill. And then there was the picture of the girl, Jody Hulfinger, with her dorky glasses and awkward smile....

* * *

Two hours later, I called Ralph. "They have Hummers in Maine?"

"You want a Hummer?"

"I'm joking, Ralph."

"A Navigator?"

I snorted.

"Don't knock it, Ashbury. SUVs have the highest survival ratio on the road."

"Yeah, if you're in one." If you're in the car they hit, they're stone deadly. "Just because I don't want to die doesn't mean I want to kill."

"I'll get you a Pinto."

"Funny."

"You read it?" Meaning the file.

"How much authority will I have?"

"NTSB special seconded to the FBI. The scene is yours. Off-scene, you'll be running parallel with their investigation."

"How about face work?" Because the scene could tell you everything about the accident, but nothing about the background, the motive, the living and the dead. I'd need to conduct interviews, dig into this girl's life.

"That's cleared. Don't step on any toes, but do what you have to." Ralph had a special relationship with the bureau—being an ex-assistant director—which is how he could clear something like that.

"What if I have to stomp on a toe?"

"Trying stepping first and if that doesn't work, call me." He didn't sound distressed at the prospect. "And Brigid? You'll do your *thing?*"

I sighed. "If I still can."

"You can. The ticket will be waiting for you at the United counter."

"Just give me a few hours notice. It's five miles from here."

I listened to dead air on the phone. Then, in a voice strained by something I couldn't identify, Ralph said, "You're not going to walk to the airport?"

Yeah. I was going to walk to the airport.

The Cumberland County Jail was not on Aaron's list of places to see. Still, no reason to be unpleasant. So he smiled at the woman and said: "You are not. Get out of town."

She showed her ID. Agent Dellgarda, FBI. Augusta, ME.

"The FBI has agents in Maine?" he asked.

"Only four of us."

"Must be lonely." He asked about the work, making conversation. They'd release him as soon as his lawyer arrived and explained everything—not that there was anything to explain. Meanwhile, he was happy to chat. Dellgarda was stocky and sallow-skinned, but she had this perfect impish face. Like a pixie in *A Midsummer Night's Dream*.

She said, "You're not going to talk your way out of this one, Mr. White."

"Call me Aaron," he said. "And I'll call you Titania."

"Last time you saw Jody Hulfinger alive was that Friday?"

He shook his head. "I thought you were only taking the vital stats."

They'd wanted to interview him, but he'd seen enough TV to know he ought to have a lawyer present. The two State Police detectives let him call a lawyer he knew in New York, who referred him to a criminal lawyer in Portland. Then they called Dellgarda over to process him. Said she was gonna take background information. None of this where-were-you-on-the-night-of stuff.

"Well, I beg your pardon, Mr. White." Her tone said she was hurt by his refusal. "I'm only trying to—"

"No, no. That's okay." He had nothing to hide, anyway. "Yeah, it was Friday. We drove around for a while… Jody was upset, she'd had a fight with her father. I guess she wanted to talk."

"Had you ever…driven around before?"

"No. The thing is, I'd been sitting on the patio…" He told the story, except about the clearing five minutes from Fire Road 26.

"That's the last time you saw her alone?"

"Yeah."

"And alive."

He nodded. It had all happened so fast, too fast. Jody was alive. Then dead. "She was… I don't know. Vibrant. One of those people who is just absolutely outraged by injustice. She got punched in the face once, you hear about that?"

"What happened?"

"She was at a bar, saw some guy with a Confederate flag on his truck. In *Maine*. She asks him if he's a Civil War buff or just a racist asshole. So he and his buddies call her some names back, I guess there were three or four of 'em—"

"Where was this?"

"C'mon, Titania. This was years ago. You think one of them tracked her down to avenge the insult to his racist flag?"

Dellgarda's pixie face became stern.

"Okay," he said. "I don't know where. Her brother, TJ, he went through some kind of macho stage—though you wouldn't know it to look at him now. Hung out at biker bars and worked for a lumberyard. I guess she'd tagged along with him somewhere."

"So she's yelling at these guys..."

"And one of them pops her in the face. It's a better story without the interruptions."

She didn't quite roll her eyes. "You know her whole family?"

He gave her the rundown of what he knew. Cate and Jody. Small and his "lady friend," Gayle. TJ, the oldest Hulfinger child and only son, who'd given up trying to be a townie and had become a clean-cut corporate type.

"That all?" Dellgarda asked.

"There's Maureen, Small's first wife. I guess she died young. Phillipa, his second wife, and her daughter, Nile. Nile's apparently some kind of academic prodigy. I never met her, but I think she and Jody are close. Were close."

"You met Cate in Boston?" Dellgarda asked.

"At the Museum of Fine Arts. She was looking at a sculpture, and backed right into me."

"Sure she did."

"I was sitting on a bench," he said. "She about fell in my lap."

"Uh-huh."

"What? You think I was stalking her, waiting for her to take a step backward?"

"Are you for real?"

"What?" he said. "What?"

She sighed, glanced back down at her form. "Employment?"

"I'm retired. But really, I wouldn't try to pick up women at a museum. I mean—"

"Retired from what?"

His turn to sigh. "Internet business."

"You're thirty-one. Kinda young to retire."

"I had a good year."

She gave him that look all women have, to tell him he was being a juvenile ass. He'd seen it before.

"I started a company, Mark It," he explained. "An intellectual property service for trademark holders. I know, you thought the boom happened ages ago. But the idea was—well, it doesn't matter, because it turns out the whole thing was—and this is the legal term—crap. But I sold it for a tidy sum and—"

"It was crap, but you sold it."

"It was getting hits." He shrugged. "So I sold out and retired. Wish I'd come up with YouTube. Then Google would've bought me for billions. Now I'm back at the drawing board, looking for the next big thing."

"Oh, really?"

"Yeah. I figure I'll know it when I see it, but turns out I like the quiet life."

"Sure you do."

"I'm excitable," he said. "I need calm."

"You looked pretty relaxed in the hotel room. The bed-and-breakfast."

"I was terrified into immobility." He looked at her, tried to picture her with a big-ass gun in her hand. "You were one of the guys in the room?"

"Hardly one of the guys."

"Jesus. What a way to make a living." The anger suddenly made itself felt. "You burst in, guns fucking everywhere, screaming off your heads. Were you always a bully, or is this a new thing?"

"Hey, settle down."

"You settle fucking down. Anyone ever come into *your* bedroom with a gun?"

"We had a warrant and a reason it was issued."

"I'm serious. Anyone ever do that to you?"

"No."

"Try it sometime, you think it's no big deal." He took a breath. "So what's the reason? The reason it was issued?"

"First you tell me—you like the lifestyle of the rich and famous?"

"Who doesn't?" He said seriously.

"Don't have enough money to put you on the cover of *Forbes,* though, do you?"

He didn't say anything.

"So you met Cate, got invited to the summer home and decided there was an easy way to cash in. Looking for the next big thing."

"What?" he said. "Like I'm Jody's insurance beneficiary? I'm inheriting the Hulfinger zillions?"

"Your fingerprint on the kidnap note."

"My fingerprint—? Jody was *kidnapped?* She was in a car crash—"

"You were seen with her the afternoon she disappeared. Leading her to her car."

"That was the day *before*—and she was leading me. She wasn't kidnapped. She was kidnapped? She was—" He realized he was babbling, and shut himself up. And noticed the whir of the tape recorder the two detectives had left on the table. "That's still on?"

"As Detectives Trake and Friedrick informed you, the recorder will remain activated until you ask us to turn it off."

"So when I said I didn't want to talk without a lawyer, they figured it was something personal. I didn't want to talk to *them,* but I'd be happy to talk to you?"

"Aren't you?" She batted her eyelashes in a faux flirt.

It bruised his faith in the kindness of strangers. He refused to say anything else, and eventually his lawyer came and made a fuss.

No good.

They had his fingerprints on a kidnap note. They had some chronologically impaired witness. And he was pretty sure they knew he had a juvenile record—it was sealed, but that'd only make them more curious.

Aaron wasn't going anywhere.

The knocking finally stopped.

I waited five minutes, then let myself out of the bathroom, back into the quaint and antique-y sitting room of my suite at the Pierce House Inn. The tremors came in waves. Beginning at my knees, moving up my body until my shoulders shuddered like a car with a fouled intake.

I sat on the edge of the rosewood couch, put my head between my knees and gulped air. Back on the horse—and it had given me a hoof in the gut.

I shuddered, breathed, shuddered, breathed.

Breathed. Okay.

All those cars. An endless line of rolling coffins with tempered glass windows and exploding pistons and molded cup holders. I'd found a woman's pinkie in a cup holder once. Snapped off during impact, the vamp manicure not even chipped. Hadn't bothered me at the time. Now I could smell it.

The bittersweet scent of gasoline and roasting meat on a backyard barbecue. It brought a metallic tang to my mouth, making me swallow. I'd never covered my nose or breathed through my mouth around carnage from an accident. The less you resisted, the faster you acclimated.

That was then. Today, the whole drive from Portland to Searsport had been a scratch-and-sniff horror film.

The flight to Maine from Santa Barbara had been fine. I didn't mind flying. Even despite the threat of terrorism, my chances of being killed in a plane crash were about one in eleven million. I actually found it sort of relaxing.

And Len Ganapi seemed nice. He was a young, skinny Omar Sharif type. Dark, handsome and suave. In his late twenties, he was fairly new to the NTSB. At least, I'd never worked with him. He'd met me outside the terminal and I'd wanted to ask him if he'd run into trouble with homeland security, looking like an Arab with a name other than Olsen or Smith. But then I'd seen the Crown Vic, blue-and-white with the seal of the State of Maine on the side and forgotten all about it.

It was a good choice for a vehicle—must've been Ralph's—because people drive a hell of a lot safer with a cop car behind them. But when I sat in the passenger seat and snapped the belt home, it was like being buried alive. I couldn't breathe, couldn't move. I'd started sweating before Ganapi even turned the key in the ignition.

Two hours in that car.

Ralph must've warned Ganapi, because he drove slow and steady, both hands on the wheel, dead center in the lane. After fifteen minutes, he tried talking to me. First saying how I'd been an inspiration to him, then filling me in on the case.

His voice had been faraway, like Charlie Brown's teacher going "waah-waaah-waah-waaaah." Instead of listening—or responding—I'd burrowed into myself. Tried to maintain control. Tried to keep my hands from shaking. Keep from screaming at him to pull over, pull over, pull over before—

The knocking started again.

Voices outside my door calling my name. I sat up and was facing the mirror. God, I looked old. I didn't answer the door. Couldn't face people, not yet.

I dragged myself to the chair by the lamp and pulled the file from my bag. Reading about the accident wouldn't cure my fears, but I was hoping the distraction would at least stop the shakes. The Traffic Homicide summary came first:

Case #:	02-08-A16534
Victim:	Jody Hulfinger
Subject:	UNK
THI:	Trooper Chester Cowan #812 SMP/THI
Location:	South of Causeway—Closest Address 113 Sears Island Road Sears Island Causeway Searsport
Incident:	Unattended Death
Times:	See Report

This Investigator received in the interoffice mail a copy of the Maine State Police Medical Examiner's Autopsy Report #02-G214, issued in conjunction with MSP Homicide Investigation Report #02-B214. The name listed on the report is that of HULFINGER, Jody. I reviewed the report and found the following:

1. A vehicle registered to a missing person, Jody Hulfinger, was found in Sears Harbor, approximately 20 feet south of the Sears Island Causeway.

2. In the vehicle after it was removed from the bay was found the remains of a Caucasian female, later identified by NoK as Jody Hulfinger.

3. Dr. Walter MacRoule, MD, of the SMP M.E. examined the remains and determined that cause of death was drowning. NB: CoD not traumatic injuries sustained during accident. See ME's report, attached.

4. This Investigator responded to Belfast Towing Impoundment Yard in Belfast to examine the vehicle that had been recovered. Damage to the vehicle appears consistent with a single vehicle accident.

5. Although the MSP Crime Scene Unit, Dive Team, Criminal Division, and ME's Office all had personnel present at the scene, Traffic Homicide was not informed until after the remains were recovered and transported to the SMP Crime Lab for evaluation.

The knocking continued outside.

I continued to ignore it and scanned numbers six through ten.

It was mostly jurisdictional stuff and explanations of exactly
how the standard and correct response to a presumed SVA—
single-vehicle accident—had corrupted the scene and disrupted
the ongoing investigation. The trooper who wrote the report was
obviously pissed that he hadn't been called on-scene while there
was still a scene to be called to. Good man. Traffic Homicide
always got the short end, despite being the single most common
cause of violent death in the country.

I smiled when I saw number eleven—must've been added after
I spoke with Ralph.

11)   MSP Crime Lab reports the injuries sustained by vic-
      tim match the damage done to the interior of the re-
      covered vehicle in every particular. Tissue samples,
      damage to steering wheel and column, and glass shards
      embedded in victim all support the preceding.

So they knew this was the car Hulfinger died in. Not that there'd
been any question, but it was nice to keep them on their toes. And
apparently I did carry some weight, if my offhand suggestion re-
sulted in a rapid and official response.

The final number read:

12)   This case is pending active.

More than active, with the FBI called in and the NTSB consulting. The thing was positively frenzied.

The knocking outside stopped again, but I barely noticed. I

flipped to the initial Event Report. Classification type was listed as unattended death. Victim was Jody Hulfinger of Somerville, Mass. Housing Advocate. Brown/brown, five-two, 139, no distinguishing marks.

I flipped ahead to the narrative, written by Officer Mitchell Pomerleau of the Searsport PD.

I responded to the area of 113 Sears Island Road, namely the Sears Island Causeway. The emergency call originated from Henry Prentice DOB 050462 of 81 Gurleyville Rd., Storrs, CT 06268. I met Prentice at scene. He stated he was tossing a ball for his dog from the south side of the causeway embankment when—

There was a scratching at the door. As I looked up from the report, the knob turned and the door opened.

Len Ganapi stood in the doorway with a guy who must've been the innkeeper—the Pierce House Inn was high-end enough so the guy looked like an innkeeper instead of a desk clerk—hovering behind him.

I saw the concern on Ganapi's face and my stomach tightened. I was afraid I'd start shuddering again. You don't go far in law enforcement if you're a woman who shows inappropriate emotion. So I held myself tight and stared at Ganapi hard enough that he took a step back.

"I was knocking," he said. "I didn't know if you were okay."

"You have a warrant to open my door?"

"I was worried, ma'am," Ganapi said. "You didn't look so good in the car, you didn't answer the door...I was out here ten minutes."

I took a deep breath.

"I'm fine," I said. Then stood and swung the door sharply closed on Ganapi. He was probably on the other side mouthing "bitch" to the innkeeper. I felt a headache beginning and pressed my palms to my temples. I wanted to be back home. To be smelling the Santa Barbara chaparral, sitting on the steps feeding the juncos. I wanted to be anywhere but here. Forcing myself through the terrors, trying to figure out who killed Jody Hulfinger.

I put my hands on the dresser and stared at myself in the mirror. "Suck it up, Bridge."

I breathed until the dizziness was gone. Then realized the telephone had been ringing for some time. I waited for it to stop. Just because they weren't here in person didn't mean I wanted to talk to them. I was supposed to check in with my liaison, FBI Agent Van Huut. But I believed in starting at the bottom and working my way up.

Like a reconstruction: check the tires before the roof.

The Principal's Daughter sat in her lightless office and caressed the button on her BlackBerry, fumbling in the darkness.

Her first memory was of being suffocated with a blanket of darkness—her second was a nightmare of waking up blind. She'd hated the dark—its threats and secrets, its empty coldness. And its loneliness.

She'd slept with a night-light until her early twenties—and despised herself for it. On her twenty-third birthday, she spent the night in the darkest patch of woods within an hour's drive of her apartment. The creeping darkness had smothered her. She'd wept and trembled. But she'd survived.

Once a week for the next two years, at dusk, she closed herself in a closet, a basement, a claustrophobic hole that admitted no light—until she could sit for hours without dreaming of the quiet footfalls that had never come.

Some nights—when the loneliness became unbearable—she still did it. Not tonight. Tonight she had work. She sat back in her chair and considered the names in her mental Rolodex. She made a call. Then another. An hour later, she could see the outlines, dimly. It was worrisome. An accident reconstructionist being called in.

She didn't know how careful *he* had been. How painstaking. She'd watched his face for three weeks, and it was a mask. A solid, shining mask. She could not detect a single sign of uncertainty— or even triumph. She approved. He was strong.

But so was this woman—this reconstructionist. They'd asked for her by name. Brigid Ashbury.

She'd have her own darkness. That was the price of strength.

Searsport PD Officer Mitchell Pomerleau perched on the antique chair in my sitting room as if he was afraid he'd break it. He was a beefy guy with a smudge of a mustache and a flawless peaches-and-cream complexion. I spent fifty bucks a month on beauty products and my skin wasn't half as good. I could probably grow a better mustache, though.

"—and then, uh, the guy was waiting there," Pomerleau said,

continuing his disjointed report. "Henry, Mr. Prentice, the one who spotted the car, the vehicle, and, um—" He was like a kid who'd been called to the principal's office. Either someone had warned him I was a hundred year bitch or he was afraid of the alphabet soup—OHS/NTSB/FBI. Or maybe he was just uncomfortable around women.

"Let me ask you a question, Officer," I said. "I reviewed your report. You're telling me this guy lives on a road called Gurley-ville?"

He nodded. "Up for two weeks vacation."

"But *Gurleyville?* That's how he pronounced it?" I let him see I was amused.

"Uh-huh. Girly-ville." He grinned—uneasily, but it was a start. "I made him spell it because, y'know...Gurleyville?"

"I had a guy one time," I said. "This is in Ventura, in California, two weeks after I'd joined the force. He says his name is Dickhead. Stanley Dickhead. I asked him three times, he said, yeah, Dickhead, Dickhead. He had this accent, Eastern European, I think. Turned out it was spelled *D-I-C-K-E-T,* but I spelled it, y'know, *Dickhead,* in my report."

Now Pomerleau was grinning for real.

"My captain calls me in and tells me there's exactly one dickhead in my report, and it's not Stanley." I smiled, and Pomerleau smiled and I thought there was no way he wasn't using some kind of deep pore cleanser or facial scrub. "So the guy from Gurleyville gives you a ring...?"

This time he was comfortable enough to be fluent: "I responded to the call and—have you seen it? Sears Island. It's not two miles from here. There's the causeway, maybe fifty yards long, two lanes. Breakwater rocks on both sides, then from zero to twenty feet of beach, depending on the tide. And Prentice was walking his dog out there at low tide, he tosses a squash ball in the water. Guy thinks it's a rock his dog is standing on—"

"Jesus," I said, with a little spin.

"A-yuh. Like he was walking on water. And the dog's found something, working it back and forth with his head. Turns out he's got a human jawbone in his mouth. Man said there was still meat on it. Looked closer and saw the rock was an upside-down car."

"You were first on the scene?"

"Correct. Couldn't see much by then but the guy said there's a body in there, so we called the state. We're a small department—any kind of body and we kick it up to the MSP."

"How'd they retrieve the car?"

"State dive team hooked up cables and towed it out."

"They remove the body on-site?"

"Nope. Put the whole shebang on a flatbed, the vehicle still upside down like it was in the water, covered it with a tarp and drove it down to the lab in Augusta. 'Course, the body was half out the car already. I said something about it looking like she'd tried to get out, but one of the troopers said probably not." He shifted in his seat, and the chair creaked beneath him. "Probably bloat and float, that's what he said."

Because as the gasses in the body expanded—what they called putrefactive gasses—it had worked itself upward through an open window or door. Not too uncommon. "They use a screen?"

"A screen? In Augusta?" Pomerleau's brow furrowed.

"When they towed it out.You get a car with the windows open, you put a screen under before removing it from the water. Otherwise when it breaks the surface, water flushes out the interior, back into the bay or whatever. Scrubs it cleaner than a car wash."

"You'd have to ask them. I didn't see a screen."

Of course not. "Okay. Back up a second. After the dive team arrived and got to the car…"

"They brought up the tag—number's in the report. Teletype was advised to the info. Came back registered owner Jody Hulfinger, reported a missing person with the Camden Police. We brought the State Criminal Division in, got a crane from Transportation Service and that's all she wrote."

"You know the family? The Hulfingers?"

"Nah, they're summer people and live a couple towns south."

I clicked my pen and watched Pomerleau, waiting to see if he had anything to add—and wondered if the other guys made fun of his complexion. Probably not. In my experience, men had two categories for skin; horrific, and unremarkable. Unless it was cratered like the surface of the moon or had a birthmark the size of a six-pack, they simply didn't notice.

Pomerleau looked more uncomfortable as the silence wore on, until I took pity. "You bag the jawbone? The one the dog had?"

"Tide got it." He shook his head. "Or the dog. By the time I rolled up, it was gone."

I kept him another ten minutes, filling in some of the details, then thanked him for his time. He shook my hand as if he meant it and headed out the door.

"Oh, and Officer Pomerleau?"

He turned.

"Strange question, but...what kind of soap do you use?"

This time when the phone rang, I answered it. "Ashbury."

"Give Ganapi a break." It was Ralph. "He thinks you hate him."

"We need the dive team back out there. Today."

"It's been almost three weeks, what do you think they're gonna find?"

"If I knew, I wouldn't need them back. They didn't screen the car."

"No one does."

True enough.

"You done your *thing?*" he asked.

"I haven't even visited the scene yet."

"You'll have Ganapi drive you?"

"Sure."

"He's one of the good guys, Brigid. I'm telling you."

"I believe you."

"Theresa sent him special. She's worried about you."

"You should talk to my mother, you want to hear someone worry."

"Theresa says Ganapi's the young Turk she has to watch for, now that you're gone." He paused for a moment. "Except she didn't say Turk, she said rookie of the year."

"Uh-huh." That was vintage Theresa. First with the sports talk, which I thought she did in a transparent—and successful—attempt to appeal to men. And second, implying in a half-complimentary fashion that I was the young competitor and Theresa the old pro.

Problem being, she was only five years older than me, and only ninety percent as good. But with Theresa you had to let the little things go, and she'd come through on the big ones.

"He's excited to be working with you. Not much of a case—a single vehicle, nothing tricky—but he didn't hesitate when he heard you'd be running it."

"He seems great." I gave it a second. "He married?"

"Len? No. No, he's not." Ralph had always wanted to set me up, and couldn't keep the interest out of his voice. "I guess he hasn't had time, what with going to Yale then straight to the Board. He's a mover. Women around the office tell me he's a looker, too."

I laughed. For a guy with a subtle mind, Ralph's matchmaking had always been over the top.

Ralph made a noise in his throat. "Ah, soak your head, Ashbury. Termagant."

"Termagant? Is that some kind of firebrand?"

"How about Special Agent Van Huut? Talked to him?"

"Not yet. What's his story?"

"You know the size of the FBI presence in Maine? Count it on one hand. He's from Boston, up special for this. Aggressive, smart and overconfident, that's what I heard. He's some friend of the Hulfingers. Conflict of interest, et-legal-cetera, but what the Hulfingers want, the Hulfingers get."

"He's a friend of Jody Hulfinger's?"

"Papa Hulfinger's. Did some consulting security work."

"Wonderful."

I could almost hear him shrug. "Live with it. And keep me informed."

"The dive team?"

"I'll make the call."

"Today, Ralph. And tell them to stay off my scene until I personally invite them on."

"I'll warn them what happened to that highway patrolman in Ventura."

"That was completely not my fault."

This time, it was Ralph who laughed.

"Mr. White. Hey, Aaron." It was Dellgarda, with at least enough grace to look slightly abashed. "You okay in there?"

There being a cell in the Cumberland County lockdown.

"All it needs is Swiss Miss," he said, "and it'd be like home."

"Yeah, well." She fiddled with the class ring she wore on her right hand. "I was wondering—as a point of interest..."

"What?" It came out sharp, even though most of his fear and anger were gone. He tried again: "Sure, Titania. Which point?"

"That's it." She gave him a sideways look. "Why Titania?"

"Queen of the pixies in *A Midsummer Night's Dream*."

She watched him warily.

"You look like I picture her," he said.

"That's Shakespeare."

"Yeah," he said.

The blush started at her neck, hit her cheeks a couple seconds later.

Maybe the bench he was sitting on didn't get any softer, or the room any warmer—then again, maybe they did.

Sears Island Road extended a half mile from Route One before it became the causeway. On the left was a sixties-looking trailer with a yard full of decomposing kitchen chairs. On the right, an old-time schoolhouse, its blue-green paint faded and peeling.

I had called Trooper Cowan, the guy who wrote the THI report, and asked him to meet me on-site. He'd offered to pick me up. No, thanks. I'd rather be functional than prompt.

Turned out I got there before him. I'd slipped silently past Ganapi's door and out to the street. Wasn't a bad walk, considering. I'd even glanced in the windows of a couple antique shops, so relieved not to be inside one of the cars driving past that they barely bothered me.

I passed the schoolhouse and crossed a set of railroad tracks. A hundred yards ahead of me, the road became causeway. The ocean—part of Penobscot Bay—was almost silver. Definitely not the Pacific Ocean I was used to. It was more imposing than inviting and it looked cold, even in summer.

I stopped at a sign welcoming me to Sears Island, hoping I'd enjoy this beautiful coastal setting. There was a tortoiseshell butterfly hair clip—$0.99 at a drugstore near you—clipped to the signpost. I considered bagging it as evidence, but it was nowhere near the crime scene and obviously unrelated. I bagged it anyway. Made me feel as if the investigation had officially begun.

A State Police Jeep arrived then and parked twenty feet away. He stayed off the scene, and away from me. I was liking this trooper more and more.

"Trooper Chester Cowan," he said as he stepped from the Jeep. "Glad to meetcha."

Cowan was a couple inches taller and a couple decades older than I was, but he probably fit into the same tuxedo pants he wore at his high-school prom. Not the cummerbund, though; his stomach ballooned over his belt like a scoop of ice cream on a sugar cone.

"Brigid Ashbury," I said. "I read your report. Nice to find someone else keeping the faith with Traffic Homicide Investigation."

He grinned, suddenly boyish. "Don't get me wound up on that, Agent Ashbury. Every other violent unattended death gets an investigation—traffic homicide, we've got to fight to get the scene intact, forget about getting new releases of the CAD software."

I was surprised. Usually a guy his age on a not-exactly-urban force wouldn't be complaining he didn't have sufficient software.

He must've seen my expression. "I'm new to reconstruction. A recent convert, you might say. But I figure it's best to start with the state of the art." He hitched up his belt and gave me a looking over. "I read in the A.R.T. newsletter you're top five in the country, maybe you can teach me some things."

"That was three years ago," I said, lightly. This was the first case I'd taken in over a year. And I wasn't even sure if I could still do my *thing*.

"Prettier than my old schoolteachers, too," he said.

I smiled, unable to take offence. Nice to hear the flirting, actually, considering I was looking twenty years older than...shit— maybe he thought we were the same age, he was seriously coming on to me.

"You want to walk me through it?" I asked, a little abruptly.

"Forward or backward?"

"Can you place her vehicle on the road?"

"Some of the skid marks look good for her car."

"I want definite only." Nothing obscured an investigation as much as assumptions.

"Definitely, then, I can point to where it went into the bay and the final position. And even that isn't so clear."

He led me onto the causeway. The island itself was ahead of us, an expanse of oak and birch and pine in the middle of the bay, surrounded by pebbled beaches. An old stone fence tumbled out of the woods and fell apart as it approached the water.

"How many people live here?" I asked.

"None. Used to be farmsteads, until back in the forties or fifties. Nine hundred and fifty acres of God's green earth. They wanted to put a nuclear plant here in the seventies. It's a protected environment now. The road turns to gravel halfway through, ends in a parking lot. They're thinking of closing it at the causeway, keep all motorized vehicles out."

"My kind of place," I said.

He gave me a look, but didn't press for an explanation.

"What was she doing here?" I asked.

"No idea. Nice view. Nice trails. Probably out for a drive." He pointed over the edge of the causeway, where the water lapped gently against breakwater boulders. "That's where she ended up driving. Can't see it now, but at low tide there's enough beach to walk on. Man with the dog was here. Car was over there."

"I guess." I shook my head. Even from where I was standing, forty feet from the shore, I could see tire furrows crisscrossing the shoulder and gouges on the earthen embankment. I'd bet money they were from official vehicles. "You got a list of rescue vehicles on-scene?"

"I can have one for you this afternoon. Why do you want—?" He looked at all the tracks, made a silent whistle. "You're gonna measure all the treads and eliminate ours."

"*Someone* is." I grinned at him.

"On-the-job training, huh?"

"That's right. We'll treat 'em like fingerprints." Any other crime scene would be inviolable, but with traffic homicide you get civilians literally driving over the evidence; and cops were even worse. "It's a *homicide* investigation and it gets all the attention of a vandalized mailbox...and do you see any police tape?"

Cowan held up his hands. "Preaching to the choir, Agent Ashbury."

"Sorry. Five minutes back on the job and I remember why I left it." Which was a lie, but a good one. "And 'Brigid' is fine—I'm a lot of things, but an FBI agent isn't one of them."

"Thought you NTSB people went by 'agent,' too."

"Hell, we're—*they're* not even LEOs." Law-enforcement officers. "No power of arrest, no license to carry. We're nothing like those CSIs you see on TV. Though I was a cop in California for a couple years." I looked at the road. "All right. Let's get started. Tape off this lane, seventy-five feet in either direction."

"They're not gonna like that."

"Then tape off both lanes, and let them convince me to compromise."

I hung my camera around my neck. Took the notepad from my bag and fiddled for my sunglasses: Giorgio Armani with polarized lenses. They'd cost a fortune but made me look a bit more Jackie O, and a bit less Buddy Holly.

I slipped them on and walked the line, a foot at a time, with Cowan following silently behind. Most of the marks would be gone. Many—such as squeegee marks and soft-material smears— were gone minutes or hours after the accident. Forget about the days or now weeks since Jody Hulfinger had disappeared. Other signs, like tire prints and debris, bituminous smear—you could never tell. Might get lucky. Might not.

Still, there were three primary sets of skid marks along the stretch of road in question. If any of them belonged to the Hulfinger accident, I could determine the minimum speed, the direction of travel and the location on road both pre- and postcollision.

I could track the movement like those feet on the floor of an Arthur Murray Dance Studio.

Fact is, most LEOs think skid marks are the whole reconstructionist bag of tricks. Well, skid marks and equations: *The radius of a critical speed scuff or a yaw mark is determined by locating the crossover mark to measure the chord, using the chord to arrive at the middle ordinate... S=3.86 √R(f±e), where S is speed, R is radius of yaw mark, f is the drag factor adjusted to level, and e is superelevation of roadway.*

Boring, right? And it looks complex, but any high-school math class could do it. Which is why saying skid marks and equations are the only way to reconstruct an accident is like saying ballistics is the only way to identify a gun.

Only way? No. Solid start? You betcha.

I dug into my bag of tricks: a giant caramel suede hobo sack I'd picked up from Lucky years ago. It was light and roomy and fit crossways across my shoulder for those long walks. Problem was, it was so big, finding things in it could take awhile. And once you rescued the longed-for item, you never knew what was going to come up with it: desiccated Tootsie Roll, feminine hygiene product, leaky pen. Still, it was a lot prettier than the tech bags other investigators used.

"Eureka!" I'd finally located the can of paint I'd been searching for. It came up solo, no Tootsie in sight. Actually, I lied about the Tootsies, I never gave them a chance to go missing: they had their special place in my thighs.

"Regulation bag?" Cowan asked.

"I'm a professional," I said, and began marking the beginning of the skids. Then I snapped a picture, triangulated the location from two utility poles and sketched them on my pad. That's when I noticed Cowan giving me a quizzical look.

Must look to him as though I was marking the road a good eight or ten feet from the start of the shadow skid—a pavement mark that precedes the skid itself. Most people think skids are rubber left from the tire, hence the expression "burn rubber, baby," or whatever it is. But they're actually melt marks caused by the heat of friction burning into the tar. And before a skidding tire generates enough heat to melt asphalt, what you see, if anything, is a shadow. On a road cold enough, shadow might be all the skid you have. To Cowan, it probably looked as though I wasn't even close to the shadow, let alone the skids. I decided to let him wonder, and tell him when I was done.

I walked back over the skids one at a time.

Skid one: light marks, possibly months old, but there was no way to tell. Only one wheel had locked up—a not-uncommon malfunction of the brake system—probably the right front. And the marks were—

"Underinflated tires, huh?" Cowan said. Because the skid was darker on the sides than in the middle.

"Overdeflected," I said. "Same mark, but my money says it's weight shift." When the driver stomps the brakes, it causes the vehicle's weight to shift to the front. The weight bears down, the tires overdeflect and it looks exactly like an overloaded vehicle or underinflated tire. "Or could be a little of both. How's that for definitive?"

The skid rode toward the shoulder, hit the gravel and turned into a furrow for twelve feet. Then tire prints showed the driver regained control and steered back onto pavement. All of this about forty feet from where Hulfinger's car had most likely left the road. Involved with her accident? Not a sure thing, but a possible one.

"Those are the marks that match her tire ribs," Cowan said.

"Mmm." I'd checked that myself. I put a paint dot at the end of the mark, snapped a photo. Triangulated and sketched.

Skid two started farther from the scene, but led directly toward the spot I'd picked for Hulfinger's exit location. The front tires had locked up first, which meant the car had front-disk brakes and rear-drum brakes. Saw that a lot. The skids stopped halfway to the exit location. Then the car went into yaw—the driver overcompensating, fishtailing. The dark rear tire marks tracked outside the front marks, showing she'd still been sliding, though the tires were no longer locked up.

The yaw marks stopped abruptly, and I walked the line looking for furrows and gouges, coming up empty. Well, not exactly empty, more like too full. Too many marks, most of which I put down to the vehicles of those damn, know-nothing officials. I put off that aggravation, though, and took the measurements. Then I went back for the third skid.

Skid three was a truck. Oil truck, or parks department. Or a long-distance trucker looking for a scenic spot to eat lunch. Under-deflected marks, so either the tires were overinflated or the truck was underloaded. Skip skids, too—the mark looking like a dotted line—which often occurred when the braking system of an under-loaded semi locks the wheels of the trailer before those of the tractor to prevent jackknifing.

One thing I knew, though, Jody Hulfinger hadn't been driving a truck. These weren't her skid marks. Didn't matter. I was going to work the scene the way I always did. Gather too much information then discard what was useless. And there was no lack of useless: acceleration marks, scrub marks, striation marks and tire prints. Pavement grinding, too. Probably nothing, but I'd check it all then walk the line fifty yards in each direction to get a sense of the normal wear on this stretch of road.

What I wanted to see now was the location I'd mentally marked as the exit point, where the Hulfinger vehicle left the roadway. It was mangled. The rescue vehicles had used it as an on-ramp. Any useful marks had been crushed into nothing. Wonderful. I looked at Cowan.

He raised his hands. "You don't have to tell me."

"Sorry." I was going to turn away when I saw he had a question. "What?"

"What's with the sunglasses?"

"What makes you think they're not just a fashion accessory?" I gave him my best movie-star smile.

He gave me a jowly, amused look. "Call it a hunch."

"Here, try them on. Careful with the frames though—they're Armani, darling." I started to remove the glasses, but stopped when I heard cars approaching. A blue Chevy Lumina with Massachusetts plates—obviously FBI—and an official-looking van I figured was the dive team.

The Lumina started to pull over on top of my scuff marks. Christ. Who were these people? I stepped beside the car, slammed on the hood and pointed to a spot down the road where the driver should park.

A clean-cut man with thinning hair and narrow lips looked out the driver's window. "I'm Special Agent Van Huut—"

"I don't care if you're the Men in Black. Pull it fifty feet either way and park on the other side of the road."

He stared at me long enough to let me know he'd do whatever he chose—then drove on. The van driver nodded once and followed the FBI agent. I waited until they were past the danger zone, then steeled myself for a confrontation with Agent Van Huut. The smell of hot engine oil was viscous in the air as I approached. Battling my phobia didn't exactly make me want to play nice.

"I don't want a pissing contest." Van Huut wasn't halfway out of his car before staking his claim.

"I thought we could arm-wrestle," I said.

"I'm in charge of this investigation, Ms. Ashbury. And this scene."

"Good," I said, trying for a more subtle approach. "Did you have the M.E. check for Meniere's?"

He straightened up—he was six-two, midthirties and made an undistinguished suit come across better than it deserved. He stared silently down at me.

I managed a straight face. "Or how about cataplexy?" I asked. "It'd be new to me, but you never know. That and hypnagogic hallucinations, you know what you got?"

"Do you have a point, Ms. Ashbury?"

"SVA due to narcolepsy," I finished. I spun toward a diver who had exited the rear of the van and was headed toward the bay. "Hey! Wait—let me establish a route in and out first, okay? Won't take ten minutes."

The diver shrugged and went back toward the van.

"I bow to your superior knowledge of crash sites, Ms. Ashbury," Van Huut said. "It's why the NTSB was called in. But I do expect three things. One is that you——"

He was saying nothing I had to hear, so I walked away and checked the route into the water. Took a couple pictures of the path—probably unnecessary but better to waste film than miss something—and called the divers over.

"Any of you here the other day?" I asked. "When they recovered it?"

"This is the team." The guy who answered looked more like a plumber than a diver; chunky, solid and competent. "We were all here."

I asked him to describe the state and location of the vehicle. I'd gone over the photos in the file, but God alone knew what they'd done to it after dragging it from the river. I wanted to hear what they saw before I inspected the car myself.

"Upside down, probably twenty-five feet in," he said. "More than a little marine life active. Crabs, bloodworm, fish. Even had a lobster who didn't mind the shallow water."

A skeezy guy with no ass spoke up. "And sea roaches."

"Sea roaches?"

"Gotta excuse him," the plumber said. "He's studying marine biology at UMaine."

Skeezy looked as though the only thing he studied was how to get a joint to burn evenly. I couldn't have been more surprised than if he'd been a neurosurgeon. I tried not to let it show. "Uh-huh," I said.

"Amphipods," Skeezy said. "We call 'em sea roaches. Scavengers, they come in swarms. You know pill bugs, the ones you find under a log? Marine amphipods look about the same, the deep-sea species get a couple inches long. That's what was at your body, along with everything else."

Ick. More than I wanted to know.

Skeezy was just warming up. "Worst thing is hagfish. Slime eels. Find a warm hole to crawl in and eat their way out. Not a true eel. They got cartilaginous skeletons like sharks, not bony ones like fish. You know eel-skin wallets and—"

"Hey, Aquaman," the plumber said. "Nobody wants to hear your slime-eel speech again."

To my great relief, Skeezy sputtered and shut up. I asked about the windows and doors.

From the descriptions, both rear windows had been closed at impact. The driver's window had been half-open and the passenger window all the way down. The doors were all closed, except the passenger door was cracked approximately two feet.

"The car was buckled on that side," the plumber said. "Looked like the door had popped."

"Right side buckled?" I hadn't heard that before. Induced damage to the side could open a door, no problem. But so could a passenger. "And the body?"

A quiet came over them, and it took me a second to realize it was respect for the dead. They weren't used to it. Probably never would be, which was a good thing. "She was still in her seat belt," the plumber said. "It was—" he made a motion across his chest "—cutting into her. But she'd shifted, like she was floating toward the surface."

"Looked like she was trying to get one last breath," Skeezy said.

There was another silence. I let it last a moment before asking the rest of my questions. I learned nothing new; nothing I needed to solve this thing. Then I told them what to look for. "Two things," I said. "First, another body."

They looked surprised.

"I've seen a man thrown through an open car window without making a mark." I shook my head, remembering. "Guy had three daughters. We told them it was their lucky day, Daddy hadn't been in the car. Turned out we left him in a ditch by the side of the road overnight. I'm the one who informed the family. I'm never gonna do that again. Now, I don't know squat about ocean rescue or diving." I caught each man's gaze in turn. "But I want every one of you to be able to assure me nobody else was in that car. Understand?"

They did.

"Second. I want everything. If it's not a fish and it's not a rock, I want it bagged and tagged. You find a Coke bottle that's been there since Creation, bag it, tag it, and if you're lucky I'll give you the nickel when I redeem it. Got it?"

They nodded.

"And thanks for coming out again. The woman's name is Jody Hulfinger. She died here and her family wants to know why. I think they deserve that."

The Principal's Daughter's face was a sheen of sweat, her triceps and lats burned. She felt the muscle exhaustion, the deeply satisfying bottomed-out weakness, yet her breath was steady.

One more. She pulled the weights down, full extension. Smooth, on the exhale. She chose weight training and the treadmill, instead of aerobics, to avoid the abrasive music, the humiliating outfits and the constant cloying competition for firmest thighs and smallest size. A competition she would never win. No—she would win. For *him.* He preferred skinny women, so she would become one.

One more. Brigid Ashbury, accident reconstructionist. The best of the best at the NTSB. But the "best of the best" was always a facade. The Principal's Daughter knew about pretense, about the fear of discovery, about needs unmet and unmeetable.

One more. She didn't look particularly strong. It pleased her; she liked being underestimated. She did not like being unloved, overlooked—*the quiet footfalls never coming, the—*

She shook her head, felt drops of sweat land on her straining shoulders. No. Back to work. She'd placed some calls. Retrieved some documents, patched together the story—she'd always been a gifted amateur psychologist. Ashbury had left the NTSB under less than auspicious circumstances. After a car crash—heavy-handed irony—that had left her shattered. Now she was receiving disability pay, seeing a psychiatrist and barely functioning.

One more. The Principal's Daughter could imagine the guilt, the paralyzing dread—an accident reconstructionist destroyed by an accident. Ashbury had been the best. Written up in magazines. Invited to speak at conventions. Attention and admiration—the men hadn't crept past *her*—and then it had all fallen apart.

She exhaled in a hiss. Brigid Ashbury, with her delicate psychology, trying to track him. Trap him.

One more. The slightest pressure, and Brigid Ashbury would snap.

* * *

I made sure the divers knew where *not* to step, and asked if any-one had questions.

"I have two," Van Huut said. He'd crept up behind me. "One—what's your title?"

Oh, here we go. Trying to reassert his control. "You can call me *ma'am*, Agent."

A couple of the divers stifled laughs.

"Your title is accident-reconstruction consultant, NTSB, seconded to the FBI. And I'm the FBI. You need something done, you do it through me. This may be a go-nowhere traffic accident, but I intend to treat it professionally, and I hope you do, too."

What made him think I was being unprofessional? Maybe he just wanted me to call him *sir*. "What's your second question?"

"You're from California?"

"That's right."

"Well, you're not in California anymore. You can lose the shades."

I didn't wear the sunglasses for the movie-star effect. That was a mere perk. I wore them because the lenses were polarized.

Skid marks show up far better through polarized lenses. I didn't know why. I didn't care. But if I walked the line in daylight, I wore sunglasses. It wasn't much of an edge—just the eight or ten feet that had confused Trooper Cowan—but sometimes, it was enough.

I'd explained all this to the trooper as we walked back up to the road, pointedly ignoring Van Huut. Cowan held the glasses delicately to his face, glanced at the marks and made a deep, satisfied grunt. He checked the skids from six or seven angles before he handed back my glasses.

"They have to be Armani?" he asked.

"Only if you want to be beautiful."

"May I see?" Van Huut asked, standing behind me.

I gave it a second. "Sure."

He held the sunglasses to his eyes, crouched over the skid marks. "Really brings them out." He straightened, handed the glasses back. "Do you want an evidence team on top, too? The locals said they'd be more than willing."

"Not until I go over the scene myself. But then, yeah. And I need an '85 Jetta—a match to her car. Need to interview the family and friends, too."

"You want to interview them yourself? For a noncollision accident?"

"You sure it's noncollision?"

"The way I see it, the unstabilized situation began there, where she lost control—"

"You think there was an unstabilized situation?"

He grinned. He had pale lips. "The car crashed, Ms. Ashbury."

"A crash doesn't necessarily mean an unstabilized situation. There are four basic possibilities here—that is, if we're only talking driver's intent and vehicle stability. One, it was intended and stable."

"That'd be suicide, right?" Cowan asked.

"Most likely, yeah. Two, it was intended and unstable. She wanted to suicide, and also lost control of the car. Three is unintended, unstable. That's ninety percent of what you see. Like falling asleep at the wheel, heart attack, losing control on a turn. Last is unintended and stable. Like running a red light or gaze nystagmus, you're in full control of the car as you wrap it around the tree." She turned to Cowan. "What'd you get on the pretrip?"

"Nothing," Cowan said. "I never saw the interview notes. Maybe the agent can help you."

"The pretrip?" Van Huut asked. Law enforcement was like that; each specialty had its own jargon.

"Pretrip series of events," I explained. "Vehicle defects, shitty driver, illness or emotional state. Whatever might have affected her driving."

"Well, Jody's driving record was good," Van Huut said. "I don't know about vehicle defects or illness or—"

"I'll handle it."

"You want me to find out, I'll find out."

"Easier to do it myself. Then there's trip events. Did she stop anywhere? Anyone see her driving erratically? Any reason she was fatigued, stressed?"

"No idea." Van Huut shook his head. "You've seen the event report, the M.E.'s report and the missing person's. There's nothing there." He looked out toward the cold silver water. "Except…have you seen the photo?"

"Yeah."

"She was a—let's say she was a handful. Born twenty years too late. She would have given Jane Fonda a run for her money."

"A firebrand, huh?"

He looked as if he wasn't sure if I was making fun of him. I wasn't sure, myself.

"I suppose," he said.

"She have skeletal and dental X-rays?"

"Dental, yes. Skeletal, no. Never broke a bone. Until this." He was silent a moment. "But I could fill you in on the family. Ralph Nicencio must've told you I know them."

"I'd rather do my own groundwork, get a fresh perspective. If that's okay."

"Fine with me." But he said it as if it wasn't.

I chose the road as a baseline and a utility pole as the zero point and walked the exit path, snapping pictures and drawing sketches of every gouge and furrow and pit. Every scraped boulder, every bruised shrub, every spray of dirt.

First thing I found of interest was the fire pit. A dozen stones in a circle around a pile of ash, scattered with green shards of broken beer bottles. Nothing out of the ordinary—except it had been built *over* a smeared furrow I was ninety-percent sure was Jody Hulfinger's. And *under* the tracks of what was almost certainly a rescue vehicle.

Which meant it was built after the crash and before the rescue. If the local cops could determine when the fire had been made—and there couldn't be that many kids around building fire pits and drinking Rolling Rock—I'd be able to narrow down the date and time.

I examined the bushes surrounding the pit. Scattered in a twenty-foot radius were: a crushed and empty plastic container of Odwalla fruit juice; a squash ball; a pair of scissors; a small yellow canvas shoe; two pens; and a black leatherette daily planner along with a couple dozen sheets of loose paper.

I bagged and tagged it all. I both loathed and adored this part of the investigation. On the one hand, it was tedious and time-consuming and required a meticulous personality usually only found in sociopaths. On the other, you never knew what you were going to find, maybe the key to the entire case.

Most of this was probably crap, although the squash ball was marginally interesting—maybe the one Gurleyville man had thrown for his dog. The sheets of paper were covered in blue scrib-blings, apparently from a class or seminar. I looked at the top page: trepca mines, 2,180, geneva convention—1949, baku-ceyhan, rambouillet accords. Lower on the page: broccoli rabe, cashews, toothbrush, envelopes, oranges. Underscored five times, in the margin just below a doodle of what appeared to be a three-legged horse, was a messy "11$11" in black ink.

So far, nothing. Unless *broccoli rabe* was going to crack this sucker wide-open.

A flash of white caught my eye. Another sheet of paper, stuck in a bush three feet off the ground. I worked it gently free from the twigs and leaves and glanced at it.

"Yahtzee," I said.

I climbed up the embankment and knocked dirt off my shoes while I waited for Van Huut to get off his cell. "Remember what you said about a go-nowhere traffic investigation?"

He must've seen something in my face, because he glanced at the paper in my gloved hand. He stood over my shoulder and read it. The sheet was torn and smeared with moisture—and pasted with letters cut out of a newspaper:

t to See YoURE dAUghtEr agaIN hULFi...weNty mILLiOn DOllArs toO bOStOn & WEiGHT aT BEARSFord arms hotEl for...eLse she wIlL DIE diE DiE diE Die!!

The FBI had been invited in at Hulfinger's request. If they'd had to justify it, they'd probably have said something about the Maine death of a Massachusetts resident—that made it interstate, which gave them jurisdiction.

Nonsense, of course, for a single-vehicle accident. They'd been here, because Van Huut was a personal friend of Hulfinger's. But it wasn't nonsense for a kidnapping.

Van Huut had read the note calmly. Then he'd read it again, still cool.

"So?" I'd asked.

"Twenty million dollars to Beresford Arms Hotel," he'd said. "Guess it wasn't narcolepsy."

He put the note into an evidence bag and drove away.

He probably thought my job was done. But I was just warming up. I walked back down to the beach to see what the dive team had found.

Detective Trake sat across from Aaron in the interrogation room, his face a portrait of skepticism. "That's your story?" he said.

"What's wrong with it?" Aaron said. "I like it. It has a beginning, a middle and an end."

"Mr. White," Meredith said, warning him not to sound flippant. Meredith was his lawyer. She had a birdlike manner and an upturned nose that made him try to think of the fancy word for upturned noses. *Retroussé?*

"Plus," he told the cop, "it's the truth. You checked her bedroom. My prints are everywhere, right? The doorknob, the laptop, her copy of *Z Magazine*. You confirmed I was with Cate in Boston the day Jody disappeared—you know I had nothing to do with it."

"Prints in her bedroom are one thing," Trake said. "On the kidnap note is another."

"All my prints mean is that the note—the paper, before the note was on it—must be from her house. I touched it before it was made into a note." Aaron was pretty impressed with this deduction.

Trake wasn't. "Then you fled the Hulfinger summer camp because…?"

"I didn't flee." He'd already told them three times. "I left, because nobody wanted the boyfriend around for a family crisis. I don't know what you'd do, Detective, but I promise Emily Post is with me on this."

"How about your juvenile record?"

This time Meredith was on Aaron's side. "Detective Trake," she said.

"Okay, okay," he said. "He doesn't have to answer."

"I don't mind—" Aaron said.

"Keep your teeth together, Mr. White," Meredith said, "and we'll have you out of here today. You want to stay, keep talking."

So he kept his teeth together—about his juvenile record, at least—as Trake grilled him for another forty-five minutes.

"I have to tell you, Detective Trake," Meredith said, when he was done. "If I didn't know you, I'd advise my client to seek legal remedy. Was there *any* cause to arrest him?"

"It was a good-faith arrest." Trake colored. "A fingerprint, an eyewitness, a criminal record."

"A sealed record I'd advise you not to mention again." Meredith froze on him, and her birdlike manner seemed suddenly less like a chickadee and more like a hawk. "It may have been good faith, Detective, but it was a bad arrest. I want that made perfectly clear to the press and to your colleagues. All the evidence—the print and the witness—was misconstrued and not sufficient grounds for arrest in any case."

"The witness was very convincing," Trake said.

The witness was Gayle Cornell, Small Hulfinger's current "lady." She'd seen Aaron and Jody drive off, and remembered it being on the day Jody disappeared, not the day before. At least that's what she said.

"Witnesses," Meredith said, scornfully. "It'll be made clear?"

"He's still a suspect."

"Irv," she said. "This is me you're talking to. You don't suspect him any more than you suspect every other person who had contact with Hulfinger. You want to make me break out the mascara and call a press conference?"

Trake grumblingly agreed he'd make it clear Aaron was no longer the prime suspect. He told Aaron he was free to go, but immediately asked that he stick around for a couple hours to speak with another investigator, from something called the NTSB.

"Oh, sure." Aaron stood to leave. "Love to help."

"Mr. White," Meredith said. This time invitingly, as she opened the door for him. She had a nice profile. It was definitely retroussé.

"You want to go, fine." Trake said. "But if you don't talk to us, who does that hurt? Not me. Not this NTSB investigator. Only people it hurts is the Hulfingers."

Aaron hesitated in the open door. But no, all he wanted was to leave.

"It's only a couple hours," the detective said. "I'll bring you— I'll have Dellgarda bring you a cup of coffee. You said you liked Jody Hulfinger." Trake half smiled, and looked almost human. "That much I believe. So why not give her a couple hours of your time? Maybe you can help."

"Yeah, well——" Aaron said, on the verge of a shattering reply. Hard to see the flaw in Trake's logic, though. "You've got a point."

"Mr. White. As your legal advisor, I have to inform you that——"

Meredith informed Aaron of a bunch of stuff, but all he could think of was Jody. She'd never be warm again. Her glasses would never flash, her dog-brown eyes were forever closed. Her smile— the coy, self-confident smile he'd only seen once—he'd never see that again. Nobody would. Guilt and grief. He felt them both, and couldn't distinguish between the two.

Someone killed her. Someone killed Jody, and there was nothing he could do. Not yet.

"I'll wait," he said, and told Meredith he'd be fine without her.

Len Ganapi arrived at the causeway a couple minutes after Van Huut left with the ransom note. He updated me and I—graciously, I thought—invited him to help me process the scene.

The divers left three hours later. They'd retrieved a wide assortment of trash and shattered car pieces, including one of the headlight lamps. But they hadn't found another body. They hadn't found much of the shattered window. They hadn't found Hulfinger's jawbone. Still, I thanked them warmly, making a California joke at my own expense, and went back to walking the line with Ganapi. Looking for paint transfer, scrape marks— gouges, dents, grind, scratches, tracks and furrows. We finished before the sun set.

"You want a ride back?" Ganapi asked. Saying it diffidently, as if he was asking to carry my schoolbooks.

"No. Thanks. I'll walk." Then, to make up for that morning: "You're welcome to join me."

To my surprise, he did. Someone from the Inn would bring him back later for his car.

"What's your next step?" he asked, as we cut through the field leading from Sears Island Road to Route One. But I was distracted by the lights of the oncoming traffic. Dusk and dawn were the most dangerous. Drivers lulled and half-asleep, the sun low and blinding—

"Brigid?"

"Hmm?" I said. "Oh. Inspect the car. Talk to the M.E. Then the investigation begins."

"The family?"

"The family. Although with this kidnap note, I guarantee the FBI will get there first. The thing is—" I paused as a rust-mottled '78 Dodge one-ton, towing a lawn mower, sped past. I tried to keep my voice steady. "The thing is, how does the note affect what looks like an ordinary single-vehicle accident?"

"Well, it raises some questions. . . ."

"Was it really a single? Was she alone? Was it a kidnapping gone bad? Too many questions to count."

"So how do you coordinate it with the feds?"

"The feds do a better job than us on everything except reconstruction. They'll dig into her associates. We'll dig into her driving record. Most reconstructionists—"

I was hit by a wall of air as a tanker drove past—it sucked the oxygen from my lungs. I bent over, hands on my knees, unable to catch my breath. I couldn't move my legs—and Ganapi was about to wrap a manly arm around me, and I couldn't take it. If he touched me I'd…*goddammit.* Suck it up, Bridge.

I forced myself to straighten and stared a moment at the faint scars on my hands. My voice sounded thin. "Most reconstructionists—we forget an accident isn't just physics and engineering. No equation tells you who the victim was. No equation gives you the human factor."

I felt Ganapi watching me, gauging if I was okay. I resisted telling him I was fine, because I wasn't. And because I couldn't trust myself not to snap at him.

"That doesn't overlap with the FBI investigation?" he asked.

"Of course it does. Addiction, abuse, anger—whatever causes any particular driver to fail on any given day." I started walking again, as if nothing had happened. "I don't know if the FBI's Kidnap Team gets called in for a failed attempt, but if they do, what're the chances they'll ask who was her most recent passenger? Did she drive with one hand or both? Did she use cruise control? Did—"

"So they'll use us like they use the CSU," Ganapi said. The Crime Scene Unit. "For the technical details."

"Difference between us and the CSU is simple. When an officer talks to a suspect, it's an interview. You know what the NTSB calls it."

"An interrogation." He smiled. "Nothing like an agency with direct Congressional empowerment."

I didn't respond. I was watching the road, which had started to narrow, but traffic hadn't slowed. An old K-car passed with a fucked alignment—it was a funeral-on-wheels looking for a chapel. A black half-ton Chevy with a racing stripe tailed it. And next came a diesel Ford with Greg's Glass written on the side, and sheets of plate glass strapped to an unstable-looking frame.

I froze. It was too much.

Plates of glass. Shards of broken glass. Sixty miles an hour, an explosion of glass, a thousand tiny barbs cutting skin. The sudden whimpered cries.

Jon, dead.

Jon, who I had no longer loved, dead. And the boy. His wet panting whimpers—I'd been hyperaware, hearing every tinkle of glass, every heartbeat and eyeblink, hearing the deadly breathless breathing of the boy, unable to lift a hand, unable to...

Ganapi touched my shoulder.

9

I toweled my hair dry and inspected my face in the bathroom mirror.

Not good. I twisted my auburn hair back into a braid, but that made things worse; drew attention to the bags under my eyes and the deep crow's-feet that were my worst feature.

I'd have to wear it loose today. I rubbed my styling stick on my hand and mussed my hair into what approximated a style. Then I put on foundation, checked the mirror and slathered on more. Chanel, liquid natural—lay it on thick as asphalt and it still looked okay.

I was applying mascara when I felt a twinge in my elbow. It was bruised a faint yellow and tender to the touch. Probably not as painful as Len's face, though.

"Could've been worse," I said. Yeah. Could've been fatal.

I was so out of here. Gone. I longed to be back in Santa Barbara, sitting on my steps feeding the juncos.

I threw on an old DKNY suit that looked businesslike and packed my suitcase. "Get back on the horse," Ralph had said. Fuck the horse. Did you tell a stab victim to get back on the knife? *Oh, you had a root canal? Well, you gotta get back in the chair.*

Fuck the horse, and the horse it rode in on.

I grabbed the phone to call Ralph—to tell him to book my return flight—and it beeped with messages. I hadn't picked up last night, not after talking to my mother. I'd called her because I'd needed to cry. A good cry, a cleansing cry—and I wasn't about to call Dr. Kugelmeyer three thousand miles away just to sob into the phone. I should have. My mother was always supportive—except when I was needy. Then she'd tell me what she considered "difficult truths," confirming all my self-doubts and cataloging each shortcoming. Well, I'd wanted a good cry, it just hadn't made me feel any better.

The phone beeped again in my hand. Three messages waiting.

One: Van Huut. "Hey. Agent—Officer—Ms. Ashbury. I'm pretty tweaked, you can probably hear it in my voice." He did sound excited, though I didn't know anyone who used the expression *tweaked*—except maybe meth addicts. "They lifted a print from the note. Belonged to a guy with a record. He was dating Cate Hulfinger. Day after Jody went missing, he disappeared. Got a wit who places him—anyway, the dumb schmuck is still using his credit cards. We get any break at all, we'll bring him in tonight. First day on the job, you crack it wide." A compliment? Okay, I'd forgive the *tweaked*.

Two: Ralph. "I heard about the latest, Ashbury. Good job with the note. Bad job with Len. He's not gonna press charges, 'cause for some reason he still respects you. And his tooth isn't broken, only loose. You have to get beyond this. You already let it end your career, you can't—" And, as Ralph would say, et-concerned and disappointed-cetera.

Three: Trooper Chester Cowan, saying he had the tire prints for elimination and asking if he should proceed to scene. Said he'd bring his own sunglasses. "Ten ninety-nine at Christy's and twice as polarized as any pair of Armani shades."

I smiled. It was easy to smile, now that I was gone from the case.

The phone rang in my hand. "Ashbury," I said.

"Morning, Bridge." It was Theresa Udall. "I heard about last night."

"Theresa. Long time no talk." I could've gone longer.

"Well, you're not one of the all-time-great phone-call return-ers. Just checking in, as the ostensible IIC here. And I wanted to tell you not to sweat last night."

"I'm not. I was about to call Ralph and tell him—"

"Not sweating it? Bullshit, Bridge. I know you too well. But you're the best. I have complete faith. And if you need, give me a ring and I'll be on the next plane out."

That was complete faith?

"It'll be like old times," Theresa said. "You and me against the world. Like that case in Missouri."

I opened my mouth to say I was off this, that I was calling Ralph and cutting my losses. What came out was: "That case in Missouri was me doing my fucking *thing*, driving over those bastard marks a dozen times before I *knew* that Escort had its brakes stomped until the linings faded." If brakes are applied for too long, the brake linings can become so hot it causes fading—and untraceable brake failure. Usually happens when the vehicle is going down a grade, but in Missouri the brakes had been applied for thirty miles by a college textbook the driver hadn't noticed was in the footwell. "That case was me. Driving my ass back and forth until only one thing made sense."

I expected Theresa to bring up my final case. The case I'd walked away from, the case I'd handed to Theresa after the crash that had ruined me.

But she just chuckled. "Now you sound like yourself, Bridge. You own that pissant causeway crash. Some dinky SVA, even if it is tied with a kidnapping. But if it turns out more than you can handle with, you know—" she paused "—whatever's going on in your head, you take it as far as you can and pass the baton."

Pass the baton?

"I've got it under control, Theresa." And just like that, I was no longer gone.

"That's what I figured. You're a living legend here, you know that? The Accident Hall of Fame."

"They gonna retire my number?" Which I said to show Theresa I could talk sports, too. Though I had to dig pretty deep for that one.

"Nah, they're just gonna put a big marble statue of you riding an engine block in the lobby. I keep telling them you weren't that good," she said, in a faux-overwrought tone. "People still read your old reports like gospel. They actually fought over your desk when you left."

"Oh, yeah? Who won?"

"One guess," Theresa said, and laughed.

So. No longer gone. One call from my rival, Theresa Udall, was all it took. I bet Ralph put her up to it. Which meant I had to forget about what I'd done to Len and get to work. Van Huut was following up on the suspect, which left me two things to do today. Inspect the car and speak with the Medical Examiner.

The M.E. I'd deal with over the phone. It was over an hour to the crime lab in Augusta, and there was no way in hell I was subjecting myself to that.

But the car was at an impound lot in Belfast, a fifteen-minute drive. I could walk it in three hours. Except that'd waste the whole day, walking there and back. I sighed, wishing I were Nero Wolfe. Then I could stay in my room and water orchids while Archie went out to do all the hard work. Only thing is, Archie didn't know how to examine a car—well that, and the fact that I had no Archie. So I'd have to call Cowan, ask him to pick me up. I could bear fifteen minutes in a car. No problem. I could do fifteen minutes, easy. Definitely. Do it now, get it over with, and talk to the M.E. this afternoon. That was my plan.

I grabbed the phone to call Trooper Cowan. Dialed. The woman who answered said I'd reached the M.E.'s office, and should hold for Dr. MacRoule. So I'd call Cowan and do the car later, so what?

"Let's see," Dr. MacRoule said after I'd introduced myself. "Ah. I'm free today at five, or tomorrow morning. You know where the office is?"

I told him it had to be now. On the phone.

"Is this necessary?" MacRoule asked. "It's all in the report."

"Yes, but now I'd want to hear it like it wasn't commissioned by the American Legal Association."

"We all work for the lawyers, I'm afraid," he said.

I was afraid, too. Of a lot of things, lately. But right now, I was afraid he wouldn't be completely forthcoming if I came across too hard. And I wasn't in the best mood to soften him up when I was still freaked from last night. But I had to try.

A woman investigator has three basic ways of dealing with male coworkers: flirt, flatter or fight. Unfair and sexist, but there it is. I'd known women who wasted their whole careers on a single one of the *f*'s. I didn't make that mistake. I preferred the fourth way: all of the above, in no particular order. Otherwise known as *F* for *fluster.*

"I know what you mean," I said warmly to the M.E. "Some days I go to a restaurant, I order what appears to be a steak consistent with rare."

MacRoule was silent for a moment, either appreciating my charm and vivacity or wondering what the fuck I was talking about.

"It's a good report, Dr. MacRoule. I can see every injury she sustained. But I want to know what you think happened."

"Ah. Is that what you want? I think she drowned."

"Right, she drowned. But how?"

"It's not so easy, Detective." I didn't correct the "detective." People tended to reveal more information if they thought you had a badge—well, people on the right side of the law, anyway.

"Drowning is a diagnosis of exclusion—at autopsy, there are no pathognomonic findings to specifically diagnose it. It's based on the circumstances of death, plus a variety of generalized anatomical findings."

"But that was the diagnosis, so you found—?"

"Hemorrhagic edema fluid in the airways. Hemorrhagic foam in the lumen of the stomach, mild dilation of the right ventricle. When the brain was examined, it was swollen, with flattening of the gyri due to nonspecific brain swelling and—"

"Wait, wait. Okay. So she drowned."

"Ah. Well, immersion of a body in water for days, or weeks in this case—"

"She was definitely in for weeks?"

"Between one week and three. No way to pinpoint it further, unless you can match her stomach contents to a meal."

I looked at the folder. "Onion rings and beer. That narrows it down."

"In fact, it does. There aren't more than ten restaurants in an hour's drive of her house that serve onion rings."

I made a note to follow that up, though I was sure the FBI was already on top of it. "You were saying—immersion of a body in water?"

"It causes leaching of blood from antemortem wounds. What appear to be bloodless postmortem wounds—say, propeller cuts—may actually be antemortem, and the cause of death."

"I feel safe in presuming, Doctor, that's a mistake you wouldn't make."

He cleared his throat. I couldn't tell if it was a sign that flattery was working well or had failed entirely.

"No," he said. "Hulfinger's wounds were antemortem, during the crash."

"But not fatal. You listed the cause of death as drowning."

"If she would have survived extraction from the vehicle and transport to the hospital—and, ultimately, treatment—then cause of death is officially drowning. In my judgment, she would have survived."

"So the accident caused the drowning, the drowning caused the death. Question is, what caused the accident?"

"Nothing anatomical, I'm afraid."

I'd get back to the facts in a moment. First, I'd try for more opinion. "Forget the cause, then. Can you look at the body and tell me what it went through?"

"All the classic signs of drowning, with the exception of hemorrhaging in the petrous or mastoid bones, but—"

"No—I mean, what it went through kinetically, the motions of the body inside the car before Hulfinger died—antemortem."

"Ah. I am not a criminalist."

"Indulge me."

"She drove off the causeway, rolled the car at least once and smashed into the water. There are—"

"At least one roll?"

"In my opinion. The left side of her face bore the brunt of a forceful impact, there were abrasions possibly consistent with— Let me rephrase. The seat belt cut into her right hip, showing she'd been thrown rightward. And she'd been thrown to the left—there were glass shards, presumably from the driver's-side window, embedded in her left cheekbone and temple. She could have been in a multiple car accident, but it's listed as a single vehicle, which leads me to believe there was at least one full rotation."

"Interesting theory." I'd wait until I inspected the car to decide if it was a good one.

"Thank you." His tone was dry, as if he knew what I was thinking.

"Drugs and alcohol?"

"If there had been, it would've been in the report."

"Other toxins?"

"Not that we found. Unless you have reason to suspect she was into some esoteric recreational activities..."

"Heart attack?"

"No anatomical signs of any antemortem distress not consistent with the accident."

"Nothing lodged in her throat?" I had investigated a crash once caused by a peanut.

"Not by the time I saw her."

"But there could—"

"Nothing in her throat, Detective."

"How about an aneurysm? Stroke? Any kind of brain pathology?"

"No, no, and not that we found."

"Meniere's Syndrome? Other inner-ear problems?"

"Ah. Hold a moment." And he was gone.

I waited and noticed I needed to file my fingernails. I inspected them more closely and felt another twinge in my elbow. Poor Ganapi. He'd been trying to be supportive, give my arm a squeeze, and look what it got him—an elbow in the face. Least I hadn't broken his nose. Just busted his mouth.

I heard rustling on the other end of the phone.

"Meniere's doesn't show up physically," MacRoule said. "At least not on a submerged body. Other inner-ear problems…who knows? Nothing evident."

"How about her eyes? She wore those Coke-bottle lenses."

"I didn't examine her eyes."

"What do you mean you didn't—" Oh, right. Two weeks in the water, with marine pill bugs swarming. Not much of her eyes left to examine. "Right. Okay. I'll check with her optometrist."

I made a note to do that and flipped through the rest of MacRoule's report. I stopped when I came to the photos of the body. It was barely human.

"We're sure it was her, right?"

"It's not Mary, Queen of Scots, Detective."

"I'm looking at the pictures." The body was fish-belly white, a featureless mass of tissue and organs. "You're telling me the next of kin identified this?"

"Right car, right clothes, right age, weight, sex, height, race. Right prescription in the glasses. No counter-indications—appendix intact, no surgical scars, no old broken bones. You aren't seriously suggesting this isn't Jody Hulfinger?"

"No." But I hesitated. "I'd just like to be sure. How are the prints?"

"Only got partials. Very partial partials. Apparently the fish were—partial—to the fingers."

"Dental charts?"

"Yeah, it's a good match."

Then why hadn't he brought it up before? "How good?"

MacRoule sighed. "Eighty-five, ninety percent good. I've got no lower jaw. The upper left was shattered beyond… I've got a quarter of a mouth of teeth, and I can tell you it's almost certainly her. Thing is, she hadn't had a dental X-ray since she was eighteen. Her wisdom teeth came in since then and shifted everything around."

"So there's no one thing that tells you definitely yes, this is her."

"Detective Ashbury, I've been doing this twenty-five years. There's never one thing. But this is Jody Hulfinger."

"I want a DNA match."

"Talk to the crime lab."

Good advice. "I'll do that. Thanks. You've been a big help."

"I'm extremely pleased to hear that. And Detective?"

"Yeah?"

"Next time, make an appointment."

10

"Give me a minute," I said to Cowan as we pulled into the Belfast Towing Impoundment Yard.

It took me three just to get out of his car. I'd held up pretty well on the ride over, even though I'd left fingernail prints in the vinyl seat. I waited until I could breathe normally, then picked my way through the maze of demolished cars, which looked like rotting metal corpses. The battered red '85 VW Jetta was encased in a shroud of whitish silt.

I circled it slowly from ten feet away as Cowan watched me. I didn't know how to tell him this wasn't part of my phobia, it was technique. I'd always done it. I needed to look at the big picture before I focused on the details. But it wasn't something you could train people to see; not everyone had the ability to walk around a car until they began to understand what it went through. I could.

What I could train him on, though, was the Mechanical Inspection Guide and Evaluation Report. So when I'd finished staring at the car, I ran through it with Cowan.

"First, there's vehicle description," I said. "Plate, make, year and model, color, registration, VIN, mileage."

He gave me a look saying he knew all that.

"Okay. Second is the accelerator. Check the linkage, freedom of movement, the pedal tread and the retrieval."

"The retrieval? That's the spring?"

"Yeah." It was how much the accelerator bounced back after having been depressed. Which, when I thought about it, was pretty apropos. I ought to check my own retrieval. Oh, who was I kidding? I didn't need to check—I was flat out of spring.

"Then the brakes," I said. "Are they hydraulic, power assist, air? Is there an antiskid device? Two-wheel or four?"

I worked through the initial exam as I spoke, clicking away with my digital camera, making sure I got clear shots.

"Wheel-brake assembly. Caliper movement, disc runout, drum service…" It took us an hour to get from the master cylinder to the pedal reserve. "Frame and doors. Exhaust system. AC. Horn—"

"Horn?" He was leaning against a gutted van, his skinny legs under his big gut. "You honk it?"

"Honk the horns that still will honk," I said. A Leonard Cohen paraphrase. *Ring the bells that still will ring. Forget your perfect offering. There is a crack in everything. It's how the light gets in.* Apropos again— I hoped. But probably wasted on Cowan.

"And if it won't honk?" he asked.

"Check the switch type—ring, button, shroud or spoke. Horn type—electrical, vacuum, air. Condition. Audibility. Then—"I ran down the list: Lights. Power train. Reflectors. Safety equipment. Windshield and windows. Suspension. "And the all-important steering."

"I know steering," he said. "I'm the kingpin of steering."

Funny. I gave him a look. "They teach you that in Accident Reconstruction class?"

"No, my puns are all original."

"You must be proud. All right, so we're almost done. Defrosters and speedometer and windshield wipers. And I always save the best for last."

"Tires."

"You got it." I smiled, remembering. "A bunch of the guys had this band, when I was with Highway Patrol in California. Called it Lugs, Seals and Rims. They wanted me to join so they'd have someone to wear a little black dress."

Cowan eyed me up and down, trying to picture me in the dress, I guess. "Did you do it?"

I shook my head. It seemed like a lifetime ago. "They wouldn't pay for the dress. I found a Helmut Lang that looked good, too, but they wouldn't shell out, and I wasn't going on stage in some cheap-ass Gap."

"Sure, Helmet Lang," Cowan said. He consulted his notebook. "For tires, I get serial number, sidewall type, load capacity, pressure, tread type—"

I considered explaining Helmut Lang to him, but decided against it. "Right. And you've got to determine if damage occurred before, during or after the accident. Half the time a driver says a blowout swerved him into the other lane, he's lying. His tire got popped because he hit the other vehicle, not the other way around."

Cowan made another note.

"Okay, we're finally ready to start," I said. "Damage inspection. First, the tires."

I measured the treads, duplicating work that Cowan had already done. He managed not to say *I told you so* when they matched.

"That's the skid that drove off the roadway." Cowan checked the file. "Made that furrow, then the driver recovered control sufficient to regain the roadway."

"Looks like," I said, and continued the inspection. Front right tire showed sidewall scrubbing, caused when the vehicle slid sideways and the sidewall got tucked under the rim. I pointed it out to Cowan. "More evidence the car slid to the right."

"Which means what?" Cowan asked. "She was either impacted on the left side—which she wasn't, 'cause there's no paint transfer—or she'd been in a hard enough rightward skid to fold the sidewall, huh?"

I didn't like hearing there was no paint transfer before I checked it myself, but I couldn't imagine he'd miss it. I nodded. "And maybe that tire was underinflated."

I snapped three pictures of the scrubbing and moved on. The hood, grille and front fender showed massive scraping and was deformed inward ten inches. "Not enough for a head-on impact," I told Cowan. "Not at the speed the car was going, based on skid length."

"You already calculated the minimum speed?" he asked. You

could do it based on skid length and drag factor and vehicle and roadway.

"Not yet. But my guess is she wasn't going more than forty. The skids will show a minimum of, oh, around thirty-one or two. No paint transfer on front, either. Point match for the scraped boulder, though."

I moved to the right side and found it scarred and scraped. No paint transfer and no frame damage. But there was one long scrape I should be able to match to a tree or rock on-site.

On the left side, there was a thick band of scrape marks that ran along the top half of the car. It must have flipped to that side and slid for some distance. The rearview mirror had been shorn off.

The hood and roof showed some metal folding, induced when the front smashed the boulder. There was some contact damage on the hood from hitting the water, but that was it. The car hadn't slid on the roof.

There was one impressive impact scar on the windshield, caused no doubt by Jody Hulfinger's head, although the blood and tissue had been washed away. I forced my brain not to replay the image in my head—in my imagination the blood and tissue were still there, like a horror movie.

The tempered glass of the left front window was shattered; most of it lost in the sea, some lodged in Hulfinger's face and neck for the M.E. to find. The right front window had been open during the crash. The left rear was shattered and the right rear intact but showing stress fractures.

Last stop: the undercarriage. There were marks from the crane, some scrapes, but no gouges. I didn't expect any; there weren't any on the scene associated with skid number one. Not finding what I shouldn't was almost as good as finding what I should.

"Okay. We're done," I said.

"That was it?" Cowan asked.

"No way. That was just the first round." I wiped my dirty hands on my pants—I always wore gray or black suits for this reason. My heart was beating fast and I was surprised by how easily the skills came back to me. And how much I enjoyed it. I grinned at him. "Now comes the good part. We start to understand what happened."

She swiveled in her chair and stared out her office window. It was a sunny morning; might as well have been dark.

The so-called investigator had not been removed for assaulting her fellow officer. Instead, she'd been assigned a new driver to help inspect the girl's car. They'd poke into the innards, extract the fluids and weigh the organs.

The Principal's Daughter watched the shadows of clouds glide over the sunlit grass and felt her jaw clench. She was unable to monitor Ashbury's reconstruction at the Belfast Impoundment Yard, and she did not like what she couldn't see.

Which was why she took her research seriously. She'd downloaded a photograph of Ashbury, attached to one of several magazine puff pieces about the inspector's act of courage. The article itself was colorful and unenlightening. But she did learn one thing. At least before her accident, Ashbury had been physically brave. The easiest kind of bravery. A purely physical threat to Ashbury would not only be obvious, but counterproductive.

She spun back to her desk. So many men, and only a handful who might be useful. She found the number she wanted and dialed.

"Yuh," was how Sol O'Keefee answered his phone.

"Han," she said. That's what they called him, on account of his name: *Sol O.* "Han" Sol O. She identified herself—misidentified herself—as a woman on staff, and asked after his wife.

"You'd know better'n me," he said.

"As good as can be expected," she said. "For now. Are you available for a short job?"

He pretended he didn't know what she meant.

She impressed upon him that he did.

"Fuck no," he said, after she explained her requirements. "No fucking way."

The conclusion was foregone; she only had to explain why that was so. In two minutes, he'd agreed to do the job. "Could be sugar in the gas tank," he said. "Even if they trace it, it looks like a juvie prank."

And probably not fatal. Excellent. All she wanted was to spark another of Ashbury's outbursts.

"Where am I supposed to meet this car?" he asked.

"The Belfast Impoundment Yard," she said. "Get it done today."

"Belfast? Shit, that's a two-hour drive."

"So leave now."

I squatted a foot from the shattered right headlight of the Jetta and ran my fingers over the ruined grille. What was the external damage telling me?

I ran down the big five in my head: light, weather, road, vehicle, driver. All told, that included glare, darkness, rain, ice, potholes, gravel, traffic and flaws both mechanical and human. But it was too early to tell *why* it happened. Only question I could halfway answer now was: *what happened?*

Hulfinger had been driving; she slammed on the brakes, went into a skid, digging a furrow. The car flipped to the side and slid until the grille smashed a boulder, then cartwheeled ass over headlight, coming down hard on the left side without touching the roof. But no, it must've spun in the air and come down on the other side, facing the same direction. Convoluted, but I'd seen stranger things. Then the car pivoted off the breakwater rocks or the tree stump—whatever the left side had impacted—and landed in the water on its roof.

"Damage on both sides, but not the roof," Cowan said. "Wasn't for the absence of paint transfer, I'd say it was at least a two-car."

"Not unprecedented for a single-car to show this kind of damage. But me, too." And it worried me. I went over the whole car again. Inch by inch. Looking for the smallest paint flake. The slightest smear. I even asked Cowan to back me up, give me a second pair of eyes. An hour later, we found what looked like grind from the boulders and bark from the trees—and a bunch of dead sea bugs that had to be amphipods—but no paint, no bumper smear, nothing to indicate a second car.

I stepped back, confused. Time for a different tactic. I reached down next to the driver's seat and popped the trunk. Inside was a jug of antifreeze, a bag of saturated potting soil, a bicycle helmet, a paddle, a mound of soggy pamphlets, some textbooks and a hefty roll of black plastic—four feet wide, like a hugely oversize roll of plastic paper towel.

I took three photos, before fiddling with the contents. "Any idea what this is?" I asked Cowan, gesturing to the roll of plastic.

"A roll of plastic," he said.

I grunted. "Gimme a hand with it."

Wedged underneath were a dozen wooden stakes, four feet tall with blazed orange tops. I took another picture.

"And those," he said, "are stakes."

"Think she used them to stake the plastic?"

"Nah. They're markers, like if you have rocks in your field you want to mow around. Can't imagine she did much mowing, but—" he indicated the bicycle helmet and paddle "—suppose it could be a kayaking thing."

Ah. Not a bike helmet, a kayak helmet. "What kind of kayaking thing?"

"No idea."

The headline on one of the pamphlets read Nonviolent Action Training! and it made me wonder: "Maybe it was for a demonstration. Like a roadblock. String the plastic across the road, attached to the stakes on either end."

"Could be." Cowan looked unimpressed.

I couldn't blame him. I was pretty unimpressed, myself. I thought about it a moment longer, decided I had no clue and closed the trunk firmly.

"What next?" Cowan asked.

"Lamps. Check it wasn't due to impaired vision, see what time the accident occurred."

I moved to the front of the vehicle and knelt in front of the shattered left headlight. There was only a fragment of the lamp left, a centimeter shard of the bulb and base. No filament. I noted the trade number and manufacturer and checked the contact and lug pin. The other bulb was in the FBI or MSP evidence bag. Damn. I should've had all the evidence the ground crew collected delivered here. If I hadn't been so worried about that fifteen-minute car ride I would've—

"Looking for this?" Cowan produced a labeled film canister. The other bulb. "Thought you might want it while you did the car."

"Ah! You're a prince."

He yanked on his belt in satisfaction. "You know it."

Bulb filament could tell a story. Bulb filament was better than a lie detector.

A filament break that occurred when the lamp was not incandescent was called cold shock. Meant there was no current running, the lights weren't on at the time of impact, despite what anybody said. Hot shock indicated the opposite—that current was flowing and the bulb was on.

Hulfinger's left front bulb showed hot shock. The high-beam filaments, which meant her brights had been on. So, presumably, it was nighttime. And presumably there was no traffic—unless Jody was fairly rude or habitually rode with her brights on, which I would check.

I took four photos; one from each direction. Checked the position of the headlight switch: on. Checked the taillights and side lights but they didn't tell me much. What I really needed was to speak with someone who knew the car—and how Jody Hulfinger drove it—before the accident.

"Did you track down her mechanic?" I asked Cowan.

"She didn't have one," he said. "Took it to whoever when it broke."

"How about someone who'd know how she drove?"

"She didn't drive much. Didn't log two thousand miles a year. Last couple weeks before she disappeared, though, she was taking the car out a lot. Van Huut said she'd gotten interested in kayaking. She'd drive to the rental place, go out for the day."

"That's how you knew it was a kayak helmet?"

"Plus it says KayakSports on it."

Oh. "She always drove by herself?"

"That's what I hear."

Frustrating. Who could I ask about Jody's driving if she never took a passenger?

"Except one time," Cowan continued. "Day before she disappeared, she took her sister's boyfriend."

"Sea kayaking?" Then I remembered. "You mean, the suspect?"

He nodded. "Not kayaking—just for a drive."

"I'll need to talk to him."

"He's not going anywhere. You done here?"

"Wish I was." Because there was still the interior.

The interior. Every significant vehicular accident consisted of a minimum of two collisions. The first was the vehicle colliding with whatever it hit. The second was the occupant colliding with the interior of the vehicle.

You traced the second the same way you did the first. Except you were looking for tissue smear, blood splatter, shoe polish, clothing transfer, strands of hair...

In this case, blood splatter and tissue smear were easy; after two weeks in the water with the fish and lobster and sea roaches, there were none. It made figuring out what happened more difficult, but I was grateful not to have to face the blood.

Instead, I ran my fingers along the moldings, seats and cushions and doors, feeling for indentations where Hulfinger might have impacted. I looked for any windshield bulge I might have missed from the exterior and checked for instrument panel and sun visor damage. Then I examined the lap and shoulder belt, the steering assembly, the hood release and parking brake and the headrest and didn't learn much.

I took a deep breath and said, "Okay."

"What's that?" Cowan asked.

I ignored him, because I didn't want to voice what I had to do. I pulled a small blue plastic tarp from my bag and unfolded it, laid it on the driver's seat and lowered myself into the car. And suppressing a shiver from sitting on the ghost of a dead woman, I let myself go.

I was Jody Hulfinger. Driving along the Sears Island Causeway. Everything is fine. Then, in less than a minute, I smash my head against the windshield, glass shards are embedded in the left side of my face, I take a blow to the jaw that almost severs it from my body, smash the steering column, crack my face against the windshield, and get flung left and right in the overturning car....

I righted myself in the seat. So what happened first? She slammed the brakes. Why? She was afraid. Of what? Maybe the engine made a grinding noise. Or she felt a stabbing pain in her head. Or there was a moose, or a squirrel. There was just no way to tell yet, except...

I shook my head. No, I was missing something. I made myself relax into the seat, ignoring what I knew had been there before—what I could still smell on the upholstery, mixed with the seawater and the mildew.

I was driving down the causeway. High beams on. Going where? Good question. Going somewhere, then slamming on the brakes and skidding, digging a furrow, frantically steering—

A woman's voice interrupted me. "I'm looking for Brigid Ashbury."

"She's in the driver's seat," Cowan said. "In more ways than one."

I came back to myself. Stepped out of the car before the woman could see me sitting there with glazed eyes. She was about my age, early thirties, and maybe an inch shorter, five-eight. She had an angular, almost hatchet face—with extremely unfortunate flyaway mouse-colored hair and unfriendly eyes.

"I'm Noreen Wash. IIC Udall sent me. I'm your new driver."

"I don't need a driver," I lied.

Wash didn't quite sneer. "You're going to walk to Portland?"

"Portland?"

"You haven't heard?" Wash said. "The prints on the note? They matched the last passenger—"

"The sister's boyfriend."

"The arrest didn't take. He walks this afternoon. Van Huut asked State to let you talk to him."

"This afternoon?" I heard the tremor in my voice and hated myself for it. "Why can't we meet up here?"

The woman didn't say anything.

"Why can't— I'll prep Cowan. Why can't I send him down?"

"Christ," Wash said. "How about because you're the lead investigator and you're a professional?"

"I'm a civilian." And I'm falling apart, you skank-haired bitch.

"You *used* to be a professional."

"Used to be a Girl Scout, too, but I don't sell fucking cookies anymore."

Cowan colored and muttered something placating, like a man does when women argue. We both ignored him.

"Theresa said you might fold," Wash said.

"Is that what she said?"

"She said you were the best investigator she ever saw—as if that gives you the right to attack Len—but you've got some issues with traffic. Which is like an agoraphobic airline pilot, for chrissake." She looked away, as if I was beneath her notice. "Get over it or get a new job."

"She tell you to drive me, or lecture me?"

That brought Wash's attention back. "I told her maybe splitting Len's lip was your way of saying goodbye. She said until she heard it from you, she'd presume you were still on. But if you folded, you folded." She stared at me, considering. "Two days at the outside. That's my guess."

What the hell brought this on? I could only think of one reason. Something about the way the woman said *Len*. "What do you do? Stare all misty-eyed from across the office and hope he notices you?"

Wash paled, and I immediately regretted saying it. I regretted everything: my phobia, hitting Len, failing at my job. But if I apologized to Wash, I'd only make it worse.

It took a minute for her to regain her composure, and when she did her eyes cut into me. "I'll drive you," Wash said. "But if you touch me, Ashbury, it's assault."

The Principal's Daughter kicked her shoes off under her desk and flexed her toes in satisfaction. She couldn't believe she'd done it—that it had gone so seamlessly. But it had.

"Sugar in the gas tank?" she'd asked when she got Han on the phone.

"Nah. Something a little different."

"It'll work? Your wife hopes it'll work."

"It'll fucking work. Easy as popping the hood and making a few score marks."

"And the...defect will become apparent between Belfast and Portland?"

"Ain't rocket science. Somewhere between halfway there and halfway back."

"Just as long as it happens."

"When it does, I won't hear from you again, will I?" Some tenuous bravado in his voice.

"Not unless I call you." She liked how that sounded. Confident. Active, not passive. She hung up.

Wash drove with one hand.

She asked me some pointed questions, which didn't bother me. But she looked at me—and away from the road—when she asked them, which made me cringe. Cringe more. Cringe until the skin on my face grew tight, stretched to the breaking point.

Wash took her other hand off the wheel to gesture, to emphasize some point in a monologue I hadn't been tracking. It was intentional. The fucking woman with her nasty-ass hair and her one fucking hand on the wheel and her—

A truck horn blew ten feet away.

When Detective Trake entered the interrogation room, Aaron greeted him with a smile, pleased with the company. He'd been waiting two hours.

"So where's this investigator?" he asked.

Trake pulled out the chair opposite and settled in. "You understand you're free to leave?"

Aaron nodded. He was still willing to wait if it would help Jody.

"Good. Then I was wondering—how's the hand?"

There was no reason for Aaron to pretend he didn't understand. It was the hand he broke while getting his juvenile record. A sordid tale—always more fun when you're not one of the main characters.

It had happened when he was in high school. He and his mother had lived on Bissel Street. Next street over was Spring, and off Spring was a little cul-de-sac called Fairweather. She'd lived on Fairweather, in a split-level ranch. Mrs. Polk. Louisa. She was twenty-five and radiated sophistication, at least when it came to sex. She made Aaron weak-kneed and willing. In retrospect, he was lucky he'd gotten away with only a broken hand, not a featured story on *Extra* and a broken life.

She hadn't been some blond, husky-voiced *femme fatale*. She was dark and angry-looking and collected Lladró figurines and Beanie Babies. But she had *it*. Aaron hadn't known what hit him. He hadn't cared.

Her husband was ten years older. He worked in an office. His first name was Patrick. That was all Aaron knew about him. Until, in true soap-opera fashion, he came home early one afternoon.

Aaron left.

Patrick stayed.

But Aaron was young—he'd crept to the side of the house and

peered through a window. It was ugly. This was before he'd ever heard the phrase *marital rape*. His memory is that he stood there, face pressed to glass, unable to move. It'd felt like an hour, but probably wasn't more than a minute. He remembered the sensation clearly—his stomach went numb and frozen, as if he'd swallowed a pitcher of ice water.

Then he broke two bones in his right hand against Patrick's forehead.

They'd arrested him, although the more serious charges were later dropped. Charges against him, that is. There were no charges against Patrick. Aaron had ended up doing a hundred hours of community service. For trespassing.

There. His darkest secret.

And hardly a secret at all, apparently. He fluttered his fingers at Detective Trake. "The hand is as good as new."

"Still have that temper problem?"

"You saw my record."

"I'm not asking about your record, I'm asking about your temper."

He considered leaving or calling back his lawyer, Meredith. But he was bored. So he told the truth. He didn't have a temper problem. He'd lost it exactly once in his life—and it landed him a broken hand and a hundred hours in an orange vest.

Aaron had been in situations, one or two, that might've called for him to lose it. But he never had. Not since Louisa. Not since his first love, at fifteen years old. He told Trake the truth, and Trake seemed satisfied.

"You need anything?" the detective asked, as he rose to leave.

"Still waiting for that tea," Aaron said.

"Brigid Ashbury," I said. "To speak with Aaron White. He's being held for me."

The Cumberland County Jail was just off Hwy 295 in Portland, Maine's largest city. It was a two-story brick complex that could be mistaken for nothing but a jail. Wash had dropped me off—and had sped violently away—over an hour ago. I spent the hour in the bathroom of the café across the street. Nothing like ruminating in a public restroom to make you wonder where you've gone wrong in your life. But it had taken me that long to recover—or nearly recover—from the two-hour car ride.

A gray-haired man in a rumpled blue suit came to meet me and introduced himself as Detective Trake. "You'll want to speak to Agent Dellgarda first," he said.

"Why? Did Agent Dellgarda go for a drive with Hulfinger, too?"

It came out harsher than I'd intended; maybe an hour in the bathroom hadn't been enough.

Trake paused, as if he was silently counting to five. "No, because you're a civilian attached to the feds. She's a fed. Far as I'm concerned, you're on their chart somewhere, let them figure out exactly where."

I forced a smile. "Good point. Maybe once they know, they'll tell me."

"Anyway, it's no glamour assignment." Agent Dellgarda looked like one of those troll dolls kids used to play with. Five-two and portly, with short hair that stuck almost straight up. "FBI in Maine. Couldn't be happier, though. It's home."

"It's a lovely state." I was still on my best behavior, trying to demonstrate, at least to myself, that I wasn't folding, wasn't finished, wasn't paralytic with fear. "Where's White from?"

"Massachusetts, mostly."

"Yeah? I was born in Boston, myself."

"I think Aaron—White—lived in western Mass. You're gonna like him." Dellgarda stopped at a framed picture of the Academy Class of 1997 hanging on the wall and floofed her hair in the reflection. Was she primping for White? "He's a piece of work."

"I'm not sure I understand."

"Looks as if he had nothing to do with this, even though we got his print on the note," Dellgarda said. "And turns out there's something in his file."

"Yeah?"

"Juvenile, so it's sealed, but some phone calls were made. About fifteen years ago, he was up on assault. And you hear about the witness?"

"To what?"

"Gayle Cornell, Stanwood Hulfinger's girlfriend. She saw him leading Jody to her car the day she disappeared. Said something looked funny."

"Like he forced her into the car?"

"Yeah. Except it was the day *before* Jody disappeared. Which he said all along." Dellgarda half smiled. "And the idea of him forcing a woman into a car..."

"Wouldn't be the first time?"

Dellgarda smiled. It was an appealing smile that seemed to change her looks. "Wait till you meet him," Dellgarda said. "Anyway, we track him to a B and B outside Portland. State Tac Team did a knock-and-enter with me being FBI presence. Rammed the door and we're inside in three seconds." She shook her head. "There he is, sitting on the balcony, sipping from a mug. Two of the tac guys are four feet away, fingers on the trigger. Aaron—White—doesn't even flinch. He says, 'Can I finish my cocoa?'"

She waited for a response, so I said, "Can I finish my cocoa?"

"Yeah. He says, 'You think the Swiss call it American Miss, like the French call them American Fries?'"

"The French call them *pomme frit*," I said, mostly because I had no idea where she was going with this.

Dellgarda snorted. "Anyway, the guys are freaking out—you know?"

Of course I knew. I'd been a cop. Nothing worse than a suspect not following the script. It was scary as hell unless everyone did exactly what you expected—then it was still scary as hell. "So what happened?"

"So he puts the mug down and they cuff him, but the thing is... I didn't mention, he's only wearing his boxer shorts this whole time." Dellgarda gave me a look I rarely saw on a woman. "Anyway, one of the guys grabs him a pair of pants and a shirt from his bag. White tells the guy, 'No, not that shirt with those pants. You wear plaid with stripes? Who dresses you?' he says. 'Your dog?' But it's clear he's kidding around, so the guy—this is the good part—holds up shirts until White approves one."

"You're kidding."

"Boys will be boys." Dellgarda shook her head. "So we bring him in, but he wants his lawyer present. Detective Trake asks me, will I talk to him? Because I'm a woman."

I looked at her. Nice personality and a cute smile, but there was no denying she was a troll doll. How hard up was this guy?

"I know what you're thinking." Dellgarda flushed, and for the second time that day I felt like a deeply shitty person. "But Trake said...you ever hear of Alton Mistle?"

I shook my head.

"He's one of those kids you read about. Had an affair with his eighth-grade teacher, she got him to shoot her husband. He goes up. Four years later, he marries a woman guard. She gets fired, he's transferred to another facility. Three years after that, another woman guard dresses him up in a uniform and escorts him out the prison. Said she felt sorry for him. He was dopey-looking, too," the agent said. "Like Elmer Fudd."

"What's the connection with White?" I asked. "He looks like Daffy Duck?"

"He's a smart guy, Trake." Dellgarda shrugged. "He said there was something about White that reminded him of Mistle. Said if I interviewed Aaron, he'd open up. And he did." Dellgarda glanced at me, apparently taking in my DKNY suit and size-ten figure I could never, no matter how little I ate, cut down to a size eight. "The way you look, he'll confess."

When we opened the door, Aaron White was sitting at a gray metal table, in a hard-backed chair. With one arm over the back, he gave the impression that he was reclining. An easy smile appeared on his face when he saw Dellgarda.

He was wearing a charcoal-gray long-sleeved V-necked T-shirt that was just tight enough to see he was fit beneath it. It brought out the color in his eyes, too: light baby-blue. Aside from the eyes, he wasn't as handsome as I'd expected from Dellgarda's description. Lanky build. Nice shoulders. But an average face under his tousled dark brown hair—so perfectly mussed I figured it had been expensively cut. I couldn't see his pants, and found myself wanting to after Dellgarda's story.

"Titania," Aaron said, and stood. He looked at Dellgarda with a sort of directness that could be threatening, but wasn't. "Any word on the tea front?"

I moved farther into the room and my eyes flicked downward. Olive cords. I wondered briefly what color shirt didn't go, then realized: It would have been light blue. It'd match his eyes, but clash with the pants.

"Mr. White," Dellgarda said. "This is Inspector Ashbury. She's an accident reconstructionist. She wants to ask you a few questions about the drive you took with Jody."

"Inspector Ashbury." His voice was the clincher. Deep, but not too deep, smooth and calm, as easy as his smile. He stood and held out his hand. "I'll do whatever I can to help."

"Good," I said, my own voice clipped. I shook his hand. It was warm and firm and I found myself responding to him, wanting him to like me. It'd been a long time since I'd felt that way about anyone, but I shut it down. There was no place for it in an investigation. "Sit."

From the glint in his eyes, he understood exactly what was happening. But he sat, looking into my face as if he found me fascinating. I forced myself not to respond and thought of my friend who'd been ten years on the Fraud Squad. He'd told me the key to a good con operator was not that he came across trustworthy. It was that he came across trusting. He didn't take trust, he gave it. Hard to defend against someone trusting you. Aaron White would've made a terrific grifter.

It made me want to prove him wrong, to somehow betray him, show him I wasn't worth trusting...but that was bullshit. I wasn't going to play his game. I wasn't out for approval or disapproval—the way my life was going, at least that much was clear. I sat down across from White and stared for a long moment. Telling him with my expression that I didn't care one way or another whether he found me attractive or not.

Still, they were eyes to die for.

The tea never came. Instead, Aaron got Inspector Ashbury. She was a tall woman, maybe five-nine or -ten, who held herself gracefully. As if she'd been raised by a governess who made her walk with a book on her head. He knew better than to stare, but he couldn't help noticing her figure. It reminded him of Jennifer Lopez. In Aaron's experience most white women thought Jennifer Lopez was fat. Brigid Ashbury seemed no exception. She dressed to minimize, though when she walked toward him, he noticed her hips swayed side to side. He liked her auburn hair and her hazel-brown eyes and the deep lovely crow's-feet, at the edges.

Women—Aaron hated to generalize, but thought the multibillion-dollar beauty industry would back him up—go to about any length to hide what they think of as blemishes. Wrinkles, crow's-feet, double chins, bushy eyebrows. Big noses, small noses, average noses. He had a friend once who thought she had ugly wrists. She was ashamed of them. Of her *wrists*.

Inspector Ashbury had tried to cover up those crow's-feet and make her figure something it wasn't. She had a pretty, smart face—a well-preserved fortysomething. There was something about her eyes, though. A look that was vulnerable, almost wounded. He looked deeper, and the look was gone, and he got nothing back except the impression she'd give nothing back.

"You were the last person to ride in her car," she said. "The only person, as far as we know, in the several weeks preceding the accident. I'm going to ask you a few questions about her driving and the state of the car."

He nodded.

"You drove with her in the late afternoon. Did she use her head-lights?"

"No, it was still light."

"You're sure?"

"Yes. No. Pretty sure." He thought back. "I think I'd have noticed if she put them on, because she didn't need to."

"It was a warm day?"

"Yes."

"She use the AC?"

"The car doesn't have one." But the Inspector would know that. "We rolled down the windows."

"Which ones?"

"The front two, I guess." He tried to remember, couldn't get much beyond Jody's warm and intense presence in the driver's seat. "Um, the driver's side was halfway down, I think. Yeah. And she wanted it cooler, so I opened mine."

"What kind of driver was she?"

"Not so bad that I noticed."

She nodded. "Was there anything wrong with the car? Noises, tremors or shuddering, anything?"

"No." He tried to remember. "No."

"She say anything about it?"

"The car? I don't even remember what it was. A Rabbit?"

"A Jetta." She asked if Jody drove with both hands or one, if she leaned her left arm out the window, if she braked with the pedal or the clutch. She asked if he'd noticed the tires, if he thought Jody was acting normally, how well the radio worked. She asked about the windshield wipers and if he'd smelled anything funny, and on and on.

"I'm sorry," he said, when it looked as if she was winding down. "I wish I could be more help."

"You can. Where'd the two of you drive to?"

"Oh—" he waved a vague hand "—around."

She pressed it, but he didn't say more than Jody wanted to talk, which she kinda had. And that she'd had a fight with her father, which he gathered wasn't the rarest of occurrences at casa Hulfinger.

"What was the fight about?"

"I'm not sure."

She tapped her pen a couple times against her pad. Waited. Clicked the pen and waited some more. He got uncomfortable, which he guessed was the point. He was about to snap when he noticed her hands. They were faintly scarred, with several patches of too-smooth skin where the scars had healed. Looked like burn marks. But they didn't seem to bother her. Those blemishes she didn't try to hide.

She was younger than he'd first thought. Early thirties. The fear and tension—the sense that something inside her was torqued—made her appear older. He wondered if it was because of whatever had caused those scars.

She broke the silence. "You're not sure. You drove around talking, but you don't know why she was upset?"

Good point. "She didn't like the way her father ran his company."

Ashbury made a note on her pad. "I listened to the tapes. Of your interrogation."

Aaron didn't know what to say: "Oh."

"That story about the Confederate flag. That's true?"

"Catie said it was."

"You don't like her father, do you?"

"I like everybody."

She gave him the look.

"Not much," he said.

She asked for a rundown on the Hulfingers, and he told her he didn't know more than he told Titania.

She glanced to the door, as if she was making sure Titania wasn't still in the room.

"Calling her Titania," she said. "You being cruel, or only manipulative?"

It was the first human thing she'd said to him.

"What?" he said. "What?"

"Forget it."

"Her face. She looks sort of…elfin. Like a pixie."

She stared at him for a moment, then gathered her papers.

"Guess I haven't been a lot of help, huh?"

"No," she said.

I hesitated on the sidewalk outside the jail.

Noreen Wash wouldn't be picking me up. I could call a taxi…but letting a cabbie drive your car is like letting a butcher perform your open-heart surgery. I had a case once where a taxi had—

But no. Dr. Kugelmeyer said I had to stop doing that to myself. Stop replaying death scenarios every time I thought of a car model. The ones I made up seeing random reckless drivers on the street were bad enough.

I could call Theresa. I could call Ralph. I could call Cowan. No, no and no. I wasn't going to drag my professional life down with my psychological life. I would keep these things entirely separate: my fears and my abilities. I had a job, and I always did my job.

Except once. Except that last case.

But this wasn't like that. I would get back on that horse. Something was wrong about this accident. I didn't know what, but I was going to find out. For Jody Hulfinger.

For me.

A handful of cops walked past. I pretended I was comfortably waiting for a ride. Maybe I could charter a flight. Sure, from Portland to Searsport, with fifteen minute's notice.

I looked at the café across the street. Maybe I'd live in the bathroom.

"Hey, Inspector." The voice was deep and smooth and amused. "Wanna ride?"

I'd tagged him for a BMW. Maybe a Porsche SUV, or—if he wasn't afraid of looking middle-aged—a Lexus. I turned to find Aaron White sitting behind the wheel of a green Subaru Outback.

"No, thank you," I said.

On my list of people I wasn't gonna let see me fall apart, a guy like him would always make the top five. Even if he only drove a Subaru.

"C'mon," he said. "I'm a free man. The fatted calf awaits my triumphal return, and you're headed my way. Back to Camden, right?"

Top five after Ralph. And Theresa. And an unknown cabbie. But who else was there? Ganapi was gone. Wash was gone. There was still Cowan. I should have called him a half hour ago. Except he'd be going over the debris the evidence team collected. And following up with the fire pit and the onion rings. Talk about unprofessional—I wasn't about to ask him to leave work to chauffeur me around like a soccer mom.

"Or Belfast?" White asked.

"Searsport. And I have a ride," I said.

"Liar."

I stared. Who was he to call me a liar? Even if it was true, he was a ringworm for saying it. Rude as hell, and a guy like that never apologized.

"Hey, I'm sorry," he said. "I apologize. And you *do* have a ride. I'm a free man, I can drive whomever I want, wherever I want, and—"

The way he drove Jody Hulfinger on their mysterious outing.

He must've seen it in my face. "I didn't drive Jody anywhere."

I watched him, giving him room to continue talking.

"I liked Jody. She was—she was the kind of person..." He became still, as if that would let me weigh his words more precisely. "She left things better than she found them."

It took me a moment to realize he was finished speaking, that was the extent of his eulogy. *She was the kind of person who left things better than she found them.* I don't know—it sounded pretty okay. More than anyone could say about me.

His eyes were guileless, and I became even more suspicious. But hadn't I just wished for a driver not connected to my professional life? One ride. I could do it—I had to. Besides, he had information I wanted.

"How's your record?" I asked.

"That's supposed to be sealed," he said, but not as if he cared. "Juvenile records—where do they seal them, front page of the *Times?*"

"Your *driving* record."

"Oh." He laughed, then caught the expression on my face and sobered. "I've never been in an accident, Inspector, and I'm not going to start today."

I strapped myself in, my heart beating too fast. Felt as if it was bruising itself against my ribs.

White reached for the radio. He was gonna turn it on. I knew he was. I couldn't take it. Music in the car? It would distract him, distract me. Distract my awareness of the traffic, the car, the road. I was terrified that if I couldn't see the accident coming, I wouldn't be able to stop it. Magical thinking, but the extra noise would—

He ejected a CD. Glanced at me, but didn't say anything. He did not turn the radio on, but put the car into First and drove.

Thirty seconds was all it took for me to start hyperventilating. White was going to start talking. He was going to ask me what was wrong. And I'd be cool. I'd say something along the lines of: "You're a manipulative, self-impressed ringworm, watch out for the traffic, it's merging—you're in an exit lane, slowdownslowdown, trucks are fucking merging toward the Mobil station, *goddammit,* they can't see us, they won't know we're here until they hear the crash, feel the impact...."

But he didn't say a word. He pulled into the Mobil and filled the tank, even though it had been three-quarters full. He wiped the windshields and said he was going inside for a minute.

I waited until he disappeared into the minimart, until I was sure my legs would support me. Then I went inside and found the women's room. I managed not to be sick, which seemed a major triumph, but didn't trust myself to leave. Not yet. Although I was definitely through with public restrooms.

Twenty minutes later, I found White sitting on a bench outside. He glanced at me, and for the first time his eyes were uninterested. He looked unchallenging and incurious—trying to put me at ease.

"I've never heard of an accident reconstructionist."

I had nothing to say to that.

"You ever take those tests," he said. "The career tests they give you in high school? I always got 'middle-management' as my best career path. That and retail sales."

Sure he did.

"You got astronaut, right?" he said. And when I didn't answer: "Or architect. Marine biologist? How'd you get down to Portland?"

Finally, a question I could answer. "I had a driver."

"What happened to him?"

"Her."

"Her, then."

"I told her what I thought of her hair."

That startled a grin out of him. "Bad?"

"Catastrophic."

He cleared his throat. He was going to ask about it. About my problem with cars, with traffic. "Rosemary, right?" he said.

"Excuse me?"

"Your shampoo. Unless it's perfume." He looked at me. "You don't wear perfume. Rosemary shampoo. I smelled it in the car."

"Rosemary-mint." I was impressed, despite myself. Then, uneasy that I was so easily impressed. So, I said, "You get a lot of women that way? Telling them what shampoo they use? It's a pretty good line."

* * *

A pretty good line. How good could it be? It wasn't working on Inspector Ashbury. He didn't even know her first name.

Aaron had found a raccoon once, when he was a kid, that had been run over. It was a mess, its hind legs twitching, a pool of blood under its mouth. But it was alive, the miserable huddled thing. He was gonna put it in a box with a blanket and a saucer of milk, have his mom nurse it back to health. Instead, it took a pretty good-size chunk out of his arm. Inspector Ashbury reminded him of that raccoon.

"That's not my best line," he said. "You wanna hear my best line?"

"Not particularly."

When you've stepped in quicksand, they say the worst thing to do is struggle. So he waited.

She eventually sighed. "Okay, tell me."

"What's your name? Your first name?"

She hesitated, then shrugged. "Brigid."

"Brigid." He leaned back. "Pretty painless, huh?"

"*What's your name* is your best line? Stick with the shampoo, Mr. White."

"Aaron."

"Mr. White, let me tell you my line. You drove around. You and Jody." She caught him with her gaze. "Then you had sex with her."

Wasn't the faintest hint of a question.

"I'm seeing her sister," he said.

She gave him that same look Dellgarda had, only hers was harder. "You're afraid it'll get back to Cate?"

He looked at her. There was something about her. He didn't

know——something that said she was hurt and she knew she was hurt but she had no self-pity. The raccoon, again. But he thought he could trust her. He crossed his fingers that this time he wouldn't need a rabies shot.

"Not really," he said. "It's not that kind of relationship."

"You have a——what——an open relationship?"

"We've been seeing each other three months. It's not like I asked her to wait for me to return from the war." He didn't mention the whole "living together" thing.

"Then why say——? Forget it. Question is, why lie about your drive?"

"I didn't lie. But… Jody wouldn't want to hurt Cate's feelings."

"She fucked her boyfriend."

Was she trying to shock him with her language? "It wasn't like that——"

She held a hand up. "Where?"

"A clearing in the woods. Ten minutes from her house."

"The day before she disappeared?"

"Yeah. Jody said she'd always wanted to, but…she was shy about it being outdoors. Funny, because she was fearless in every other way."

Ashbury looked toward the gas pumps. "So the day before she disappeared, she finally got the courage, huh?"

He didn't follow, and he told her so.

"We have to get back," she said. She stood and walked to the car. He liked the way she moved under her suit. And if he hadn't been watching, he might've missed how she steeled herself to open the car door.

* * *

I caught myself biting at a hangnail and forced my hand back to my lap.

White drove okay. He kept quiet, and he'd stopped twice more, saying he needed to stretch his legs, which gave me time to collect myself. He was doing it for me, I knew, but doing it with no affect, so flatly that all I had to do was be relieved.

But I could tell, each time we stopped, that he was measuring my weaknesses. He remained cool and unthreatening as he dispassionately graphed the fault lines that ran through my life. It was worth it for the good information: Jody Hulfinger wanting one final screw in the woods. It made me think suicide was an option. Jody's last hurrah.

I still didn't know how it'd work, though. Especially with the kidnap note. Plus the skid marks would show Hulfinger wasn't driving that fast, while most suicides tended to overestimate the speed at which a car crash became fatal. And why did she brake? If she was set on killing herself, why—

A siren sounded behind us. The ululating whine of an ambulance stopping my heart.

White slowed, glancing in the rearview mirror. The siren crept up and I felt pain in my knee where I was digging my nails into skin. I tried to relax my hand, and couldn't, as if it wasn't a part of me. An arterial-red Suzuki Sidekick swung in from the left lane, ten feet in front of us, and White braked slightly, and I saw it all before it happened with a piercing clarity:

The Sidekick braking hard—White swerving to avoid it—and locking up, skidding into the ambulance. The Subaru tapping the Sidekick's back end, almost gently; spinning once, twice, three times. A door shooting open, a scream—and the '79 Mack Superliner that'd been on our ass for twenty miles grinding us into the asphalt, smearing us over twenty yards of broken glass.

Then the ambulance was past us, and the Sidekick was back in the left lane and nothing had happened. Except to me. I heard ragged breathing and felt the pain in my knee only distantly.

"Brigid," White said.

I didn't even bother turning my head. I didn't know if I could. I simply let vent the fear. It wasn't pretty.

14

Stanwood Hulfinger was a bull of a man. When Van Huut introduced him, Hulfinger put his head down and I thought for one surreal second he was going to charge. Instead, he grabbed my hand and shook it vigorously.

"Walter tells me you're the best, Ms. Ashbury," he said. "Can't tell you how pleased I am to have you—given the nature of the circumstances. This is a terrible thing. No one can know what it's like to lose a daughter. Jody said I was reactionary, sexist—I suppose I'll prove her right, because she always was my little girl."

He came across like a beefy carnival barker, emoting his lines without hearing them, using his girth and volume to indicate the depth of his feeling.

"Mmm," I said, glancing at Van Huut. *Walter?* He looked unembarrassed by Hulfinger's transparent show.

"Here, sit." Hulfinger waved me toward a stool. "Walter tells me you have another round of questions. Would you like a drink?"

We were in what could only be the billiard room. I sat on the stool, feeling like Miss Scarlet confronting Colonel Mustard about the candlestick. "All I want, Mr. Hulfinger, is to ask some questions about your daughter's death."

He didn't exactly flush, but I got the impression he considered retiring the jolly innkeeper and producing the grieving father. "Afraid I've been looking for answers at the bottom of a bottle too long. Oh, and call me Small. Everybody does." He sat across from me. "Shoot."

"Well...*Small*..." and I led him through my standard questions: vehicle condition, driver ability, unusual circumstances. Unsurprisingly, nothing emerged I hadn't heard before. Then I started on some less-standard questions: "Do you have any idea why Jody would have been driving to Sears Island?"

"Not a one. She'd bought a Maine atlas, probably wanted to get reacquainted with the state is my guess. Not that unusual, when we're all at the camp, for her to make herself scarce. She needs— needed to get away, sometimes."

I looked down at my notepad, then back up into Small's eyes. "Is there anyone you can think of who might benefit from Jody's death?"

"It was a car crash, an accident."

"It was a car crash." I didn't say, *not necessarily an accident,* but I saw that he understood.

He studied me. "And the kidnap note?"

"Was written on paper from this house, possibly from her room.

Who had access to the house?" His family, that's who. Same people who might benefit when the girl died, by increasing their share of the inheritance.

"I went over this with the FBI. I'd always intended to leave everything to my children—my three *real* children—no steps. Except Jody would have taken the bequest and torn down what I'd built. We all knew that. She admitted it. So all I left her was a trust, a small one. It's no secret. She was proud, bragged that she'd been cut out of the will. Walter, you knew, didn't you?"

Van Huut nodded. "TJ mentioned it."

"No secret. Besides, she predeceased me."

"May I see the will?"

I finally got a reaction from the man, and it was disbelief. "It lists all my holdings, Ms. Ashbury. I keep it close to the vest."

Fair enough. I was already out on a limb. "And there's no one else who might've...disliked Jody?"

"Jody was my favorite," he said, not answering the question. "Walter tell you that?"

"We haven't spoken about your family."

"A father's not supposed to have a favorite. But Jody—" He shook his head and half smiled. "She was like her mother. Maureen took the train out to San Diego once. This is before we were married. She gets off in Chicago for some fresh air and puts her bags in a locker. One of those where you take the key and drop a coin in when you unlock it. She goes walking around Chicago and sees this woman, with a baby, on the streets. Homeless, a druggie—who knows? It's winter, the woman barely has a coat. Maureen gives her the fur she's wearing and what money she had on her."

He shook his head again, and the smile grew. "When she gets back to the terminal, she doesn't have any money to get her bags out. The train's leaving in five-minutes' time, her bags are locked away, so Maureen had to run around asking strangers for change. Panhandling."

He told the story so fondly that I found myself grinning.

"That day on," Small continued, "anyone with a hard-luck story—they needed money for the bus, their sick grannie—she'd look at me and say, 'I'd still be in Chicago, Small, and by golly, I don't like the wind.' Then she'd give up every cent she carried, except one quarter. 'Course, I never let her carry much.

"Jody's the same. She'd do anything, if she thought it was the right thing. TJ's a good man, don't get me wrong and Cate's gonna turn out okay. Even saw her smile a couple times in the week before…before it happened. You met the White boy? No ambition, but he's a good influence on her. Loosens her up."

I kept my expression neutral—I didn't want to think about that car ride, what I'd just finished saying to "the White boy."

"But Jody, she was something else. Just like her mother. She used to come to stockholder meetings. Jody, I mean. You hear about that?"

I nodded.

"Embarrassed the hell out of me, no denying." He chuckled, and for a moment I thought he might cry. The crack in the carnival-barker facade made me warm to him. Then I remembered his fortune—the backroom deals and the boardroom coups—and I was certain he could cry on command. "But she was my little girl. She was ninety percent me, even if she did grab the wrong end of the stick every time she closed her hand. She told Phillipa to divorce me. Wrong end of every stick. Turned my stockholder meetings into a circus…" He kept talking under the weight of his own personality. Glib and overbearing. If I wanted to get a straight answer from him, I'd have to stem the tide.

"Why did you let her into the stockholder meetings, Mr. Hulfinger?" I finally interrupted.

"Anyone who owns a stock is legally—"

"You encouraged it," I said. "Why? Because she disrupted meetings you wanted disrupted. She catalyzed your support by showing the depth of the opposition. Or she undermined the opposition by representing a straw man of some sort."

Van Huut opened and closed his mouth without speaking.

"Did I miss something?" I asked. "I'm not familiar with corporate affairs."

Hulfinger stared at the tabletop as if he was hoping it'd tell him what to say, then shook his head. "Sometimes you get so used to shoveling manure, you think everywhere you go is a stable. I apologize, Ms. Ashbury. She *was* my favorite. I did—I do love her. You're right, I learned early to use the tools at hand. But Jody was… Nothing is more important to me right now than finding what happened to my little girl." He met my eyes. "She's gone. Can't turn back time. But I have to know why. I have to know why. And with this note you found…"

I let it hang there a moment. "I understand you fought."

"Like cats and dogs." He exhaled, an obvious effort to compose himself.

"I mean, the day she disappeared."

"Day before," he said. "Hell, maybe the day of, too. Over break-fast, but that was nothing. That was about milk. She wouldn't drink milk with hormones in it. I'd picked up a gallon of the wrong kind."

"This was normal? She seemed to be acting normally?"

"Normal for Jody wasn't the same as normal for you and me."

I glanced down at my pad, again. He'd be surprised to know what was normal for me.

"But in retrospect I think, no, it wasn't normal. Sometimes ar-guing was our way of…" He shrugged. "Our way of relating. That morning, I think she took it a little hard. She might've been on edge. I don't know."

If you're planning on driving into the bay, do you spend the morning fighting over milk? "And the argument the day before?"

"Jody has a list. Pharmaceutical companies. Biotech firms. Weapons, oil companies. Logging, though Lord alone knows if she'd rather wipe her nose with birch bark. And prisons. She thought I was the evil trifecta." Hulfinger made a noise that wasn't quite a laugh. "Started managing a paper mill in my twenties. Bought out the owners, turned around and sold it. Took the profits into biotech. Sold that off in the early nineties and started HulCorp. We're now the third largest privatized corrections corporation on the planet. And I believe in it, Ms. Ashbury. It's a lucrative business, no denying, and it's what this country needs. You know what the taxpayers pay per inmate per year? Almost thirty grand. That's more than the average workingman's salary. That's an abomination, to pay criminals more than—" He started to slip into carnival-barker mode, then caught himself. "So Jody had read some article in *Lenin Today* about Greenville Bay, that's our largest facility—"

"Lenin Today?"

"That's what I called 'em. *Lenin Today, Stalinist Sun, Mao Monthly.* All her magazines. She used my credit card to subscribe, too."

"You didn't cancel them?"

"If I did, she woulda paid for them out of her salary." He shook his head. "She lives in a slum already."

"The argument was about this article?"

"The title was 'Privatized Prisons, Modernized Slavery,' you can imagine how objective it was. Jody wanted me to sell HulCorp. Divest, she called it. She'd been at it for years. Wanted me to divest from my own company."

"What'd the article say?"

"Nothing new. That HulCorp in particular, and privatized prisons in general, is a reinstitution of slavery. They whine 'cause we do what's called 'creaming.' We only take nonviolent offenders—an inmate acts up, we ship him back to state. Never was sure why that's a bad thing, separating the nonviolent inmates from the violent. You know what it's really about?"

I took the bait, though this was nothing I needed to know. "What?"

"Stock is up from six dollars to sixty-five. In five years we grew from nine thousand to almost sixty-thousand beds. It's a knee-jerk reaction to a profitable business. If organic farming made that kind of money, the knee-jerk liberals would boycott broccoli...."

"Was that necessary?" Van Huut asked me as we waited in the billiard room for TJ to show. "Given the direction of the investigation."

"The bureau is following up the note," I said. "I'll follow up everything else. Only five people lived in this house, and were around her vehicle, in the time that counts. The three Hulfingers, Gayle Cornell and Aaron White. One of them may be able to give me the information I need."

"Exactly how is knowing about her relationship with her father gonna tell you if her carburetor was clogged?"

"Her carburetor wasn't clogged."

"Why don't you stick with the vehicle, Ms. Ashbury?"

I looked at him. "Do you know the single most important component of a 1985 VW Jetta?"

He didn't answer.

"The driver," I said. "I *am* sticking to the vehicle, *Walter.* The driver, the car, the crash. They're all the same thing."

"Talking about HulCorp stockholder meetings will tell you what kind of driver she was? That's crap, and you know it. You have the transcriptions of our interviews. You're not asking anything we didn't." He shook his head. "No. You're off this end of the investigation."

"Am I?" I hated these confrontations. Hated playing the moody, I'm-always-right detective to the bureaucratic numbskull boss, but Van Huut was beginning to piss me off. "If you were a judge, you'd have to recuse yourself due to conflict of interest. You're a personal friend of the Hulfingers."

He stood abruptly, his chair scraping against the floor. I wondered what nerve I'd hit—there was something more than just a personal friendship going on. He carefully sat back down and caught my eyes with an unwavering glare.

I wasn't about to get into a staring contest. I took a nail file from my bag and went at the nail I'd broken on my left middle finger, while clawing my knee in White's car. I wasn't a woman who filed her nails in public, but the alternative was sitting like a schoolgirl waiting for Van Huut to reprimand me.

I had the nail halfway fixed when Van Huut spoke. "I'll get you the transcriptions if you don't have them already. Stay with what you know, Ms. Ashbury."

"You should talk to Ralph Nicencio before you try telling me who I can speak with."

"Nicencio is no longer an AD. The problem is, Ms. Ashbury..." Van Huut laced his fingers together. "And correct me if I'm wrong—but you busted your first driver in the face."

I didn't correct him.

"You attacked an NTSB investigator. How far do you think Nicencio is going to extend his neck for someone who apparently has an impulse-control disorder?"

My face flushed. "I am very good at what I do, Agent Van Huut. If I'm allowed to do it." I wondered if he heard the supplicating tone in my voice, and prayed that he didn't. "I need to conduct these interviews, I need to understand who Jody Hulfinger was, not just as a driver. I need to take the interviews in any direction I want, to see if I stumble on the question I didn't know I had to ask."

"It's all in our transcriptions. You got under Small's skin. You got him talking. I think he even liked you. But what do you honestly think you can learn that we didn't?"

"There are questions about her car—"

"You don't really believe someone's gonna say, yeah, her car was making a funny crunching sound, they just didn't think it was important enough to mention before now?"

"No."

"Then unless you can tell me one thing you learned from Small you couldn't have from the transcription, you're off this end."

"That a promise?"

He looked disgusted. As if I was being a child, saying *is that a threat or a promise?*

"I'm serious," I said. "If I tell you one thing I learned, you won't try to keep me off this?"

"Sure."

"The milk. They got in a fight that morning about milk. Because it wasn't organic or whatever—"

"Bovine growth hormone," he said. "And I meant one *useful* thing."

"It is useful. Was she allergic to the hormones? Lactose intolerant? I had an airline shuttle bus one time drove through the plate glass and into the terminal when the driver's allergies kicked in so hard he couldn't see."

"What's the chance the milk has anything to do with anything?"

"Almost nil. But if it does, it's the key to the whole thing."

Van Huut closed his eyes and pinched the bridge of his nose between his thumb and forefinger. It was straight out of a bad cop movie.

"Good," I said, as if it was settled. "Now can I ask you something?"

Van Huut shrugged.

"You know Hulfinger pretty well. How much of what he said was bullshit?"

For a moment, I thought Van Huut would defend Hulfinger, or attack me. He did neither. "One hundred percent of what sounded like bullshit was bullshit. Ninety percent of what didn't sound like bullshit, wasn't. That's his way. I've never seen him as upset as he is now. She really was his favorite. But he's got his show, the Small Hulfinger show. Can't help himself."

"I guess we all have our shows, huh?" I wasn't sure if I was apologizing to Van Huut or thanking him. "Mine's a dramady."

TJ Hulfinger stepped out of a Thomas Pink catalog and into the billiard room. Blue button-down shirt with French cuffs, lightweight twill khakis…looked as if he wished he were in a necktie and sport jacket, too.

There were echoes of his father in his build and the shape of his head, but they were faint. Short hair, high forehead, long straight nose. Quiet and watchful was my first impression. Where Small had a powerfully oversize presence, TJ was the opposite: unobtrusive and withdrawn. Probably just a different road to the same destination.

He sat in the chair across from me and was attentive and deferential, as if he were meeting the Chairman of the Board.

He was not the type of man I had a lot of use for and I had to make an effort to equal his politeness. "I appreciate your agreeing to speak with me. I know this is a hard time for you, and I won't keep you longer than I have to."

"Of course, I'm happy to help. I—I don't want to sound callous, but the truth is, it's important to my father to know how this happened. To me—" he fluttered his hands "—it doesn't matter how so much as, well…she's gone."

"Not callous at all." Over the years, I'd seen every kind of response to death. "Some people have to understand, to grieve. Others can grieve without knowing."

"It's probably a control thing." TJ offered a weak grin. "My father is big on control."

Seemed inappropriate to agree with him, so I made a noncommittal noise before taking him through my standard questions. He was even less helpful than Small had been. No carnival-barker facade, no tall tales to pick apart, looking for the truth.

"I'm afraid Jody and I haven't spent much time together recently. I can't remember the last time we were in the same car."

"You didn't get along?"

"Well, Walter must've told you. No? Jody has—she *had* strong opinions, and was very concerned with being seen to do the right thing." He fiddled with his cuffs. "And my plan has always been—for the past eight or nine years—to follow in my father's footsteps. Our interests couldn't have been more different. We didn't argue, though." He stared blankly out the window. "We ignored each other fairly completely."

I allowed him a moment of quiet, and was surprised when he began speaking again. "We weren't close, but we were very much the same. Only opposite. Does that make sense?"

"Your father said something similar."

TJ looked startled. "I—really? I'm surprised to hear that."

His reaction came across almost rehearsed. I wondered if I could shock him into spontaneity. I said, "Did Jody commit suicide?"

He didn't hesitate. "She would've sacrificed herself for the greater good, maybe. But she would've left a note." He smiled, a little grim and a little sad. "A manifesto."

I was taken aback to hear the same word applied to Jody Hulfinger that Ralph had used to describe me. I withdrew to my cabin in the woods, and Jody withdrew to what? Her politics? But TJ made a good point. Not all suicides left notes, but someone like Jody had a lot to live for, a lot to fight against, and it was hard to believe she could resist firing a parting shot.

"Except..." TJ said. "She'd been different lately. Distracted. Maybe Nile would know."

"Your stepsister?" The one not in the will.

"Yeah. She knew Jody better than I. Even my father knew her better, and all they did was argue. We mostly ignored each other." He twisted the button on his shirt. "I wish we *had* argued more. Isn't that strange?"

"So you *can* be polite," Van Huut said as TJ closed the door. I thought I heard the hint of a grin in his voice.

"Can't always use the same tack," I said. "The trick is figuring out what gets the best results." I hadn't gotten far with TJ. Did learn one thing, though. "His father doesn't like him?"

"Where'd you hear that?"

I shrugged. Wasn't it obvious?

"TJ went through a rebellious phase," Van Huut said. "I think Small's finally getting over it."

"A rebellious phase? What, he bought his clothes at Wal-Mart?"

"Drugs, drinking, the usual."

"And the girls have always been angels?"

"Jody was pot and politics. Cate was coke and clothes. But TJ, being the eldest and the only boy…"

"No understanding for the prodigal son? How serious was he into it?"

"Not very. He had a kind of roughneck lumberjack high-school buddy, and the feeling in the family is TJ followed him off the straight and narrow."

"He seems to have regained his footing." It was hard for me to picture him as a rebel.

"Very much so. He's the acting COO of HulCorp. He's not a showman like Small, but he's sharp and methodical." He looked at his watch. "Cate will be ten minutes late."

"In his rebellious phase—was TJ political like Jody?"

"More he wanted to sow some wild oats."

For some reason that reminded me of Aaron White. "Speaking of which, Aaron White slept with Jody. The day before she disappeared."

"He *what?*"

I told him what little I knew.

"Took her for a ride?" Van Huut headed for the door. "I'm gonna take *him* for a ride."

Good. It worked. Now I'd be able to interview Cate without Van Huut breathing down my neck.

"She was very attached to that car. It was a terrible beater, an accident waiting to—" Cate Hulfinger heard what she'd just said, and paled. The whiteness accentuated her blue-gray eyes and elegant cheekbones. She was taller than I, and moved with the sort of careful grace you don't see anywhere but fashion runways. I disliked her on sight.

"I know what you mean," I said gently. "It's okay. I hadn't heard that about her car before. That she was attached to it."

"She bought it herself, first year of college. Took the bus until she could afford a used Jetta with her own money. As a...y'know, a symbol of her separation from Small."

Hmm, she called her father by his nickname. What had TJ called him? Father? "How long ago was that?"

"Ten years." Cate considered. "Almost eleven."

Tracing the car that far back to the original owner wasn't worth bothering with, but I used it as a bridge to ask the rest of my vehicle-related questions. It quickly became obvious Cate wouldn't have noticed a strange noise in her own car—a silver convertible BMW—much less in Jody's.

I moved on. "When you last saw her, say in the week before she disappeared, was Jody acting strange?"

"*Acting* strange?" Cate stifled what might have been a laugh or a sob. "Jody was always acting strange. She *was* strange. Smart as a whip but she had no idea about anything. Was she acting strange? She was—she was—" And Cate fell apart, weeping and apologizing and wiping her eyes and in her grief looking like a painting of a medieval Madonna. "I'm sorry, I'm sorry..."

I lifted a hand to comfort her, and let it fall back onto the table. Cate's tears were the loveliest things I'd seen all day.

"Hey." It was White's voice. I hadn't even heard him enter. He knelt beside Cate and gathered her into his arms. "Go on," he said. "She doesn't care if you cry."

He held Cate as she shuddered, and I felt rigidly uncomfortable: intrusive and voyeuristic. I watched White murmur to Cate, acting like a different person than he'd been with me. He was masterful and gentle. Either would've set my back up, but Cate responded, taking a few deep breaths.

"Sorry," she said again. "I thought I was done crying."

"Y'know, Catie," White said before I could respond, "there's no need to broadcast your feelings."

He put a strange emphasis on the word, saying it *broad*cast, and for some reason, this brought a tentative smile to Cate's face.

"Although I'm sure the inspector is a *broad*-minded woman," he continued, "and won't hold it against you."

The smile grew, and became genuine. But I don't think it was a smile for White. More for Jody. The kind of smile you see at a wake, when a mourner forgets the death and remembers the love.

Well done, White. I let some fractional approval show in my eyes before telling him I needed to speak with Cate alone. "And I think Agent Van Huut has some questions for you," I added.

He nodded, squeezed Cate's hands and padded silently away.

Cate watched the door close behind him. "She had been acting strange," she said. "Well...strang*er*. Have you heard of FTA?"

I shook my head.

"Free Them All. It's an antiprison group. Jody's kind of thing—nose-pierced hippies carrying a torch." She grinned. "Of course, she'd have said my friends are diamond-ringed sorority sisters carrying a Coach."

I smiled, surprised Cate could laugh at herself.

"She was mother's little girl—I suppose I take after Small." Cate considered for a moment, didn't seem pleased. "Did you hear about her and the bobcat?"

"Jody?"

"My mother. She found this kitten, brought it home. Didn't know it was a bobcat cub. At least that's what she told Small. Spontaneous acts of unthinking kindness, that was mom. She did that Christian Children's thing, where for only thirty cents a day you can adopt a South American kid? Spent six bucks a day, I guess. Planned to have Small hire 'em all at the mill…"

I couldn't help asking, "And the bobcat?"

"A vet saw her carrying it around in her handbag. Told her she was lucky it hadn't taken a bite out of Jody or me…" She brushed her bangs back. "Jody was the same. Do for those less fortunate. She'd been in a bunch of antiprison groups over the years. But FTA was more…militant, I guess. Jody took things seriously. Too seriously—I can be the same—and FTA wasn't exactly a light-hearted romp. I think most of them are ex-prisoners."

I made a note. Nothing like a roomful of ex-cons for identifying a couple of suspects. "So what part was strange?"

"Small told her they were full of shit, and she dropped them, cold turkey."

"That does sound uncharacteristic," I said. "Is that the only thing?"

"Small and TJ think it's odd how much she'd been alone lately, driving around, kayaking."

"But it wasn't?"

"Aaron says Jody was a dumpling, like it's a compliment. But she was fat. I think maybe the kayaking—she might've wanted to lose weight. I mean, if she were appearing naked somewhere."

Ah. The lose-weight-so-you-aren't-embarrassed-to-have-sex theory.

"Kayaking's great exercise," Cate continued. "And she even went to the HulCorp gym a couple times, which is unlike her."

"Did she have a boyfriend?"

"A lover, maybe," Cate said. "It's not like she'd tell me."

"She was gay?"

"She didn't think so. But I thought maybe. Jody was…prudish, personally. Politically liberal, but, I don't know—I always wondered is all."

Much to my surprise, I found myself liking Cate. Unfortunately, sometimes you had to kick the wasps' nest to see if you got stung. "She slept with Aaron."

"Oh, that." Cate waved an unconcerned hand. "That's no indication either way."

"She told you?"

"She didn't need to."

"You don't mind your boyfriend slept with your sister?"

"Aaron is…" She shook her head. "Has he fallen in love with you yet?"

"He gave me a ride from Portland," I said.

"Plenty of time," she said. "He's sincere. That's the secret of Aaron White. He'll find something in you to love, and he'll convince you to love it, too."

"Oh. Well." Was there anything left in me to love? White would have a hard time persuading me. Not that I wanted him to.

"Hard to resist. Of course, he's an absolute mutt." At my confused look, Cate explained. "A mutt. A man-slut. But when he's with you, he is entirely focused. I've been with better-looking men, more successful, funnier men, but none of them…" She smiled, secretively. "The thing is, when he meets another woman, there's no room in his tiny pea brain for me. It's as if I never existed." One of her shoulders rose and fell an inch. "It's worth it."

"Is it?" I was honestly curious. I couldn't imagine living my life that way, but part of being a good investigator is realizing you aren't everyone. For some people, being a part-time girlfriend was ideal, or at least enough.

Cate was silent a moment. "No, not really. I'd love to find someone who—I'm twenty-eight, you know? I know it's cliché, but the clock *is* ticking. But asking Aaron to change…" Cate's voice petered out. I wasn't surprised by how much she was revealing. People who'd lost someone close, whose emotions were raw, would confide anything to anyone. "Once this is all over, I mean, once I stop weeping every night over Jody, I'm going to tell Aaron we're through. I wish I didn't have to, but he's not ready. And, you know what? I don't need him anymore. He's helped me see that."

Aaron White as therapist? Hmm. Couldn't really picture it. But once a boyfriend sleeps with your sister, it's definitely time to cut him loose. "Thanks for being so open," I said.

"You're easy to talk to. You remind me of him a little. Of Aaron." Cate brushed her long bangs behind her ear, oblivious of my stare. "Jody and I never had that. I mean, a chatty, girl-talky relationship. You know, people thought we were so different. They thought we didn't care about each other. But we're twins. There's a bond you can't explain. I've never told anyone this." Cate met my eyes. "If I could be anyone, it would be Jody."

Aaron grabbed his sketch pad and sat on the stone steps that led to the garden and back lawn. Brigid had said Agent Van Huut had some questions—which only made Aaron want to avoid him.

Sketching was his hobby. Well, his hobby was taking classes. In addition to drawing, he'd delved into clay sculpture and stone carving—aka chain-gang labor. He could almost play a scale on a violin and threw a nearly round pot. He'd taken language classes in Italian and Japanese and had learned to cook dim sum and chicken enchiladas. A Renaissance man in search of a renaissance.

He roughed out a sketch of a nearby tree trunk, admiring its sinewy shape. Sitting on the same steps he and Jody had sat on, all he could think of was Brigid Ashbury. He couldn't remember the last time someone unloaded that much venom on him. Well, yeah, he could remember—but at least Amy knew him.

With Brigid, it had been visceral. She was hurt, she was bleeding, she was holding her guts in with both hands. So she lashed out.

And yet…he found her oddly attractive.

What could happen to you to cause that kind of pain? That kind of fear? It wasn't her vulnerability that he found sexy, it was the fact that she didn't let it stop her.

Aaron was aware that he liked women. He was drawn to women. Not just for sex. He liked sex—loved sex—it just wasn't the only thing he liked about women. Still, Brigid Ashbury was different. Prickly, smart, injured, abrasive. But the way she held her head. The way her body moved under her clothes and—

"Excuse me." A man's voice interrupted his reverie.

Aaron looked up, expecting Agent Van Huut, but found two men and a woman. All wearing expensive suits and formidable expressions. The man who spoke was Latino, probably ten years older than Aaron. Handsome, trim, with thick hair and a receding hairline. "We're looking for Small Hulfinger," he said. "I'm sorry to bother you."

Aaron stood and offered his hand. "I'm Aaron White. It's no bother."

"John Iqbal." He shook with a firm grip. With the name Iqbal, maybe he wasn't Latino. "HulCorp. Glad to meet you. This is Leanne Laclaire, our CFO."

Iqbal said it as if she was Aaron's CFO, too. It surprised him, made him grin, so he was smiling when he turned to greet her. She gave him a cool glance in return.

She was about Iqbal's age, and smaller than she looked. Petite, with shoulder-length dark hair tamed into a business-appropriate coif, and a pretty, lightly freckled cheerleader's face. She shook his hand and told him it was her pleasure. Her grip was firmer than Iqbal's. Nice hands; well-shaped.

"And this is Gary Putnam," Iqbal said. "Our DOS."

Gary Putnam was a stocky man in his fifties with a salt-and-pepper crew cut. Looked as if he could kill a man seven ways with his pinkie—he just shook Aaron's hand, though.

"DOS?" Aaron asked him.

"Director of Security."

"Well, I'm afraid I don't have an acronym myself," Aaron said. "Unless you count SOL."

"We told Small we'd stop by," Iqbal said. "We came up from Boston."

Aaron nodded, and waited for someone to ask what SOL stood for. One of Brigid Ashbury's tricks, the silent treatment. But Putnam could've stood there all day without blinking and Laclaire put a friendly look in her eye that somehow disturbed Aaron. Iqbal didn't lose sight of his goal. "We should look for Small inside?"

Aaron waved toward the back doors. "Try the kitchen or the study."

They looked uncomfortable about barging into the house; then Leanne Laclaire squared her narrow shoulders and led them in.

"White." A voice from behind him.

He turned. It was Agent Van Huut. "I guess I really am SOL." Shit out of luck.

Despite having read in the report that she sat on the board of directors of a "banking concern," I expected Gayle Cornell to be some variety of trophy girlfriend. And maybe she was. But she couldn't have been a day under fifty, despite Tina Turner legs and an unwrinkled face.

I felt some grudging respect for Small—I expected him to be dating a twenty-year-old aspiring actress. It would've been an easy way to disregard his intelligence. Nothing like a man dating a woman his daughter's age to reveal the depth of his immaturity. My father was a case in point. I hadn't talked to him much since he'd remarried a woman who was really more of a girl.

Cornell made fifty look good. I doubted anyone would be saying that about me in twenty years. She sat, crossed her endless legs and ran a finger around the inside of her Christian Louboutin peep-toes. "I'm still breaking them in," she said, instead of *hello*. "Or maybe it's vice versa."

I offered a polite grin.

"They're Christian Louboutin. Worth the pain."

"Are they?" I said. As if I couldn't spot a Louboutin at ten paces. I glanced down at my pad. "Is it G-A-I-L? No?" Cornell gave the correct spelling. "Thank you. Date of birth?"

Cornell may not have gritted her teeth, but I bet she came close. She was the type who'd hate admitting her age, especially to a younger woman—despite that four out of five thirtysomething women would have traded their firstborn for her figure. She gave me the date. She was sixty-one. Christ. She didn't even have crow's-feet.

I asked my usual questions, but Cornell had none of the answers.

"I'm afraid I wouldn't know an unusual engine noise if one woke me in the night and put a mint on my pillow. I didn't even realize Jody had a car. I suppose she must have."

"What was her relationship with her father?"

"Antagonistic."

"He says she was his favorite."

"*I'm* his favorite, dear." She arched a penciled eyebrow. "His favorite child? Cate. TJ was the eldest son and heir to the throne, but he fell out of favor. Between Jody and Cate there's no contest."

"I'm surprised to hear that."

"You know that Small and Jody fought terribly, the day before she disappeared—surely you've heard this?"

I nodded. "Sounds like an argument they had often."

"With a new twist. Jody disapproved of her father's business, as if it were any of her own. But recently, he'd been considering liquidating some assets and reinvesting them in HulCorp. Instead of divesting, he was investing."

Hadn't heard that before. "What kind of assets?"

"If he wanted you to know, dear, I'm sure he would have told you. But they were in excess of twenty million dollars. Twenty-three and change."

"The company needed the cash?" People killed for much less than twenty million.

"Not *needed*." An elegant shrug. "Small smells an opportunity, and it's Pavlovian."

"So he was going to sell some other—" what had he called them? "—holdings, and put the money back into the prison business?"

"He wanted to expand. Diversify. There's a...oh, I don't know the details. A food-service company that specializes in correctional facilities, and the price is apparently...substantially marked down." She glanced casually at my suit. "Shopping the sales, you know."

I was wearing DKNY, for chrissake. A four-hundred dollar suit. How did she know I got it on sale? "How did TJ fall out of favor?"

"I'm sure I don't know."

And I was sure she did. Probably this "phase" of his. But I couldn't think of an excuse for digging into it more aggressively. I contented myself with hoping Cornell's shoes were biting like piranhas into her feet as she teetered from the room.

Van Huut entered as Cornell left, as if he'd been waiting outside. I thanked him for not interrupting.

He ignored me. "White won't talk to me. Said if we want to speak further, my lawyer could call his lawyer."

I wasn't surprised. Van Huut should've sent a woman. Maybe Aaron had sensed all Van Huut wanted to do was scold him for sleeping with Jody. That didn't make him guilty. "We're just lucky he didn't raise a fuss over the arrest."

Van Huut snorted. "You met the HulCorp Board of Directors?"

I shook my head.

"They just arrived. White was their welcome wagon. You know he's an artist?"

"Con artist?"

"No. He had his whaddyacallit, his sketch pad with him. Drawing some outdoor erotica, John said."

"Seems to be a recurring theme." I straightened my notes.

"They apologized for bothering him. He looks up from shading in the naughty bits, says it's not a problem, he was just sitting there thinking about Jody."

"Least he's honest."

"Then he tells Leanne—Leanne Laclaire, the CFO—he tells her she has lovely hands. What the hell is that?"

"A better line than rosemary shampoo."

"What?" But he thought better of it. "Forget it. You done in here?"

"I'm done." Except I should talk to the board members, get a better feel for HulCorp.

"Learn anything?"

"Yeah. But I'm not sure what."

"Anything about her vehicle or her driving ability?" he said, a little sharply.

"Not one thing."

"So it's still a single-vehicle accident. Other than the note, there's no physical evidence this is anything out of the ordinary."

I thought I agreed with him, until I heard myself say: "The scene is off. I'm missing a piece of the puzzle. I know I am, but I can't put my finger on it." I considered. "The kidnap note. And coming from this family, with this kind of money. It's something."

"I'm not sure. The lab ran the note and came up blank. There's been no surveillance on Jody—we did knock-bys all down her neighborhood in Boston and here in Maine, too. There's been no contact, no abortive contact from any possible kidnappers."

"Maybe this wasn't a kidnapping gone bad. Maybe it was something else, gone right." I looked at him. "Maybe the question we should be asking is, who benefits?"

"No," Gary Putnam, HulCorp's Director of Security, said.
It was a word—a concept—he seemed stuck on, but I main-

tained a neutral expression. Putnam had the sort of hard-ass military vibe you almost never saw in an actual hard-ass military guy. He had graying hair and maybe his body had thickened in the past twenty years, but I bet he could still bench-press the same three hundred.

"I'm sure you understand, Mr. Putnam, we always interview people individually. I'm asking you to do me the favor of letting me speak with the others, alone."

It was his decision, as Director of Security, to allow Iqbal and Laclaire to speak with me. "No," he said.

I let it sit there. The three Fs—flirt, fight or flatter—were useless with this guy. All I could do is try to wait him out and wear him down.

"Your job is accident reconstruction," he said, after a pause. "Mine is HulCorp security. I can think of no way in which permitting Mr. Iqbal and Ms. Laclaire to speak with you alone could benefit our security."

"I can think of no way it would harm it."

He sat upright in his chair, and watched me with flat, unblinking eyes.

"There's a girl dead," I said. "I'm not asking to do a body-cavity search."

"We're due back in Massachusetts in five hours. The longer you spend speaking with me, the less time you'll have with them."

I exhaled slowly. "Then would you ask Mr. Iqbal and Ms. Laclaire to join us?"

He left the room without a backward glance, and I had no idea if he intended to return.

Five minutes later, he did. "I apologize for the delay. They were with Mr. Hulfinger. John Iqbal, this is Brigid Ashbury. Ms. Laclaire will be here in a moment."

Putnam stepped aside, and John Iqbal stood in the doorway.

He was gorgeous. If he hadn't been a millionaire corporate type, he could've made his fortune posing with his shirt off for the cover of romance novels. Better looking than Aaron White by far.

"Mr. Iqbal," I said, trying to keep my voice businesslike. "Thanks for agreeing to speak with me."

"Not a problem. We're on a schedule, but we'll do everything we can to help."

"I appreciate that. The first thing is, I'd prefer to speak with you alone." Jesus. Did that sound like a come-on?

"That'd be my preference, too," he said with such sincerity I knew it was a lie. "But it's not my decision. If you want to follow up with a visit to the office or via conference call, we're at your disposal. Subject to Putnam's approval, of course."

"Ah," I said. "Good." Good? What was good about it? Problem was, all I could think to ask was, *Have you had your teeth whitened?*

Before I could, a petite woman in a business suit knocked on the open door. She had a trim body and the sort of face men would find beautiful because she knew how to apply makeup. Her hands were nothing special.

"Leanne," John said. "This is Inspector Ashbury."

"Pleased to meet you," Laclaire said. "Except, of course, under the circumstances…"

"Ms. Ashbury is not an inspector, John," Putnam said. "She's a civilian consultant."

"Thanks for clearing that up, Gary," I said. "Why don't we sit?"

They sat, and I ran though my questions and learned nothing about the car. So I asked about the driver.

"We all knew Jody," Iqbal said. "You've heard about her attendance at stockholder meetings? The trick was keeping her from bringing along—what did you call them, Putnam?"

"Props."

"Water balloons full of dye, that sort of thing," Iqbal said.

"How disruptive was she?" I asked.

"Exactly as disruptive as I'd allow," Putnam said.

I didn't roll my eyes, but it was hard. "Did any of you have contact with her outside these meetings?"

"I'm not sure where these questions are meant to lead, Ms. Ashbury," Putnam said.

"To Jody Hulfinger. She had a grudge against HulCorp. I want to know how deep it ran and who it threatened. She was involved in FTA—you've heard of FTA?" I could see from their faces they had.

"Do you know what the acronym means?" Laclaire asked.

"Free Them All," I said.

"Fuck The Authorities." The *fuck* sounded doubly harsh coming from Laclaire's pretty mouth. "That's their mind-set. It had nothing to do with freedom and everything to do with contempt."

"Uh-huh," I said, hoping for more.

"As if 'free them all' wasn't objectionable enough." Laclaire said. "But at least it's a fair measure of their seriousness. Free Them All—an infantile solution to a dreadful problem."

"Like saying the solution to war is peace," Iqbal said.

"Right," I said, disliking them both. "And outside the stockholder meetings? Was there any other contact with her?"

"I saw her from afar at several demonstrations," Putnam said.

I turned to the others. "Either of you see her?"

"Leanne and I met her socially two or three times," Iqbal said. "At family gatherings. She wouldn't come to company events, but she was at an anniversary party, once, and a—what else was there?"

"The Halloween party," Laclaire said. "She came as a fat cat."

It caught me by surprise—no doubt it riled the rich and greedy Small—and I half laughed. I was the only one. "And that was the extent of it?"

"I met her one additional time," Putnam said. "At the office."

"Not a demonstration?"

"Inside the office. The corridor outside TJ Hulfinger's office. It was after hours. She claimed she'd wanted to use the health club, and thought she'd see TJ while she was there. She had a sports bag with her."

"But you don't believe that."

He looked at me quizzically. As if saying that someone "claimed" they did something didn't imply you believed the opposite.

"No," he said. "I have no opinion. I'm simply repeating what she claimed."

"She'd been inside his office? TJ's office?"

"No. It was locked. We have very adequate locks."

"Private corrections," Iqbal said with a fairly dazzling smile. "We pride ourselves on our locks."

"And this only happened the one time?"

"Yes," Putnam said, for a change. "Three months ago. Evening."

I nodded. What did I want from these people? Jody Hulfinger was extraordinary for two reasons. She was a Hulfinger, so I was interested in her family; and she was an activist, so I was interested in HulCorp. But I didn't get the impression these three were even remotely threatened by Jody's activism. In fact, they seemed to sanction it. Following Small's lead, no doubt.

"Were you aware of any bad feelings between Jody and her family?"

Nothing more than what I'd already heard.

"Between Jody and anyone at all?"

Nope.

If I'd spoken to each of them alone, I might've played one against the other. But all together…

"I'm sorry," Putnam said. "That's all the time we have."

They stood, murmured goodbye. I got close to John Iqbal. His face was perfect. He held the door for Laclaire before following her out. I was disappointed in how he moved. He'd be flawless, airbrushed on a romance novel cover, but in motion, he lost it. Not like…

"Hey," I said to Putnam, "you have any write-ups on Jody?"

He hesitated at the door. Clearly, he had something; there was just no way he was going to hand it over.

"Fax me?" I asked.

"No," he said, and was gone.

Wonderful.

"They all want to think they're like Jody." The words came unbidden from my mouth as White sat next to me on the stone bench on the Hulfinger's front lawn. "Well, except maybe Laclaire."

"Who?"

I looked at him sideways. "The one with the nice hands?"

He nodded in recognition, and the dappled shadows of the ancient oak hanging over us glided across his face. He was watching me with some combination of wariness and warmth—which both pleased and unnerved me. Why was I sitting here talking to him anyway?

Van Huut had offered me a ride back to the Inn, but I'd refused. We had a tenuous working relationship as it was; if I bloodied his nose or insulted his thinning hair, it would become unsalvageable. Instead of a ride, I'd wandered outside to the cool stone bench, and had been aimlessly turning over the new information when White appeared.

He'd sprawled onto the bench next to me. Looking for an apology? Never gonna happen. But—for whatever reason—I couldn't keep myself quiet.

"They all want to think that, deep down, there was a little Jody in them," I said.

"She was that kind of woman. I wanted to think it, too."

"They hated her politics, disapproved of her lifestyle."

"Jody was…she was neurotic, is what she was. Yeah, she made a lot of people crazy, but she had a sort of purity. I don't know…"

"She left things better than she found them."

He nodded. "You know that feeling in college when you can see the inequities of the world so clearly? And it all seems so simple to fix everything. But then you graduate and are forced to pay rent and taxes and school loans, credit-card debt. Most of us forget all about saving the world. But Jody didn't. She only got more determined."

I could relate. I knew a few things about determination. For instance, I was determined to get back to the Inn.

"You need a ride to your hotel?"

"What?" Had I actually said it aloud?

"A ride to your hotel."

"You're kidding."

"No, I'm asking if you want a ride to your hotel."

For a moment I wondered if this was a juvenile revenge strategy. I'd say, "Yes, I'd like a ride," and he'd say, "Good luck finding one!" and would walk away.

"I weathered the storm," he said, to my silence. "Might as well enjoy the tranquil aftermath."

"Why?" And I wasn't promising any tranquility.

"I don't know." He considered. "I like your voice. I like the way you hold your head. I've never met an accident reconstructionist before and... You want to know why?"

The way I held my head. How *did* I hold my head? Something new to be self-conscious about. How I held my fucking head. "Why?"

"You must see it all the time," he said. "People slow down for car crashes. Rubbernecking. They can't look away, can they?"

I felt myself become still.

"That's why," he said.

Because I was a car crash, and he couldn't look away.

It was true, truer than he could know. And impersonal. It wasn't pity that rubberneckers felt, it was fascination. I let him drive.

It was better this time, the pressure had bled off. I made myself breathe deep and slow. Tried loosening the death grip on my knees. Tried convincing myself that I wasn't smelling the fumes, wasn't strapped down helpless and battered, wasn't trembling like an infant.

It was better. I didn't feel the shame. I'd already shown White how bad I could get—I didn't have to worry about revealing my deepest pain. It made all the difference. Plus, he'd withdrawn into himself. Didn't make a noise, didn't present a target. He drove competently but not overcautiously, as if he were unaware that I was rigid in the seat next to him.

Of course, it was only a twenty, twenty-five minute drive....

Twenty, twenty-five. Twenty-three.

In excess of twenty million dollars. Twenty-three and change—

And I knew. About the kidnap attempt. The perpetrator. The motive. All I had to do was prove it.

17

The Principal's Daughter's face hurt from smiling.

Jody Hulfinger got what she deserved. She didn't love her father. She didn't deserve her father. She didn't deserve the tears, the grief. But she did deserve one thing—and, eventually, *he* realized it and provided it. He saw what Jody was worth, he cut his losses and—

For a dizzy moment, she thought about it. The car crash. The shattered corpse in the submerged car, waving slowly in the current.

She put a hand out to steady herself. She would not have dealt with it that way. She would not have—but he did. He saw a problem and he fixed it. Simple and direct. None of the hypocrisy that made her face ache.

He did what he did, and all she could do was support him. Protect him. Listen hopefully for the soft footfall's approach.

Her head hurt, too. From seeing that woman—the so-called investigator—still on her feet. Unshaken and prying—tenacious as a rat terrier.

She took a breath. She'd put Ashbury down directly if she had to. But there were other, subtler ways.

Not through Han, though. She'd made a call to determine what had happened. Ironic: the so-called investigator had avoided the accident meant to devastate her only because she'd been too devastated already. The Principal's Daughter appreciated the irony— but not the effect.

Still, she could salvage the operation. Half of strategy was harnessing unintended effects. What had Han said? *Popping the hood and making a few score marks.*

She considered. The driver's name was Eleanor Wash. And the NTSB was only a phone call away.

Aaron pulled the Subaru into Belfast Harbor parking lot and sat looking out at the lobster boats. Sometimes he did his best thinking in the car. Sometimes he just kept the seat warm.

Inspector Ashbury—Brigid—had had an epiphany. She'd realized something on the ride to the Inn, something that took her by surprise. She'd been sitting an arm's length from him, and he'd been watching her—or not watching her, but aware of her—and he couldn't come close to imagining what she'd realized.

So he sat, quietly listening. As if the car itself would tell him what she'd known.

Worked about as well as he expected.

It had taken Aaron two hours to realize his romp in the woods with Jody would make Brigid wonder if she'd committed suicide. This time, he knew he'd spend another two hours and still have no idea what Brigid was thinking. But he couldn't let it go. He'd have to do some research.

Something Jody had said about Nile made him wonder. He'd never met her—or her mother, Phillipa, Small's ex-wife. A condolence call was overdue.

I opened the door to my private garden patio, stepped out and opened the wood gate that led to a sprawling lawn that skirted the sea. It was the kind of place where people got married in the summer. The gray light of dusk had settled over the Inn grounds, washing the color from the trees.

Okay, so I knew the kidnapper. I knew the motive. Only thing left was walking the island to confirm it all. I wanted to do it now, but I wasn't about to walk on Route One at night. Not again. Not after Ganapi.

My mind was racing, but my body ached. It'd been a long day. I went back inside and ran a bath, hot as would come out of the faucet. I lay in the steaming water, letting it leach the fear and exhaustion from my body. When the water cooled, I picked up the FBI file I'd left by the side of the tub. It was an extensive write-up on the Hulfingers, as befits a wealthy and connected family. And it was boring.

Stanwood Hulfinger was the son of a chemical engineer. He'd served in the Korean War and been honorably discharged a sergeant. Got a job at EPW Paper, in Maine, worked his way up to the proverbial corner office. Married the owner's daughter,

Maureen Winchell, and transformed the company from sixth-largest paper producer in Maine to second. Sold out, and transferred his Midas touch to biotechnology.

Got into and out of biotechnology without developing a single product—but he'd trebled his personal fortune, anyway. Found the time to have TJ, the heir apparent, and then ten years later Cate and Jody. Then his wife had died, and that'd been the end of Small's expansion into family life. Well, beyond a five-year marriage to Phillipa Lockwood—an English barrister he'd met at a conference—and being half-assed stepfather to her daughter, Nile.

I ran more hot water and flipped to the most recent addendum. The report was exhaustive. Exhaust*ing.* Even had blueprints of the Beresford Arms Hotel, the intended ransom drop spot. Also included the brochure which showed old-world charm, with iron fire escapes and art deco decor. There was even a blurb about the trash incinerator chute covers, which had been featured in a *House & Garden* article about salvaged building materials, called "Second Sights."

Even their trash cans were more architecturally appealing than my trailer back home. I dropped the report next to the tub and let my mind drift. What to do next?

Walk Sears Island. Identify the spot that had to be there.

Ask Small Hulfinger about his finances, and this time get some answers. No—I'd ask Van Huut to do that. He was bound to get further. Frankly, I had no idea what kind of assets "holdings" entailed. I was guessing more than 4K in an IRA, which was all I could claim.

Follow up the pretrip events. The optometrist, the stomach

contents, the fire pit. Examine evidence collected by the dive and surface teams. Examine the site again.

Speak with FTA. *Free Them All.* At least you didn't have to wonder about their agenda. Of course, FTA was in Boston. Boston was a three-hour drive. Maybe I'd have Van Huut take care of that, too.

It was a lot to do, but I'd soon have answers. I'd be able to confirm the motive and the identity of the kidnapper.

But I'd still have to do my *thing* to answer the one question that mattered: what caused the accident that killed Jody Hulfinger?

"You must be Aaron White," the woman said from behind him, with an English accent that brought to mind the word *plummy.*

Aaron turned from the closed front door, where he'd just knocked. Phillipa Lockwood was fiftysomething, with a round, gracious face and short, sand-colored hair. Plump in a way that radiated good health. Wearing a straw bonnet with sunflowers around the brim and blue-striped overalls and muddy gardening clogs. Hard to imagine her as a hard-nosed barrister.

"I was afraid you'd think I was selling encyclopedias," he said.

"Oh, you're easy enough to recognize," she said. "Plus, you're not wearing a tie. Dead cert you're not a salesman."

Easy to recognize? "That picture of me and Cate on the T platform?"

"I've never seen a picture. Chalk it up to a lucky guess." She was laughing at him, but not unkindly. "Will you stay for dinner? Ratatouille fresh from the garden."

He found himself wanting to say *aubergine* and *courgette* to exhibit his worldliness, but contented himself with: "That'd be great, thanks." And, with a little Eddie Haskel, "You must be Nile."

She laughed and told him to follow her to the garden, where she handed him a basket and directed him to the cherry tomatoes.

"There's a question I wanted to ask Nile," he said. "About Jody. I know it's kinda inappropriate…"

"Nonsense. We've done nothing but talk about Jody for days. It's all that's kept us sane."

"Yes," he said. *The brown eyes, the warmth of her hip cradled in his hand.*

Phillipa looked up at him from the garden patch where she was kneeling. "Has Nile met you?"

"No, but Jody mentioned her often. She gave me one of her articles."

"And you read it?"

"Sure." He tried a grin. "Well, most of it."

"Hmm," she said, and twisted a zucchini off the vine. Nile was a professor at Smith College and he supposed a proud mother doesn't want to hear her daughter is incomprehensible.

He blundered onward. "I remember she used the word *praxis*. A little above my head."

"She distinguishes affirmative from critical postmodernism," Phillipa said. "If it's the article I'm thinking of. The difficulties of political epistemology and the exchange of structuralist social science with postmodernism." Then, smiling, "Or so I've been told."

"Right. And I gather she disapproves of Derrida and Lacan."

"I'm impressed you remember their names."

Should've mentioned *courgette* and *aubergine* when he had the chance. "I had a friend who suffered from acute academia," he said. "I memorized phrases to amuse her. Intertextual dichotomy, hegemonic valorization."

Phillipa smiled again. "Bring the basket inside, would you?"

Inside was through French doors into a Martha Stewart-looking, country-style kitchen. When he'd decided to speak with Nile, he'd expected to have to drive to Massachusetts. Turned out she and her mother were in Phillipa's house in Lincolnville, the town next to Camden. They'd come up when Jody had gone missing, and were staying for the funeral.

"Have you seen the family since—" he didn't know how to say "since the body was found" "—recently?"

"Not since Jody's body was found."

Ah. That's how.

"We're giving Small some privacy. I think he feels— I think he understood that Nile and I were, in many ways, closer to Jody than he was."

The front door opened, and Nile entered the kitchen, hidden behind two shopping bags. She put them on the counter, greeted her mother—Aaron was disappointed she didn't call her *Mum*— and turned to him.

With the name Nile and a reputation as a ferocious post-post-modernist, he'd formed a detailed—and deeply flawed—mental picture of Nile Lockwood. Turned out she was what they used to call a "pocket Venus." Maybe five feet tall, with pale blond hair, vague green eyes and definite curves.

"Nile, this is Aaron White," her mother said.

He smiled and met her eyes, but he got no ping. Usually, when he met someone, he got a ping. Faint or loud, obvious or subtle. Like he pinged with Phillipa, or with Jody, even with Brigid "Quicksand" Ashbury, though she'd probably say that was a negative ping. A pong.

He didn't get one with Nile. She had a sweet smile, an open face, an Aphrodite body—and she was smarter than him by a factor of ten. He should've been pinged over. But there was nothing. Well, sometimes he had to work for it.

"Jody gave me one of your papers," he told her. "The one about political epistemology. I liked the plot, but the dialogue needs help."

"I'll have to work on that."

"You want to start with a couple jokes," he said. Because when he found himself in a hole, his instinct was to start digging. "'Derrida and Lacan go into a bar...' Something like that."

She smiled faintly. He considered telling her the punch line would be "no, he's a *de*construction worker," but he gave it a pass. Made him think of Brigid again. Deconstructionist, reconstructionist: seemed sort of the same in his mind.

"Aaron is staying for dinner," Phillipa said. "Will you two set the table?"

Nile directed him to a drawer for silverware. He'd planned to spring his question on her after dinner, but as they were arranging glasses and napkins in the dining room, she asked what he wanted to know.

"Probably it should wait until after dinner—"

"Ask me now." For a pocket Venus, she had a commanding voice. He bet she didn't have trouble disciplining her students.

"Jody and I, we spent some time together. The day before she died. Before she disappeared. She mentioned something, I thought maybe it was—it struck me, not then, but later, that maybe it was—" He took a breath and remembered:

"I've always wanted to bring someone here. But I was afraid what they'd think. You know, it being outdoors. Would it be okay?" she'd asked. "It's my one secret. Doing it outdoors. I haven't even told Nile."

"She mentioned she always told you her secrets. The way she said it—" he shrugged "—made me wonder how many secrets she had."

"You wondered."

"Well," he said. "Something about the way she said it."

"I'm confused." Nile pinned him with her no-longer-vague gaze. "Why would I tell you? You didn't know Jody. I knew Jody. You didn't care about Jody. I cared about Jody. What gives you the right to ask?"

"Well," he said.

"You're playing detective? You think you're Colombo?"

"Well," he said.

"Except this is Maine, so you're more like Jessica Fletcher—*Murder She Wrote.* I don't think Jessica solved many car crashes."

"It wasn't just a car crash," he said. He heard an indrawn breath behind him. Phillipa had entered upon hearing Nile's raised voice. "I spent two nights in jail because of the note, and I don't think—"

"What note?"

"The kidnap note. They found a note near her car. About ransom. They thought it was me. You hadn't heard—?"

Nile dropped a napkin onto the table and left the room. The French doors in the kitchen opened and closed.

"I'm sorry," he said. "I thought you knew."

"No, we hadn't heard—excuse me." Phillipa left. The French doors opened and closed again.

He shook his head. What a way to break the news. He looked through the kitchen to the garden, saw the two women deep in conversation in the backyard. Question was, what *would* Jessica Fletcher do? In the hall bathroom, he opened the window and stood in the dark, straining his ears. He heard:

Nile's voice, barely a whisper.

Phillipa's voice: "—was your decision, but you must tell someone—"

When they returned, he was hovering by the front door. He apologized and told them he'd take a rain check on dinner. But Phillipa said he must stay, so he did. Conversation was strained, and all he could hear was *you must tell someone.*

By the time dinner was finished, he'd resolved that *someone* would be him. He said he'd love a cup of decaf. Phillipa bustled off to make it and he studied Nile's face. She must've felt him looking, but she seemed entranced by the pattern on the end of her dessert spoon.

"I have a question," he finally said.

She turned her eyes on him. They were big.

"Is that okay?" he asked.

She nodded.

"What does *praxis* mean?"

She didn't smile.

Shit. Time for plan B.

* * *

Four hours later, Aaron rolled onto his side and ran a hand over her rib cage. Down the curve of her waist, back up onto her hip.

"I'm someone," he said.

She touched him. "You certainly are."

She put a hand on the side of his face. Her breath tickled his nose. She told him Jody's final secret.

There was a scratching at the door. I sat up in bed, wrapping the quilt around myself.

"Breakfast in bed." Must be the innkeeper, his voice way too hearty for seven o'clock. Still, it was an indulgence I needed before facing the traffic of the day.

"Hold on," I called. I pulled on a voluminous pale pink cotton nightgown my mother had sent me, unlocked the door and hopped back in bed. "Okay."

The door opened, and Aaron White entered with a box of doughnuts.

"White!" I sat straighter against the headboard, resisting the urge to check that my nightgown was covering me properly, though given its dimensions there was no way it wasn't. I was suddenly aware of how my hair looked, and oh God, my crow's-feet would be visible from the doorway, like the Great Wall of China is visible from the moon. "What the fuck do you think you're doing?"

"Breakfast in bed," he said. "There's coffee, too."

I gave him the same stare that had made Len Ganapi take a step back.

Didn't phase White. He offered me the doughnut box. "I figured you for buttermilk or old-fashioned."

Buttermilk and old-fashioned. He thought I was a schoolmarm. Where was the spicy cinnamon, the chocolate frosting?

"Get out," I said.

He stepped in and closed the door behind him. "There's something I need to tell you. About Jody."

I could tell from his face that my theory had been correct. But while I'd been worrying about proof, Aaron White had found a witness.

"Jody kidnapped herself," I said, before he had a chance to speak.

He didn't quite gape, but he came close. He sat heavily on the chair next to my bed. The hot sugary scent of doughnuts wafted up. My mouth watered. It wasn't as if I *disliked* old-fashioneds.

"What?" he said. "You knew? How did you know?"

"I'm an investigator, Mr. White. I'm more interested in how *you* knew." Which was as good an exit line as I'd get. I swung out of bed and—attempting dignity—dragged my suitcase into the bathroom with me.

I closed the door, feeling I'd acquitted myself fairly well considering the disadvantage. Then realized I'd left Aaron White alone in my bedroom. He was probably already going through my wallet.

* * *

Aaron went out the back door, onto the little patio and squinted in the sunlight.

Okay. Two things.

First, she knew.

From what he'd heard, nobody on the planet but Nile and Phillipa knew. But Brigid Ashbury knew. He'd planned to blow her away with his Colombo act, but she already knew. When he thought about it, he was almost unsurprised.

Second, she was gorgeous.

Her hair mussed, fanned on the pillow behind her head like a red-golden halo on a Russian icon. Her green-brown eyes had been sleepy and gentle—her terrors woke later than she did, apparently. But she was quick to anger—that look had made him want to check if the wallpaper beside his head had scorched and curled.

He went back inside and the bathroom door opened. She was wearing a fitted skirt with a too-busy pattern—looked good, though—and a black ribbed top with a fairly generous scoop neck.

"Lacroix?" he asked. He had a friend once who was a fashion editor. She'd had a half-dozen outfits that clashed and competed for attention. They were usually Lacroix. She'd put them on and do a catwalk spin for him, and say: "Lacroix, dahling." Apparently loud outfits were okay if they were French and ferociously expensive.

Brigid did not do a catwalk spin. She grabbed one of the cups of coffee and peered into it suspiciously.

"Cream, no sugar," he said.

She looked affronted, but she sipped and made a noise that might've been a grunt of thanks.

"How'd you know?" she said.

"It's a gift. I worked at Starbucks one summer and—"

"About the kidnapping."

"Oh. I had dinner with Phillipa and Nile. I mentioned something about the note—"

"They knew that Jody had planned—? They didn't think this was something they should share with the police?"

"They hadn't heard a kidnap note had been found. Jody told Nile she was going to keep her father from expanding HulCorp if she had to become Patty Hearst. Nile thought she was just talking." Then, to prove he was an idiot, he said, "You'd like them."

"What was their cut?"

"Their what?"

"Of the ransom."

"No—no. It was just Jody, trying to keep her father from the Dark Side. I guess he'd liquidated some assets to invest in—"

"He'd raised twenty-three million—the note demanded twenty. Guess she didn't want to wait for her inheritance."

"She was a wealth-a-phobe. She'd have made a donation to Greenpeace or PETA or something."

"FTA."

"What's FTA?"

She brushed away the question with a wave of her coffee cup. "Why'd they tell you?"

"Because of the kidnap note. They realized they couldn't keep it to themselves."

"But why you?"

"I don't know. I guess they realized they had to come forward, and I was—"

Something sparked in Brigid's eyes. "You slept with her."

"The day before she disappeared. I told you."

"You slept with Nile Lockwood. That's why she told you about Jody."

"What?" he said. "Absolutely not."

She carefully placed her coffee on the table. Looked at him with severe and unforgiving eyes. It was all he could do not to admit he'd been the man on the grassy knoll, but he kept his teeth together.

Brigid eventually took a breath, but her eyes did not grow one degree warmer. She thanked him for sharing the information. She told him she'd have a statement for him to sign if he would please wait ten minutes. She pulled a form from her bag and wrote. Five minutes later, she handed it to him. It was a full and accurate representation of the information he'd given. It didn't mention him sleeping with anyone. He signed it.

"I think," he said. "I think I'd better check on Catie. Fill her in before she hears it officially. If that's okay."

"You know what I think?" she said. "I think you're a disgusting human being."

So much for Colombo.

Before the door fully closed behind White, I was on the phone. The report I'd been writing was incomplete, but when Nile Lockwood came forward, it would be conclusive, and they'd need to decide how to deal with this bombshell.

Fucking Aaron White. Cream, no sugar. Lounging in my bedroom, the epitome of casual ease, while I worried over my clothes and makeup and hair in the bathroom. *Lacroix.* What did that mean, asking if it was Lacroix?

He filled the room. There'd been no space in it for me. My God, he screwed Nile Lockwood to get the information. What had Cate called him? A mutt. Who did he think he was—Mata Hari? Even worse—he'd lied about it. He could screw whomever he wanted, he could tell Leanne Laclaire she had lovely fingers, but when he lied to my face—well, I took that as an insult.

I finished making the calls. The meeting would be in the Inn's conference room in one hour. I reread my report. Then casually opened the doughnut box and stared inside for a long moment.

There were a dozen doughnuts. Old-fashioned and buttermilk, sure enough. But also chocolate glazed, and chocolate cake and two cinnamon rolls twirling on top.

"Confirmation?" I asked. "You mean, beyond the Lockwoods' statement that this was what Jody planned?"

"Hearsay," Van Huut said. "Granted, it fits, but there's no proof. I wouldn't want to bring it to Boston—or to Small—without confirmation."

We were sitting around the table in the Inn's conference room—me and Van Huut, Detective Trake and Trooper Cowan from the State, and Officer Pomerleau representing the locals and looking more than a little overwhelmed. Watching the men fall upon the doughnut box made me wonder if White had meant it as some kind of cop joke. At least I'd had first pick.

"We can get confirmation." I glanced at Cowan. "Remember the black plastic rolls in her trunk? And the stakes?"

"With the orange blazes."

"And the kayak helmet. Hulfinger was driving to Sears Island to stake out a location. That's where she was going to hide during her 'ordeal.' Run the plastic in a big circle somewhere, so she didn't get a hiker or hunter stumbling into her tent."

"Hunting season's not for months," Detective Trake said.

"A bird-watcher, then. But I'm betting she already scouted it out. Tracks maybe?" Although it had rained. Still, she could've left markers or something.

"We'll bring dogs in," Cowan said. "And forensics."

"And I've been looking at the maps." I unfolded a State of Maine map. "Her problem was where to leave her car. That's where the kayak comes in. She could leave her car anywhere from Rockland, here, to the Blue Hill peninsula. Castine, say, or take a ferry to this island. Islesboro. Then she'd kayak in."

"That's a long paddle from Rockland," Pomerleau said. "Northport, maybe."

"Fine. Doesn't matter. But it's possible we can locate where she planned to leave the car. If we get a witness, we could prove this was a dry run. The location would have to be on the coast for access, but far enough away that we'd look in the wrong direction. Maybe the parking lot of a hiking trail or a Wal-Mart. We'd never expect her there."

We discussed the feasibility of that scenario, the possible locations for the car and the campsite. Van Huut asked if I had come to any conclusions about the accident, and I said no, I was too busy solving the kidnapping.

Van Huut actually chuckled at that.

"But what about the Lockwoods?" Detective Trake asked. "Can we charge them? Anyone hear from the D.A.?"

"You haven't met their lawyer," Van Huut said. "Or you wouldn't bother asking. We'll be lucky if we don't have to give them awards for public service."

"You think they were in on the planning stages?" Pomerleau asked.

"Could be. Or it could all be Jody."

"Girl went to some lengths to raise her allowance," Cowan said. "You'd think splitting a couple hundred million three ways would be enough for her."

"It wasn't greed," Van Huut said. "Jody probably would've tossed it in a Dumpster, if she didn't give it to Earth First. Jesus H." He shook his head, disgusted. "I should've seen this coming. It is extremely Jody."

Tossed it in a Dumpster.

"Oh," I said. "Um..."

"If the actual kidnapping had gone down," Trake said. "We would've caught on that it was staged. It's only because it never happened that it pulled the wool over."

"A Dumpster," I said. "*The* Dumpster."

Silence. They all turned to me.

"What's the weakest link in a kidnapping? I mean, for the kidnappers."

"The two points of definite contact," Van Huut said. "Getting the victim and getting the ransom."

"And spending the marked bills, right?" Pomerleau said. "But I guess that's afterward."

"Or not spending it," I said. "Jody didn't give a shit about the money—she only wanted it gone. She'd have her father waiting with a sack of cash at the Beresford Arms Hotel. She was going to have him 'deliver' it down the incinerator—the art deco incinerator chute. I fucking guarantee it." I saw from Van Huut's face that he agreed. "Twenty million dollars, up in smoke. You gotta love it."

I sat back in my chair, my heart pumping. It was beautiful, in its way. What had Ralph said? *Mousy-looking, chunky little thing, but passionate.* It took balls to burn twenty million dollars. But also a certain level of vindictiveness. No one had mentioned that about Jody.

"So for confirmation, we need to look for a clearing on Sears Island and find evidence she was there," Detective Trake said, consulting his notepad. "A drop location for her car, a witness who places her at the Beresford..."

"And the print on the note," I said.

"The White print."

"It'll tie the ransom note to her room."

"What the hell was the note doing in her car in the first place?"

I shrugged. "A mock-up? We have no idea what her time frame was."

"This is all a castle built on snow," Trake said. "But—"

"On sand," Cowan said. "A castle built on sand."

"Hey, I don't tell you where to build your castles," Trake said. "But I like it. It's...tidy. And it'll help us focus the investigation back where it ought to be. On the accident."

"That's right," Van Huut said. "Ralph Nicencio mentioned Ashbury might be able to clear that up once she does her—once she finishes with the accident scene."

Once I do my *thing*. Despite making so much progress with the fake kidnapping, I felt my throat tighten. I didn't want to do my fucking *thing*. I was gonna tell Van Huut where he could stick my *thing* when his cell phone rang.

"Van Huut," he said into the phone. "I'm in the middle of a... What? Are you sure?" He was silent for a minute. Then shook his head. "But that's... You're certain?" He listened some more. "Let me put you on conference call." He asked Pomerleau to get hold of a speakerphone and gave them the short version: "The DNA tests Ashbury ordered just came back." He looked directly at me. "The body. It's not Jody Hulfinger."

Back in my room, I pored over the old reports and started new ones. The phone rang and I finished the sentence I was writing before answering.

"They want you gone, Bridge," Theresa said.

"Who? Where?" I was only half listening, my mind muddled with too much information. I didn't feel like stopping for a pep talk from Theresa Udall.

"From the case."

"Uh-huh." There were too many loose ends. The stomach contents had been used to trace Jody to a restaurant in Camden—which would presumably help the Kidnap Team—but nobody noticed anything strange about her behavior, which meant I couldn't hang the accident on driver impairment, at least not yet. Plus, despite the fact that Jody had been ID'd at the restaurant, it turned out it wasn't *her* stomach. "They want me where?" I asked.

"Gone. Dropped from the team. Fired."

That got my attention. "Fired? From the case?"

"I'm sorry, Bridge—"

"They fire me, I'll never finish this investigation."

"That's what fired means. I just got off the phone with Ralph. Now that Jody Hulfinger is redisappeared, the Kidnap Team doesn't want you involved."

"The Kidnap Team wouldn't be here if it weren't for me."

"Then you only have yourself to blame."

"What about the accident scene?" Something was wrong at the scene. No one else would notice. "I haven't done my *thing*."

"I'm sorry, Bridge. But you know the FBI..."

"Yeah, I know the FBI." I tapped my pen against my report. This was bullshit. Van Huut didn't even hate me anymore. "Why would the FBI want me gone?"

"Well, the FBI...and Eleanor Wash."

Ah. This was from the NTSB. "With the rat hair? I didn't touch her."

"How about her car?"

"What? I was supposed to ride to Portland levitating off the seat?"

"Wash had an accident. On the way back from dropping you off," Theresa said. "She lost power, going seventy on the Mass Pike."

I felt my jaw knot. Losing power at seventy miles an hour, traffic screaming past, desperate to reach the safety of the shoulder... "Oh, Jesus." It could've been—

"Don't worry. She's fine."

It wasn't only Eleanor Wash I was worried about. "Great. Good."

"She says you were hostile."

"Is she NTSB, or OC? I don't like her hair. I don't like the way she drives. So what?"

"She got a call saying her vehicle was tampered with."

"She drove with one hand."

"Doesn't matter if you drive with no hands, that's not gonna pierce your radiator hose. She said, based on your psych eval—"

"She saw my eval?" Now I was really getting pissed off.

"Based on the *rumors* of your psych eval, it was possible you sabotaged the car."

I rubbed at the pain that was growing in my forehead. "Theresa, I was in that car." It was an effort not to imagine it; the cooling system failing at seventy mph on a road thick with traffic. "I was in that car and I'm not suicidal. A break in a radiator hose could be age, natural wear."

"Could be."

"What does Nguyen say?" The NTSB's top lab tech.

"It was a new break. On the underside of the hose. Could be due to a substandard part, or preexisting stress." Theresa gave it a second. "Could have been filed thin, then blown under the load of highway driving."

"This is bullshit, Theresa. Is there any physical evidence it was sabotage?"

"Nguyen didn't rule out the possibility."

Which meant there was no evidence. So they were trying to ease me off the case with nothing. "Admit it. This is all NTSB. That was crap about the FBI."

"Yeah, that was crap." Theresa's voice changed, became more human. "It was my decision. I want to take you off the team before you end on a stretcher."

"I can do my job."

"It's not your job I'm worried about," she said. "It's everything else."

"What happened to the good old days, like in Missouri?"

"You tell me."

What was there to tell? Highway 17 in California, between San Jose and Santa Cruz. Driving down that death-trap grade.

I'd been working the Hennessey-Enslow case, a multiple. Eight people dead in a three-car in Cupertino. Two of the cars had held the board members of Softwhere, who'd been carpooling to a meeting in Scotts Valley. Six men, worth three billion dollars. The third car had been two Vietnamese high-school kids worth substantially less than three billion dollars. Everyone would've been happy if it'd been their fault.

Far as I could tell, it hadn't been. Far as I could tell, it was spontaneous human combustion—because I didn't take it far. I dropped it halfway and handed it to Theresa. I'd dropped it and fled.

The cement risers between the lanes on Hwy 17 were black with tire marks. They were warnings, like decomposing skulls on a line of spears on a jungle path. Except I was the only one who saw them.

Jon had been in the left-hand seat, his hands resting gently on the wheel. In college, I'd loved Jon with the passion of a girl who thought she was a woman. Three months we'd been a couple, then three years we'd lived in the same house, with me pretending it was over and him believing it. I was a maven of masochism.

He'd been prelaw, idealistic prelaw, and married another house-mate, Hyacinth. A Frenchwoman. A *Parisienne*. Hyacinth was everything I was not, and a good deal more.

It took another year—after the wedding, which I'd helped arrange—to stop loving him. Two more to become friends, though he'd thought we'd been friends all along. Three years after that—when he'd become a rising star at Jacopy Brice Leadbetter, the law firm at which he specialized in representing corporate whistle-blowers—I'd become godmother to their baby boy.

Satchel.

What a stupid name. I'd told them it was stupid. Hell, they asked. I told them they'd regret not calling him Joe or Alex or Mark. They didn't listen. And the way Hyacinth pronounced it—Sah-shell, with the accent on the shell—made it only barely palatable.

Satchel. I loved that boy. I loved him still.

Jon had been driving, it had been his hands resting gently on the wheel. Thank God. Thank God Jon had been driving. That's what the year had done to my grief—relief that it hadn't been my hand on the wheel, my foot on the gas.

He'd been telling a story about a client who worked for an anti-freeze manufacturer who had sent internal memos to the press, describing how the company wouldn't spend a half cent a gallon to add "bitterant" to its product, which would have prevented dozens of child poisonings a year. Talk about someone who'd have liked Jody Hulfinger—idealistic, Opie-looking Jon, who represented his whistle-blowers with a sort of Biblical righteousness.

I had been turned around in the passenger seat, facing backward, putting Satchel's sock back on his foot. He squirmed like a one-year-old. I scolded, like a twenty-nine-year-old single, childless woman who wished the baby were hers. He was winning, his face all screwed up like an old man's. He'd been cranky and fussing, waving his pudgy ineffectual arms, wearing the Blue's Clues pullover that Jon's mother had bought over Hyacinth's objections—Hyacinth saying he was a baby, not a billboard. That round unlined face squooshed up and perfect clear eyes watching mine.

Jon had been laughing at the antifreeze manufacturer's foolishness. "Try to sell that to a jury, a half penny per gallon isn't worth making their bright blue, soda-looking product too bitter for children to drink. I almost pity the—"

The impact came without warning.

The initial explosive crash, the violent displacement of air. The screaming, the torsion, the twisted metal and sickening uncontrollable speed—my body snapping forward, bisected by the seat belt. Jon—his face whipping the windshield, starring the glass and splattering blood—scrabbling feebly at the wheel and dying, his right knee pressed against my leg, still warm.

And the boy. My little boy. His wet panting whimpers, the reek of blood and exhaust, of burning plastic. He hadn't cried. The boy, who cried from ten to midnight every night, who cried at the wind and the color of the walls, had made no sound louder than a whimper.

I had been paralyzed. Unhurt. Bruised. They called it shock. But it was fear.

I scratched at the seat belt cutting into my breast, in a world suddenly without light or heat, hyperaware, hearing every tinkle of glass, every eyeblink, scratching at the seat belt, unable to turn, unable to save my little boy....

The quiet, the stillness. The whimpers became silence.

What was there to tell?

The Principal's Daughter sat in the dark room and poured herself another glass of Syrah. She breathed it in and allowed herself to relax.

The inspector was being removed from the case. She had not let Brigid Ashbury have her man. A handful of conversations was all it had taken to brush Ashbury away. Like a gnat. Violence was the last resort—leverage the first.

The phone rang in the dark room.

It was him. His voice vibrated through the receiver. Chimed through her body like a hammer hitting a low, deep note on a gong. Like her father's voice, echoing in an empty room.

He had some news, he said. He wanted to be the person to tell her.

"Yes," she said. Did he suspect what she'd done for him? Did he know what she would do, if necessary?

He told her why he'd called, and her breath caught.

His did not. His voice was as steady as a pylon, rooted as deep as a grounding wire. Was there a message in his tone? Was he asking her to act, to refrain from acting?

She wished they could speak freely.

"Thank you," she said. She hung up before him. She always hung up before him. She did not like to ask herself why.

"The body was not Jody Hulfinger," she told the empty room. Then what had he done? He had taken pains and been subtler than she'd guessed. She should not have doubted him.

Relief and anxiety hit her again. He was not a killer. Yes, he was. He had removed Jody—that was true. But her body was not in the car. Had he killed twice?

How could she protect him if she didn't know what he'd done?

They wanted me gone, so I was gone.

Jody Hulfinger was gone. This other woman—the unnamed, unknown woman in the Jetta, her neck craning for one final breath—she was gone. Jon was gone, Satchel was gone. Why not me? No reason. Why hadn't it been Jody Hulfinger dead in that car? No reason.

Dr. MacRoule's voice had sounded weak and attenuated over the speakerphone sitting next to the open box of doughnuts, but his opinions had been as strong as ever.

I had said this new DNA information must be wrong.

"No," he'd replied. "Not at all."

"But it's one test, versus a wealth of evidence that—"

"Man strangled his wife," the doctor said. "Froze and dismembered her, and introduced the remains into a wood chipper vented toward a river behind his house. All that was recovered was a single tooth—but it yielded sufficient DNA material for comparison. The man was tried, convicted and sentenced."

"That's a great story, Doctor," I said. Somehow I'd been silently nominated as the person to speak with MacRoule. Didn't know how it had happened, but if I didn't object to this news, nobody would. "But if Jody—if the DNA of the woman in the car doesn't show she's Jody, then something's wrong with the test."

"The two samples are positively and unequivocally from unrelated people."

"These things aren't always conclusive."

"We used Catherine Hulfinger as a reference—as you suggested. The subject's—the purported subject's—twin sister. The DNA test shows conclusively that the recovered body was not related to Catherine Hulfinger."

"What about lab error?" I asked. "False positives or corrupted samples or whatever you call it."

"There was no lab error. If the samples provided were from the individuals claimed, the results are absolutely reliable."

I raised an eyebrow at Van Huut. Were the samples definitely from the individuals claimed? From the recovered body and from Cate Hulfinger?

He nodded sharply, his thin lips compressing, as though he were offended by the silent question.

I shrugged. It was my job to offend. "Run it through for me, again. The specimens were delivered to your lab. Then what?"

Dr. MacRoule's sigh did not sound weak, coming over the

speaker. "We extracted DNA from the specimen and purified it. We cut it into fragments using a restriction enzyme, which divides the DNA molecule at specific base sequences. The fragments, which carry a negative charge, are then separated into bands during electrophoresis, with the distance each fragment travels depending upon its length."

He paused. Despite the fact that he'd lost me in the first sentence, I said, "Go on. Depending on the length of the fragment..."

"The longer the fragment, the slower its rate of migration. This creates a number of DNA bands in a gel, which are transferred..." and so on.

The men around the table watched me. In disbelief or respect, I couldn't tell. But this is what I did—asked all the questions, then separated the wheat from the chaff. At least that was the theory. Still, it was getting too technical.

"Would you like me to explain Southern blotting?" MacRoule asked.

"No, that's okay. Continue."

"The membrane is exposed to a DNA probe with a radioactive tag, which seeks out a complementary sequence of bases. The probe binds to the DNA pattern and X-ray film is placed next to the membrane to detect the radioactive patterns. The patterns appear as a series of bands, not unlike a bar code on items at a grocery store."

"And this bar code?" I asked.

"Is unique for each individual. Except identical twins, of course. Like a fingerprint. Hence 'DNA fingerprinting.' We do multiple probes to increase the probability for a definitive identification."

"The probability. So it's not as definite as—"

"The probability, in this case, having compared five distinct sequences, is one in a hundred...to the fifth power. That's one in a billion, Inspector. One in a billion chance that the deceased was related to Catherine Hulfinger."

One in a billion. But maybe my point had been made. "Sounds like a complex procedure."

MacRoule knew where I was going. "It is both complex and routine. We do it all the time. There was no error."

His tone did not allow for further questions along that line.

"Shit." I glanced at Van Huut. "Was one of them adopted?"

"Sure," he said. "An adopted twin."

I gave him a halfhearted glare, then addressed the speakerphone. "But all the evidence, the size and weight and...you were so sure. What happened to eighty-five or ninety percent confidence the body was Jody Hulfinger?"

"Ten to fifteen percent happened."

I had retreated to my room. Then decided I needed to think aloud, so I called Ralph. I'd filled him in, then said, "So, three questions."

"Who's the dead girl? Where's Jody Hulfinger?" Ralph's voice was as mellow as ever. "And what else?"

I rubbed my eyes. "What was the dead girl doing in the Jetta?"

"How about, what was the Jetta doing in the bay? Theresa's concerned the reconstruction is slipping into the background."

"I can't reconstruct motive, Ralph."

"Wouldn't put it past you—so what's your operating delusion?"

"Don't have any for the first two questions. For the third...an

as-yet-unidentified friend of Jody's. The same size—probably
shared clothes. Jody asked her to dress up, drive the car. Give us
a 'Jody-spotting' as far as possible from the island. To make the kidnapping look real."

"But the car was on the island, where you expected Jody to camp
out...."

"This is a nightmare," I said. "First, a dead girl due to probable
SVA, except there's no apparent cause. Second, a kidnap note is
found, except there's no indication a kidnapping was planned,
much less implemented. And—"

"How would a kidnap attempt, even a staged one, tie in with a
single-vehicle accident?"

"That's third—the kidnapping wasn't a kidnapping. It was a
prank, or started that way. Fourth, the dead girl isn't the dead girl.
And fifth and sixth and seventh—"

"Back to the first three, Brigid. Who is the deceased? What was
she doing in Jody's car? Where is Jody Hulfinger? Break it down
and follow it up."

"How about this?" I said. "Is everything part of the same series
of events? Did the mock-kidnapping and the 'accident' and this
identical corpse all result from the same point of origin? They had
to. Like a ten-car accident caused by a cat crossing the road. There's
only one series of events. Because what kind of upside-down coincidence could lead to a situation this convoluted?"

"That's the biggest question of all," Ralph had said.

Maybe an upside-down coincidence *was* the only explanation. I
sat on my packed bag in front of the Inn, waiting for the driver *du*

jour to take me to the airport. Let my suits wrinkle. I'd have the NTSB pay for dry cleaning.

I toyed with the zipper of my bag, thinking about the case. No—it was too much. I could accept a little coincidence, but this was too much.

Didn't matter now. I was gone. Back to the cabin and the dark-eyed juncos. I wondered how Teeter was getting on. I wondered what happened to the girl in the Jetta. Maybe I'd never know. Probably no one would. Not without me doing my *thing*. 'Course, that was the good news; now I didn't have to do my *thing*. Or discover I was no longer able to—I didn't know which would be worse.

A Searsport police car rolled to a stop on the gravel driveway. I recognized the peaches-and-cream complexion through the glare on the window.

"Officer Pomerleau." I stood, bag in hand. "Glad to see a friendly face. Gonna be a long drive."

"Drive? No, I stopped by to report. You waiting on someone?"

I told him I'd been taken off the case.

"Oh, well." He glanced at the notepad he was holding. Forlorn. "Oh."

"But I'd love to hear it, you want to run it by me."

"Could I? Never wrote a report for the feds before. I'm a little… I want to get it right."

"What have you got, then?" I said quickly, before he realized he shouldn't be reporting to someone no longer on the case.

"A lucky break."

"On the pretrip? Or something the evidence team found?"

"Not the evidence team." And, with a little flourish: "The fire pit."

"You didn't track that down already?" I let him see my pleasure at the news—though why I cared, now that I was gone, I did not know.

"It was nothing. Small town. We've all been through the fire-pit stage. I spent some time at the high school—my sister's girl is a senior—and I made it sound like they'd crack the case for us. Aiding an FBI investigation, I called it."

I nodded. "Make 'em think Sydney Bristow would personally pin a medal on them. Though I guess she was CIA."

"The CIA's involved now?"

Sheesh. Perfect skin and not a TV-watcher; if I were halfway smart, I'd bring this guy home. "Forget it. What'd you learn?"

"Bunch of the kids were out on the day Hulfinger disappeared. Around midnight, they said, but could have been early as eleven-thirty or late as twelve-fifteen."

"Which means the accident occurred roughly between sundown and midnight."

"How do you figure sundown?"

"I checked the filaments," I said. "Her lights were on, the high beams."

"And midnight, because the fire pit was built on top of a skid mark."

A furrow, actually, but I let it go. "What time was sunset?"

"Six-thirty or seven. Let me check." He reached into his car, popped the glove compartment. Pulled out a farmer's almanac. Talk about prepared.

"Boy Scout?"

"Troop leader." He ran his finger down a page. "Seven-twelve.

So the event occurred between seven-twelve and twelve-fifteen. That narrows it down."

"Could be earlier, given that Jody—that the driver—probably hit her high beams before the sun set. At dusk." I shrugged. "But it gives Cowan a hell of a lot more on the pretrip."

He could track Jody Hulfinger backward in time, trace her car, maybe follow her from the restaurant where she'd had those onion rings. Except it wasn't her who ate the onion rings. Wasn't her in the car. Shit. Well, Cowan could try to pinpoint when the switch had occurred, when Jody's car keys ended up in the dead woman's hand.

It made my head spin thinking about it: Jody, not Jody. Kidnapping, not kidnapping. It was the FBI's problem now. I'd give them the time frame, and they could do the footwork, check the alibis. Determine who could have been on the causeway when the car went over. I said as much to Pomerleau.

"I thought you were off the investigation," he said.

"Just put it in your report. About alibis. And take all the credit you can."

"Credit for what?"

"Narrowing it down from two weeks to six hours."

"But what's important about those six hours? If the driver crashed the car herself, it doesn't matter. No one else was there. If someone tinkered with the car beforehand, it still doesn't matter. They wouldn't have stuck around to watch the fireworks."

"Yeah. Yeah, that's true." Then what was I thinking? There was something I couldn't grab hold of. I sat back down on my bag and stared at the patrol car's hubcap. There was something....

"I mean," he said, "why would the perp stick around, right?"

The hubcap was muddy, a Spirograph splash pattern twirling around the smooth silver convexity. "Right."

I stared at the hubcap. Pomerleau waited two minutes, then said he had to write that report and left. I watched the splash pattern spin away. Why had I thought an alibi was important? Why had I assumed it was?

Only one explanation. This was not an SVA, and the car hadn't been rigged. I didn't know how I knew, but I did.

Jody Hulfinger—Jody Hulfinger's car—had been run off the road.

The news hit the Hulfingers hard. Maybe harder than the original news had.

Aaron thought they'd be relieved, overjoyed—but they heard Jody was still missing, might still be alive, and they crumpled. Instead of mourning Jody, they were terrified for her. If she was alive, she'd been missing for a month—no end of horrors a woman could suffer in a month. If she was dead, how had she died? No end of horrors there, either.

And who was this woman in Jody's place? Her presence, her resemblance to Jody, proved this was no accident. It was not swift, random, unpredictable. It was intentional, and intended to cause pain, and someone knew more than they were saying. There was a feeling in the house—there were currents and undercurrents thickening in the air. Someone knew something. Aaron intended to find out who and what.

Nile and Phillipa were due in a couple hours. He'd get one of them alone when they came. At the moment, though, he was in the living room, relaying the latest to Small and Gayle. The FBI had searched its missing-persons archives, found no hits for the dead woman. They'd recontacted hospitals and unearthed nobody matching Jody's description. And they were following Brigid Ashbury's lead, tracking Jody's movements: she'd had dinner, paid cash and walked out the restaurant into darkness.

Small listened without expression. Aaron wondered if Gayle'd been dispensing her Zopiclone—she was apparently a world-class insomniac—because Small looked, for the first time since Aaron had met him, small. He was slumped in a leather armchair, pale and sunken. He'd snapped into action upon hearing the news— asking questions, making phone calls—but then, not two hours later, had all but collapsed.

"Be a darling and get the Scotch?" Gayle asked Aaron. "The good Scotch. You know where it's kept?"

"Don't want Scotch," Small said. "Not even lunchtime."

"It's not for you." She smiled at Small, Aaron was surprised by how gently. "You only have to deal with the news. I have to deal with you."

"I'm not sure," Small said, shaking his head. "Not sure how much longer I can bear this…this not knowing."

"You'll bear it as long as you have to, Stanwood." Her voice was commanding but not unkind, almost maternal.

Small didn't like the tone. "Don't you try to manage me."

She folded herself into the love seat opposite. Crossed her great expanse of legs and watched him without visible concern. "Someone has to if you're turning teetotaler. Now will you have that Scotch or not?"

He guffawed. Gayle took it as a yes, and glanced toward Aaron. "Two glasses, then, darling."

The Scotch was in the pool room, as were Cate and Van Huut. They were in the slung-leather seats at the mahogany table, chairs pulled close. He caught a glimpse of something in Van Huut's expression that made him think of a father confessor with impure thoughts—and Cate was looking like a model-turned-actress, playing one of her pet roles. "Tough little rich girl on the verge," maybe.

Aaron supposed he was jealous. There was an intimacy to the scene which excluded him—then Cate noticed him in the doorway and flashed a smile he recognized.

The goodbye smile.

The average shelf life of his relationships was roughly that of buttermilk—though far less sour. And when women left him, they always said the same thing: *Thanks.* As if he'd held the elevator door or zipped up their dress.

Except that time when Shirley stuck a pair of scissors in his leg. But that wasn't the point. Point was, Cate gave him the goodbye smile. She wouldn't get the words out for another week, unless he helped things along. He wasn't going to, though: he needed access to the Hulfingers. Needed to see this through and figure out who killed Jody. Well, Brigid Ashbury would probably figure that out, but maybe not without Aaron's help.

"I'm on a medicine run," he said, pretending he hadn't recognized the smile. "Sent for your father's finest Scotch." He kissed her on the crown of her head. "How are you holding up, Catie?"

She started to answer, then turned toward him and buried her face in his side. He stroked her neck, and Van Huut was suddenly busy in his briefcase. Aaron felt a flash of triumph—he'd asserted ownership of Cate. Neanderthal, but there it was. He traced a line from behind her ear to her cheekbone to her lips. He'd miss her.

"Small and Gayle okay?" Van Huut's voice was a little abrupt. "I was telling Cate how sorry we are—I am—that this happened. Happened now, when they were coming to terms with Jody being gone."

Aaron nodded. "I'm sure they—"

There was a scuffing at the door, and TJ entered. He'd been wafting around the house like a wraith. Aaron had always found him kind of...glassy. Smooth and cool. But now he had welts where his eyes should be, taking it even harder than Catie.

"Dad can't chair the Yedrow meeting," he told Cate, his voice almost timid. "Should I sit in, or ask Leanne and John to deal with it?"

"Oh, TJ," Cate said, with more sympathy than the question deserved. "You poor thing."

"It's nothing. It's details. It's just Dad would want—"

"Asking *me* for business advice, I mean. You must be a wreck. Let Leanne and John handle it."

"Yes, okay. Of course." He sat next to her, and they were silent while Aaron got two glasses from the bar. Then he got four more and put them on the mahogany table and waited for someone to object. No one did. He poured.

"You know what's strange?" TJ said. "I don't know why, but—
I keep thinking about the day she was born. You were born. You
and Jody."

"Not that again," Cate said. She turned to Van Huut. "It's like
the bobcat story—you must've heard this a hundred times."

"Only a dozen," he said.

The story was a Hulfinger classic. One of Small's favorites. He
and his first wife, Maureen, were in San Francisco in 1972. She was
pregnant, due in two weeks. The pregnancy had been easy, a walk
in the park. Then her water broke on a trolley, halfway up Powell
Street. Now, if Small told the story, he already had the audience
laughing. Describing how he'd panicked, while Maureen kept
saying, "I think it's time, Stan," and TJ rode on the outside of the
trolley, blissfully unaware.

But in brief, some kind soul told Small there was a birthing
center a block away. This was before birthing centers, Small says;
he thought they meant a hospital. He rushed Maureen around the
block and found a hovel. Bright and cheery, but a hovel. The
women there—at the Sunrise Birthing Center—put Maureen in
a bright yellow room and asked if Small wanted to be present for
the birth.

That's a laugh line if you know Small.

Then they asked if he wanted a joint. That's another laugh line.

And after all that, the twins weren't born for another eight
hours.

"The thing is," TJ said. "I remember you both, the size of my
forearm, and I keep thinking, you know, from there—from then—
to here and now."

There was silence. Ice cubes tinkled in glasses of Scotch. A few minutes slipped by.

"There's something I never told anyone." TJ stared into his Scotch. "I was there. When you were born. They asked Dad if he wanted to be in the room with Mom. If he wanted to cut the umbilical cord. But, you know, they asked me, too."

"If you wanted to cut the cord?"

"If I wanted to be with Mom when she had you. They said it'd be beautiful." He grinned faintly, remembering. "I was ten, I wasn't stupid. I said no way. And then, you know, when you and Jody started coming—"

"Small sent out for cigars," Cate said, filling in the blanks.

"But before that, before the cigars. I went back in."

"To Mom? In the delivery room?"

TJ nodded.

Aaron sipped, let the Scotch burn his throat. Not him. He'd get down and dirty when it was his woman having a kid—but his mother? Not him.

"Yeah." TJ hunched a shoulder. "I don't know. I wanted to see."

"I'd have done the same," Aaron said.

"And they were very encouraging. I remember—you know, they didn't know she was having twins. You came first, and they were like, 'job well done, let's sing Kuumbaya.' Then one of them, the older lady, she says, 'Hold the reins, she's only half-done.'" He smiled. "And then Jody came, like the icing on the cake."

He looked from Cate to Aaron to Van Huut. This was something that'd been weighing on him, something he'd wanted to say for a long time.

"I keep thinking," he said. "I was there when she was born. And I'm here now, and Jody, she's just...gone."

I didn't have to do my *thing*. That was the bright and shining silver lining. But getting fired, shit. That was a dark cloud. And getting fired when I knew—when I *knew*—that Jody Hulfinger's car had been run off the road? Beyond cloudy. That was a whole rainstorm.

I squirmed on top of my bag. Where was that driver? Firing me was one thing—making me wait was another. Especially when I couldn't stop thinking.

I'd been over it and over it. Why was I so sure an impact had knocked the Jetta off the road? The vehicle path was consistent with being run off the road—but there was no paint transfer, no vehicle imprints. Unless the second vehicle was encased in a huge condom, there had to be an exchange of material.

It wasn't getting any clearer. The more I thought, the less I knew. I pulled my nail file from my purse and went to work on my pinkie again. A little obsessively, like picking at a scab, but I tried not to let it bother me.

If she'd been run off the road, then what was the initial impact? Imprints showed nothing but boulders and tree stumps. Forget it. I was off the case. There was no point—

"Ready for the postgame show?"

It was Theresa. I hadn't heard the Ford Taurus approach. Hmm. Maybe I was getting better.

"You're my driver?" I asked.

"Your personal gold watch."

I stood and put my hands on the roof of the car and looked down at Theresa. "The car was run off the road. The car—Theresa, it was run off the road."

"Bridge, you're off the case."

"You're not listening. It was run off the fucking road, and there isn't another investigator in the NTSB can tell you why."

It took ten minutes, and some degree of brutality, for me to convince Theresa. But I'd been right too many times.

"Then you're back on. Provisionally. With one condition."

I felt a flush of triumph, then realized what the condition was. Fuck.

"I'll do it tomorrow," I said. Theresa and I were in the Inn's living room—surrounded by chintz, talking about death. She'd shown up an hour ago, pretending she was here for moral support, really looking for weaknesses. "I'll do my *thing* tomorrow."

"It's still light out."

"I don't care if it's high fucking noon. It's gotta be the same time of day the crash occurred."

"One minute nothing's more important than finishing the investigation, the next we have all the time in the world."

"All the time in the world." I rolled my eyes like a surly preteen. "I'm talking about tomorrow, Theresa."

"It's bottom of the ninth and two strikes." Theresa put her coffee cup on the end table. "We need a hit."

"Drive me to the Hulfinger's. You can hit it off with Van Huut." He'd called, and said he had the alibis written up. He asked me to meet him at the Hulfinger's camp.

"Do it today."

"How long are you here for?"

"I leave at dawn. I want your report in my fax machine by noon."

I stood, walked to the window and looked outside. Don't say it. Don't say you'll do it. I'd spent the last hour not saying it. Instead, I'd stonewalled. Explained DNA testing. Called the FTA twice, left messages for Sesame Gustine, the guy in charge. Told Theresa this whole thing was rooted in Jody's family—just as if a Kennedy disappeared, you had to look at all the angles, but odds were it had something to do with being a Kennedy. Even if it was Jody's politics, that went back to her family, too. "It's not exactly a camp, either," I said. "More like a mansion." Hoping to get her interested in gossiping about the rich, if not famous.

"That's hardly news," Theresa had said.

I sighed. "The investigation of the family has been half-assed. Alibis, motives, means, opportunity—all sketchy."

"What do you expect? We don't know what crime has been committed. We don't know what happened to her car. And we won't. Until you do your *thing*."

I pressed a finger against my temple, still needing some Advil. Don't say it. I didn't need to do this. I could figure it out without... No. I couldn't.

I said it: "Tomorrow. Tomorrow evening."

And there went the silver lining.

It wasn't a half hour to the Hulfinger's house. A drive I had endured four times already. An easy drive, a pushover. All I had to do was not reveal to Theresa how deep the fractures went.

It was worse than ever.

With Theresa driving, I couldn't let myself tremble. I made myself relax into the passenger seat. Made myself feel the snugness of the belt without wincing. Made myself respond to Theresa's inane chatter in a calm and level voice.

When Aaron—when White—drove, it didn't matter. I didn't care what he thought. Maybe he made me wonder how I held my head, but I didn't have to maintain the fiction of my composure.

With Theresa, I did. Theresa now telling me a story about one of the many men in Washington who was in love with her. This one was a cardiac surgeon. David. They were all named David. They were all cardiac surgeons.

I moved my mouth into what was meant to be a smile. "Next right," I said in a thin voice.

Theresa pulled into the driveway, and I was out the door the moment the car stopped. Leaning over the bench on the front lawn, my hands on the cool, rough stone and swallowing air. I heard footfalls behind me. Theresa, who'd never had a moment's self-doubt.

"I'll find Van Huut," she said to the back of my head. "Maybe we can talk out here. Five minutes?"

"Ten," I said.

They gave me twenty minutes. Barely enough.

I looked at them with what I felt were yellowed eyes when they approached. They returned my look with bland nods. Van Huut sat on the bench next to me and opened the report in his lap. Theresa perched on the stone armrest.

"You asked for alibis for the time of the crash," Van Huut said. "Six-thirty to twelve-fifteen."

"Yeah."

"I did this as a courtesy to you—to Ralph. But I know the Hulfingers. None of the members of Jody's immediate family were party to this—"

"Does that mean you think the Lockwoods were a party?" I asked.

"Excuse me?"

"Not immediate family, are they?"

"Jody would have said they were." He flipped the page. "Nile Lockwood was at a departmental meeting from four to five-thirty at Smith in Massachusetts. Then she drove to Lincolnville. Colleagues say she was in a hurry to leave—"

"Oh?" Theresa said.

"They also say that's not unusual. Consensus is that she has a demon lover in the Maine woods—races up here every chance she gets. But racing, it still takes five hours. So the earliest she arrived at her mother's house was nine-thirty."

"She's got no alibi other than her mother for that evening?" I asked.

Van Huut nodded. "Phillipa Lockwood. Came up from Boston the same day. Puttered around the house and garden. Nile showed up at ten, according to her statement, and they went to bed soon after."

"So neither would know if the other left the house?"

Van Huut nodded again. "Or they might have left together, if you insist upon paranoia. Oh—and their statement was vague about

the hows and whys of their decision to get Aaron White involved.
I wondered if—"

"He screwed it out of Nile Lockwood."

"Jesus H!" Van Huut said. "What is it with him? Cate, Jody,
Nile. He's not even much to look at— Is he?"

"Not much," I said. But his voice and eyes, and the way he
moved...

"The more I hear," Theresa said, "the more I want to meet him."

"Take a chaperone," Van Huut said.

"How's his alibi?" I asked.

"He and Cate are the only ones who couldn't have been on-
scene. They were in Cambridge all day and into the night."

"Then it's definitely one of them," Theresa said. "Nothing more
suspicious than an airtight alibi. Ask Agatha Christie."

Van Huut smiled at her. "Or Arthur Conan Doyle."

They were kindred cheese balls. Bet Van Huut liked sports
analogies, too. "And the rest?" I asked.

Van Huut made an exasperated noise. "Gayle was in and out of
the house a half-dozen times during the target hours. Small worked
at the Portland branch office until five-thirty, then drove home.
TJ worked at same until six, spent a couple hours at the gym and
went back to work until ten."

"Well, that's deeply unhelpful."

"Especially considering we've got better questions than alibis.
Where's Jody? Who's the woman in the car?"

"Had to be done," Theresa said. "And when we get a read on the
accident scene—"

A shadow moved across the bench, and TJ was suddenly

standing behind us. He was so quiet it made me suspect a multitude of sins, but I didn't know if it was the quiet of stealth or self-effacement. I had no idea how long he'd been standing there.

"Would you like some lemonade?" he asked.

"Pardon?" Theresa said.

"I saw you out here. I thought you might like some lemonade."

Van Huut told him no, they didn't want lemonade and suggested perhaps Small and Gayle would be better people to ask. TJ nodded, drifted toward the house.

"Been like that all day," Van Huut said.

"Skulking around?" I asked.

"Disoriented. Kidnap Team says it's a common enough response. Hell, Small's turning into an invalid, Gayle into a den mother, TJ's reminiscing about the good old days. And Cate—" Van Huut cut himself off. "Well, they're all pretty upset."

"That's in your report, is it?" I asked.

He tossed the file onto the bench next to me. "Knock yourself out, Ashbury."

I would. It was better than thinking about doing my *thing* tomorrow evening.

22

"I don't want to talk to you," Nile told Aaron, still standing in the kitchen with him.

"I don't care."

"I don't have to talk to you," she said.

"Don't care about that, either."

She paused, her vague eyes brushing his. Then she slid past him, toward the dining room.

"Goddammit," Aaron said. He smacked his palm against the cabinet next to her head. That got her undivided attention, for the first time since she'd wandered into the kitchen.

A half hour ago, TJ had floated wraithlike from the pool room after unburdening himself of his story. Van Huut had bustled off to file another report. And—Aaron didn't know if this was ghoulish or reprehensible or what—Catie and he, left alone, the taste of Scotch and bereavement in their mouths, had exchanged a familiar look. He supposed they had both wanted comfort and forgetting. They had walked silently to her room.

She'd stood motionless as he undressed her.

It was their way. She liked to be still, at first. She liked to be handled, to be passive as he undressed her. She'd wait until he'd unbuttoned the final button, slid the last strip of cloth off her slender, hungry body. Then she'd pull him close—her eyes glazed, a catch in her breath—greedy and demanding, an entirely selfish lover. Nothing is sexier than that. Sex with a woman who wants to please a man is nothing compared to sex with a woman who wants to please herself.

Aaron had kissed his way from Cate's forehead to her mouth to the nape of her neck. He'd undressed her—but her eyes were not glazed and her breath did not catch. He took her oval face in his hands and he looked at her looking at him.

Then they'd smiled, together. Not a goodbye, but a kind of greeting. She'd dressed, and they'd walked downstairs to make lunch.

He'd been slicing tomatoes for the gazpacho when Nile wafted in. She'd hugged Cate, and murmured something comforting. She didn't hug Aaron.

He gave Catie the lazy eye, asking her to leave. She shot him a look. He wasn't sure if it said *Nile? You're sniffing after Nile?* or *Did you sleep with Nile, you fuckwit?* He shook his head minutely, and apparently Cate believed whatever she saw in his face. She said she'd go check on her father.

Aaron always wondered how much he could silently communicate with a woman if they were together longer than three or four months. Ten years, and he bet you could explain macro-economic theory with a lifted eyebrow.

Of course, he was giving Nile more than an eyebrow.

"Goddammit," he said again, his palm stinging from the impact of the cabinet. He leaned in close, too abruptly, and she startled. He was pleased to see he could inspire an unrehearsed response from her—all it required was brutality.

"Nile, you're the one she talked to," he said. "The one she had no secrets from. What the fuck is going on?"

I shifted on the cold stone bench. There was some baffling crap in Van Huut's report. That was my official conclusion. Question was, how did you follow up on baffling crap? Trying to block out Van Huut's and Theresa's nattering, I mentally divided it into two categories.

First category was family crap: Gayle Cornell attempting a bloodless coup—the woman staking some kind of matriarchal claim on the family. TJ drifting about unmoored, telling rambling stories of Jody's birth and childhood. Cate indulging in hour-long crying jags when she wasn't clinging to Aaron. Phillipa Lockwood being effusive and unhelpful and Nile Lockwood being mulishly unforthcoming.

Second category was factual crap:

Cate had been in rehab for a cocaine addiction. That was new.

TJ had been in a couple barroom brawls during his lumberjack phase. Old, but intriguing.

Phillipa had taken early retirement two months ago, claiming she wanted to put more time into Home of Our Own, a nonprofit that funded women's shelters.

Nile was at the center of an obscure yet growing academic firestorm.

Gayle Cornell had been married three times and widowed twice—to her great financial benefit. She came from a San Francisco "society" family, and at a time when being a debutante and young wife meant something, she'd embodied that something. At least until her first husband, twenty-five years her senior, failed to wake up one morning, nine months after the wedding. Husband number two moved to Spain after they divorced, and was apparently still alive; number three lasted seven years, then collapsed in the middle of a doubles tennis game. No sign of foul play.

Then there was Small. He wasn't reinvesting twenty-three million in HulCorp on a whim. The corporation had been under heavy fire, and not only from groups like Free Them All. Three months earlier, the U.S. Federal Institute of Corrections issued a report claiming that privatizing prison operations did not reduce expenditures. The twenty-three million invested in the contract laundry business was Hulfinger's personal guarantee of performance and longevity. He was putting his own money into expanding at a time when the company's raison d'être was being called into question. The amount was a drop in the bucket for Hulfinger, but people at his level never risked their own personal money— his doing so showed complete confidence.

I read the report, trying to discern the normal strangeness from the extraordinary. One thing in particular made me wonder. One innocent thing. No reason to doubt it, no reason to read it twice.

Maybe that's why I did. It was too convenient. If only Van Huut and Theresa would shut up, I'd be able to read it a third time. Maybe put my finger on the problem.

But they wouldn't.

Van Huut had briefed Theresa, given her the verbal update as I read the written one. Fine—until they'd started comparing life stories. I knew Theresa's well enough to ignore hers, but I hadn't heard Van Huut's, and was half listening as I read. He was a Wisconsin boy. Joined the National Park Service out of college. Transferred ten years later to the FBI and had been working his way ever upward since that time. With a little help from his friends.

The security-consulting work he did for Small Hulfinger was back during the biotech days. He'd been introduced through Gary Putnam, who'd been in charge of Hulfinger's corporate security even then. I got the impression that's why the FBI was working so smoothly with HulCorp security to cover the corporate end of the investigation. I got another impression, too: there were personal feelings involved. On Van Huut's side. It wasn't simply a professional relationship he had with...with whom? Maybe Jody. Maybe Cate. Hell, maybe Gayle or TJ, for all I knew. Maybe I needed to let him sit in on more questionings, gauge his reaction.

Listening to the story of his meritorious rise at the Bureau— and hearing Theresa's self-impressed story again—I felt the pressure building behind my temples. The two of them so sure the only direction was up—the law of gravity as applied to the bright and ambitious.

I rubbed my forehead, stood and told Theresa I'd see her for dinner, I was going inside to find some silence.

Van Huut looked offended, Theresa unsurprised.

"We boring you?" Theresa said.

"No. Annoying me."

"That's fine, then," Theresa said. "I'll go over the playbook with Special Agent Van Huut, meet back at your hotel at seven."

"Seven is good."

"Great—we'll be at the Kidnap Team incident room in Augusta, you need anything. The federal building." Then she frowned at me. "Oh, but you need me to drive you back."

"I'm fine," I lied.

Theresa raised an eyebrow.

"I'll get a ride. It's no problem."

"If you're sure…"

"I'm sure."

"You're sure?"

"I'm sure."

And I was. I'd call Cowan or Pomerleau or—no. No reason to start lying to myself. I'd ask Aaron. White. I wouldn't even ask. I'd put myself in his path, and he'd offer. I'd accept.

Because with him, I didn't have to focus on keeping it together. I could sit rigid in the passenger seat, clutching the dashboard, thinking about how to follow up on Van Huut's report. And how I held my head.

Nile was small. Girlish and soft-spoken, and even knowing she was an intellectual Olympian didn't change the effect. She inspired a kind of automatic masculine response. Made Aaron want to protect and coddle her.

He overcame the impulse. Leaned in closer, stepping all over her personal space. "Nile. Tell me."

She shook her head. "I don't know, I don't know anything about this."

"You knew she kidnapped herself. You knew that."

She turned her face away, as if she refused to admit Aaron existed.

"What was your cut?" he asked.

She raised her face, her gaze suddenly incisive.

"Of the ransom. Your mother doesn't get enough alimony? Not in the will, are you? I hear Small's got language in there says any child of his who isn't *his* doesn't get a dime. Is that it? Figure you and Mom'll renegotiate the prenup?"

"I can't imagine why you think you have a right to talk like this."

"I don't give a shit what rights I have. Someone knows something. Someone knows something, and I think it's you."

She didn't say anything, but she managed to make the silence eloquent. Still, he wasn't going to stop now.

"Jody tells you she's gonna Patty Hearst herself. Then she disappears." He made his voice cruel. "And you? You kept on teaching political-fucking-epistemology and Jacques Derrida like nothing happened while she was—"

"I didn't! I did not. I did not keep teaching like nothing happened."

"—like nothing happened, like you didn't have everything to do with it, and lo and fucking behold, a kidnap note is found. Then you say, 'oh, yeah, well, she did mention something about kidnapping herself, terribly sorry but I didn't think it mattered before,' and now she's dead. She's dead. But, oh, actually it's not Jody who's dead, she's still missing and the only one who knows—"

"I loved her." Her voice was as steady as a flat line on a heart monitor. "I love her, you asshole, like she's my twin instead of Cate's. I was up here a week, waiting. Not sleeping, not eating, and what good did it do? I was on the phone every day talking to Cate or TJ."

"You were on the phone," he said dismissively, because she'd paused and he wanted her to keep talking.

"If she'd done what she said, there would have been demands. She would have made demands. There weren't any. Why would I drag her through this when there were no demands? Don't you think I wonder—should I have said she made some remark about Patty Hearst? If I could've saved her, saved her from—whatever's happened? Don't you think I wonder where she is now?"

She turned her beautiful, crumpled face toward the floor. Tears rolled down her cheeks, and there was silence in the kitchen except for the sound of her breathing.

Aaron murmured something wordless, low and comforting.

"I loved her," she said. "I loved her like she was *my* sister. My real sister. We were both…you know, ugly ducklings—smart fat girls with glasses. Right out of central casting. But then, with two of us, when Mom married Small…it was the best thing. We were alone, then we were together."

Aaron was finally getting a ping. Nile loved Jody Hulfinger. And when she found someone to love, there was nothing she wouldn't do for them.

"I thought you left." I was sitting in Small's study, deciding who I wanted to interview when Theresa entered without knocking.

"In five minutes," Theresa said. "But I just saw White in action and wanted to say—*shee-it. Shee.*" Theresa shook her head. "*It.*"

White in action? What did that mean? "Okay, you said it."

"I'll say it again. *Shee-it.* I wouldn't mind taking him for a victory lap."

"Do I need to hear this?"

"Are you telling me to take a number?"

"I'm telling you to take a cold shower."

"You should have seen him. He was in the kitchen with Nile Lockwood—have you met her?"

"Briefly."

"Yeah, I don't like her, either. Better than Cate, though. At least Nile's carrying some extra pounds."

Yeah, like two of them. And Theresa was a size six. I pretended to hear something outside. "Is that Walter, honking for you?"

She ignored me. "I'm in the dining room, I see the whole thing. White says he wants to talk to her. She doesn't want to talk. She tries to scoot past him, out the door."

"Can't blame her."

"He puts his hands up, kinda boxes her in. Between his arms. Mmm-hmm. Starts talking low and furious. I couldn't hear what he was saying, but the way he was looking at her… He looks at me that way, I'll give up *all* my secrets."

"You don't have any secrets, Theresa."

"That's part of my charm. So he's… I don't know—it's like the verbal lambada. Takes two minutes before she gives it up, they're sitting at the kitchen counter and she's pouring her heart out."

"Well, I'm glad to hear you've been busy."

"I have been busy." Theresa let me see she was serious. "With the bus. Twelve kids, plus one in a coma and one who'll never look right again. I get the press conferences, acting Little Miss Official Sympathy to those poor fucking parents. Driver asleep at the wheel. Okay?"

"Okay."

"I'm sorry," Theresa said. "But this is like the halftime show, after dealing with that."

"I understood you the first time. You have anything constructive to add?"

"Fuck you, Bridge," Theresa said lightly. "You got a stick shift up your ass?" And on those immortal words, she left.

The verbal lambada. Maybe I would start asking my questions in the kitchen.

Nile was in love. Sick with unrequited love. She couldn't hide the symptoms.

She'd been talking for ten minutes about *men*. Talking about *men* as if there weren't one man in particular she loved. Men will treat you like a lover when you want a friend, and treat you like a friend when you want a lover. You can't make a man love you, you can't make yourself stop loving him. On and on.

Aaron wanted to tell her men weren't that complex. Maybe a mind like hers, used to delving into the mysteries, had trouble seeing the simple things. Or maybe it was just she was a woman. But sometimes it's better to listen than speak, so he kept quiet and heard all about *men*. He didn't like them much, either, the way she described them.

Her face was flushed yet composed. A tear occasionally welled up in the corner of her eye, rolled down the curve of her cheek. The tears for Jody had become tears for herself. He guessed that's what grief was. So he said the standard, inadequate things. And he thought: if the currents and undercurrents of guilt and denial weren't coming from Nile, where were they coming from?

Not Catie. TJ? Small? Maybe; he'd deflated like an old balloon, but Aaron couldn't tell if it was pose or reality. Gayle or Phillipa? Both were strong, both were smart. He liked Phillipa and disliked Gayle, but that didn't mean anything. Could be more than one of them, he supposed, or—

Nile made a sudden hiccuping cry. She stood and covered her mouth with her hand. Her eyes went wide and she grabbed a handful of napkins and was gone before Aaron could remember what she'd just been saying.

TJ was framed in the doorway. He looked better, his face less drained, his eyes more alive.

TJ? Was Nile running from TJ? Was it possible that polite, colorless TJ could inspire passion? If so, what else would he be capable of? No one could be that respectful without having some deeply buried twist. But if he was involved...why?

He had everything. But maybe he knew about Jody's fake kidnapping attempt, and felt threatened. Yeah. TJ knew, because if Nile was in love with him, she would have told him. Then he arranged to have Jody— But no, the easiest way for TJ to stop Jody was simply to tell Small her plans. And who the hell was this second woman, this dead woman?

"Hey, TJ?" Aaron said. "Is Nile in love with you?"

TJ grinned and grabbed a bottle of balsamic vinegar off the butcher-block table and hit Aaron in the face with it.

Aaron fell backward off his chair. Didn't feel anything in his cheekbone and ear—not yet—but the sound of the bottle impacting cracked through his head, and the dislocation from falling, the abrupt violence and the sick-making realization he'd been hit stunned him into immobility.

He put his hand to his face, felt for blood. The room tilted and the chair was tangled in his feet and he didn't understand what had just happened.

TJ strolled around the counter and looked down, the bottle held casually in his hand. "Don't fuck with her," he said.

Aaron said, "Okay."

TJ leaned over as if he was gonna help Aaron up, but the hand holding the bottle cocked back ready to deliver another blow. Aaron crabbed backward, scrambling and uncoordinated, until he hit the kitchen wall. TJ took two steps forward, and Aaron kicked at his knee. Missed, and hit the fallen chair instead. It pivoted, spun on its axis, and smacked TJ's shin with a gratifying *crack*.

"You fucker," TJ said, and sucked in a breath. He tossed the chair aside and swung the bottle at Aaron's face again.

Aaron raised his arm against the blow and TJ kicked him in the stomach. Aaron grabbed his stomach, and TJ punched him in the face. Not, mercifully, with the vinegar bottle—but Aaron's head snapped back into the wall. He was stunned and gasping, and TJ leaned down to his ear. Two inches away. Aaron thought he was going to bite it off.

"I heard you fucked Nile," TJ said.

"I never touched her, TJ," Aaron said.

"You made her cry," he said. "You made her cry."

Aaron said, "Men!" in the tone women use, and smashed the side of his head into TJ's mouth. It hurt like hell, but must've hurt TJ worse, his teeth splitting his lip open. TJ jerked away with a grunt and Aaron stood, and his feet weren't where he expected. He lurched, almost fell over. Grabbed the counter to steady himself, and put his hand in the pulpy mess of the tomatoes he'd been slicing.

Right next to the knife.

"You fucked my *sister*," TJ said. "You fucked my *stepsister*. There's no way you're going to fuck *me*."

TJ's lip was pouring blood, and seeing it gave Aaron a moment of pleasure between the time he said, "I fucked both your sisters, asshole," and the time TJ jumped him.

Aaron remembered thinking: *grab the knife, dumbass.* But he hesitated. He didn't know if he was afraid he'd stab TJ or afraid he wouldn't, but that temper Detective Trake had been so interested in was nowhere to be found.

Aaron hesitated—TJ didn't. It was a brief and uneven struggle, and all Aaron had to defend himself was a hand dripping tomato juice. If TJ hadn't smashed him in the face, maybe it would've been different. But he had. And TJ brought the vinegar bottle up again, and was about to bring it down when he suddenly jerked backward.

Brigid Ashbury, glorious angel of a woman, had grabbed TJ's left wrist and elbow and spun it down to her hip, twisted at a wrong angle. The rest of his body followed his arm like a marionette following a dropped string. He bent at an acute angle, his left arm held

effortlessly in her hands, his right waving the vinegar bottle inef-
fectually in the air.

They froze. It was like a strobe light going off in a nightclub;
the motion stopped, the room arrested. Then the bottle fell, shattered on the tile floor. The stain slid fast across the tiles, the smell
of vinegar filled the air.

"What the fuck is going on?" Brigid said in what must've been
her cop voice, half growl, half command.

Her face was flushed, her lips curved in what wasn't a grin—
her red-brown hair vibrant against the white of the ceiling. She was
glorious. Of course, Aaron was hardly impartial—she'd just
stopped him from getting his face stomped. But still, he thought
glorious was a statement of fact.

"Let go of me," TJ said. His lip was swollen and dripping blood.
"Take your hand off."

She pushed his elbow an inch toward the floor—he sucked air,
and the acute angle sharpened.

Aaron stayed on the floor, looking up at them, going over his
face with his fingertips. Nothing broken; everything bruised.

"I asked you a question," she said. Her gaze was on Aaron.

"Nothing," TJ said. "Nothing's going on. We had a disagreement."

"He started it," Aaron said. He thought the flippant tone came
through okay, but the attempted grin hurt like hell.

Brigid didn't smile. She stared at him a moment longer, and he
tried a shrug. That hurt, too.

"We're all calm now?" she said.

Aaron slowly stood. Considered, for a passing moment, punch-
ing TJ in the face while Brigid held him, but decided against it.

TJ breathed for a minute. "Yeah. Calm now," he said. The deferential quality back in his voice. "I'm sorry, Aaron. I just—I just blew. I don't know what came over me...all this has been, you know... I haven't lost my cool like that in years."

Aaron grabbed a dish towel from a drawer and shuffled toward the fridge. It probably hadn't been two minutes since he'd said *Hey, TJ? Is Nile in love with you?*

"There's a difference between losing your cool and assault and battery," Brigid said. She released TJ in such a way that the momentum sent him two steps toward the dining room, away from Aaron.

TJ stood in the doorway, uncertain, his eyes flickering between Aaron and Brigid. He gave the impression of being stooped. Confused and repentant and sort of feeble.

"I'm sorry," he said. "It's done."

"I'm not sure that's your decision to make," Brigid said. "From what I saw, Mr. Hulfinger, I think Mr. White could bring charges."

Aaron opened the freezer, grabbed a handful of ice, packed it in the dish towel. Shuffled back to the counter, righted the chair and sat heavily. TJ had thought he was protecting his property. Like Aaron trying to show Van Huut that Catie was his. They deserved each other, him and TJ. He thought Aaron slept with Nile, and even if he wasn't in love with her, he didn't want anyone infringing on his...

Aaron pressed the cold cloth to his cheek and realized where TJ must've heard that he'd slept with Nile: Brigid. But why would she tell him? Maybe she'd been trying to get a reaction. If so, she'd succeeded. But maybe it was nothing that complex.

Maybe she was jealous.

"TJ," he said, trying not to smile. "TJ, you dumbass. I never slept with Nile, okay?"

TJ didn't believe him, but Aaron didn't care. It wasn't TJ he was talking to.

I willed the adrenaline to stop pumping. All over now. Nothing to see here. Move along.

TJ obeyed my silent order. He ducked his head, muttered something apologetic and faded away. Aaron sat at the counter, tentatively holding a dish towel to the side of his head.

I opened my mouth to ask if he was okay, and he said, "Are you okay?"

"What?" I said. "No, I have a hangnail. Let me see your eyes."

"Why, Inspector Ashbury," he said, "I never thought you'd ask."

I pulled the dish towel from his face and looked at his pupils. They dilated normally, meaning no concussion, at least in my half-assed medical opinion.

"It's not that bad," he said. "But I'm gonna have a monster hangover."

He was lucky that's all he'd have. I brushed the hair out of my face, remembering: TJ holding the blue-black bottle by the neck, blood sheeted over his chin, a look in his eyes that was beyond reason. Aaron unbalanced, right hand on the counter, two inches from the handle of a smooth-edged knife.

I'd seen it in slow motion. Aaron's hand had twitched toward the handle, then jerked away—I saw the decision in the way he held his body. The decision to leave the knife, the decision to suffer instead of injure. Aaron White might be a reprehensible mutt—jury was still out—but at least he had the guts to lose a fight.

I wondered where he got the strength to let someone come at him with a bottle to the face. Then I knew. Introduction to Anthropology, freshman year of college. I couldn't remember the context, but the point had been clear. Men competing for resources were really competing for sexual access to women. Man with the most cattle got the most brides.

Aaron White didn't need the cattle. Didn't need to win a fight, drive a Porsche, flash a platinum credit card. He cut straight to the chase.

For the first time, that didn't seem like such a bad thing.

Aaron felt bad ten minutes later. His whole face was burning and tender. His stomach felt as if he'd swallowed broken glass. He could hardly move his neck, though he didn't think TJ even touched it. But the worst thing was remembering what he'd said: *I fucked both your sisters.*

He couldn't believe that filth came out his mouth. What kind of man says *I fucked both your sisters* as some kind of triumphal insult?

The kind of man always looking to score. To *get*. Get some. Get laid. Get lucky. Get a piece of ass. He can notch his bedposts until they're nothing but splinters, but he hates women. Not the kind of man Aaron ever wanted to be. It was like looking in the mirror, and seeing some ugliness he'd never suspected. You started to wonder, am I the only one who never saw it?

He looked at Brigid. She looked back. He'd seen disgust on her face before, but couldn't detect any now. Maybe she was so used to the ugliness she didn't notice it anymore.

"Give me your shirt," she said.

"What?" he said. "What?"

"Your shirt."

The shirt was a cotton crewneck in a color he thought they called birch. Now featuring several blotches of a color he was certain they called blood. Mostly TJ's, from his lip. Still wet.

"My shirt," he said, stupidly.

"Yes." She smiled softly. "Your shirt."

It was the first time she'd smiled at him. He would've given her—he smiled, too, painfully—the shirt off his back. He pulled it over his head, which made his neck unhappy, and handed it to her.

"Where's your stuff?" She headed for the door, shirt in hand. "Your bags?"

"Cate's room."

She paused a moment, turned her head in that way he loved. "Keep ice on it."

I was surprised to find Cate's bedroom had powder-blue walls and three picture windows. Far too "country cute" for chic Cate Hulfinger. Must've been decorated ten years ago and never redone. Maybe Cate enjoyed that it didn't fit, maybe it was like slipping into new skin.

Laura Ashley skin. The only thing that didn't match was a four-poster bed the size of a swimming pool. Tousled sheets. The duvet thrown back recklessly. Pillows strewn about in disarray. I shook my head. What the hell did I care about Cate Hulfinger's bed—or who she'd been sharing it with?

I found Aaron's bag stuffed under a chair. A canvas duffel that couldn't have been more out of place, yet fit in perfectly, as if it'd been designed to provide contrast.

A silk chiffon dress was draped over the chair, the cloth pooling on the duffel bag. I moved the dress. Nice fabric. Nice color, an expensive shade of magenta—I couldn't wear it, but it would highlight Cate's brilliant blue eyes.

I wondered... Stop. You don't care about Cate Hulfinger's dress.

I knelt next to the bag, put a hand on the zipper—and couldn't resist. I checked the dress label: Versace. Checked the size: four. Wonderful.

I tossed it aside. Unzipped Aaron's duffel and pulled it open. It smelled like him. Musk and vanilla and cloves. I snorted in disgust. What was *that?* Was I going to light him up and call him incense, or use him to close this investigation?

I grabbed a shirt, closed the bag and backed quickly from the room. I felt a tightness in my chest that I knew was shame. Sniffing around in his bag. I quick-walked downstairs and was almost at the kitchen door when I remembered why I'd offered to bring him a fresh shirt in the first place.

I backtracked to the study and tagged the evidence.

23

The blue linen button-down Brigid had brought Aaron yesterday was crumpled on the chair in Cate's room. Rummaging in his bag that morning, he happened to pull out another button-down. Happened to be another Hugo Boss. Happened to be linen, too. But it was slate-colored, and wearing it had nothing to do with Brigid's preference in shirts. Nothing at all.

He shrugged it on. Slowly, still sore. Sleep had not come easy, and shampooing his hair this morning had nearly finished him. Almost worth it, though, for the information.

TJ and Nile. Nile was in love with TJ—that much Aaron knew. And TJ knew it, too, though he'd never admit it. Why not? Because she was his stepsister? Was that taboo if you hadn't been raised together? Or maybe he didn't fancy her. Hard to imagine, with a woman like Nile.

But there were better things to think about. Brigid and the smile. There'd been two hours when Aaron had thought she was warming. Two hours when she'd been warm.

Then she'd turned to him with her magnificent barbed eyes and said: "You're fucking unbelievable, White. You're some kind of Ted Bundy."

She was a little moody.

That was yesterday. She'd brought him the button-down, asked about the fight and the conversation with Nile. Asked more about the Hulfingers, going over the same ground as before. But warmer. And when she finished with him, she gave another smile like an unexpected gift.

Then she'd rounded up various Hulfingers, and put them to the question.

Aaron went down to the lake, trying not to walk like an old man. He sat on the dock, tossing pebbles into the water and mulled it over. Came to no conclusions, but moved a few pebbles.

The sun lowered itself slowly down. It was poetry; early September, the lake, the crickets, the silence.

Then her velvety voice came from behind him. "Give me a ride."

He turned his head, and the burned-yellow glow of the sunset was vivid on the treetops behind Brigid. More poetry, more silence.

"To the Inn," she said.

"Okay." He stood with some difficulty.

"You can drive?"

He looked at her and tried to say something with his eyes, but didn't know if she heard. So he said, "Yes."

She nodded. They walked together to the car.

More crickets. More sunset. More lake. It was that kind of night.

And if she hadn't been so utterly pole-axed with terror of driving, he would have opened the car door for her. To poke fun at the Rockwellian romantic evening—and to participate in it, too. Instead, he ignored the anxiety that came off her in waves and pretended he didn't notice the terrified pause as she reached for the door handle. She was graceful even in her fear, though; the curve of her elbow, the angle of her neck—

"You can stop that," she said.

"What?" Had he been staring at her tits? What could he say? *No, I was staring at your elbow.*

"Pretending you don't know about this." Her nod toward the car encompassed it, her, and everything between them.

Oh. That. He started to say something vapid, but the glow of sunset caught her on the nape of her neck, lit the curves and valleys and—

"Stop that, too," she said, but the warmth was back.

They drove in silence to her Inn. He parked under a stand of birch trees. They got out and stood together. Her breathing was a little strained. She looked not entirely steady.

They took two steps toward the entrance, then stopped. He wanted to kiss her. That's a feeling that had never changed for him, since the fifth grade—the feeling of wanting to kiss a girl, the nervousness and anticipation. It was a terrible feeling, an intoxicating and terrible feeling. You never knew: was she waiting for the kiss, or regretting she ordered the Caesar salad?

He'd just about worked up his nerve and stepped toward her. She stepped back and said, "I wouldn't ask, Aaron, but I need to know for my report."

It was not what he'd been hoping she'd say. "For your report."

"You were telling TJ the truth when you said you hadn't slept with Nile?"

"Yeah."

She caught him in her gaze. She was after the whole truth. "Are you going to tell me?"

"Do I really have to?"

It took her less than five seconds. "Phillipa," she said. "You slept with Phillipa. You're fucking unbelievable, White. You're some kind of Ted Bundy."

The thickness of her voice had a harsh edge. The way sugar can burn your throat. She turned away, and ran into a woman with too much blond hair and too-clever eyes.

"Thought we'd have dinner, Bridge," she said. "And you're Aaron White. I'm Theresa Udall, Brigid's boss at the NTSB." The woman offered her hand and a whole lot more.

"This is all I needed." Brigid rubbed her temples. "I just lost my appetite. Why don't you two have dinner, instead?"

So they did.

"Black gold." Sesame Gustine was articulate and enthusiastic, and I was pleased to listen to him. Better than thinking about the dinner I wasn't eating. Or who was eating it together.

"Pardon?" I said. Back at the Hulfinger's, I'd asked Van Huut to swing by for the evidence I'd bagged. He'd done so, reluctantly,

and told me I shouldn't hold my breath. Before he'd left, I'd asked
for information on Free Them All. To my surprise, he'd faxed me
a brief report. The Van Huut wasn't turning out the way I'd expected at all—I think I was beginning to like him.

The report was neat and tight. FTA was a small-time organiza-
tion, insolvent and impassioned. Run by a guy with the improbable
name of Sesame Gustine. I'd called him at home and found him
surprisingly willing to talk. But there'd been nothing in the report
about black gold.

"The new black gold," Gustine explained. "Instead of drilling in
a field and tapping a gusher, corporatized prisons push through leg-
islation and tap the ghetto. You've heard of DWB?"

"Driving while black."

"Tip of the iceberg. *B*WB is how these private prisons make their
billions. Two million African-American men in prison in the
country with the highest incarceration rate on earth. The U.S. has
seven percent of the world's population, and twenty-five percent
of its prisoners. True fact. They're locked in there for BWB.
Breathing while black."

I couldn't begin to argue with him. A college friend was a
Brooklyn Public Defender. She'd told me she'd seen blacks and
Latinos serving time for offenses whites weren't even fined for, let
alone put on trial.

"The State of New York couldn't find money to build new
prisons," he said. "So you know where they got it? From the low-
income public-housing budget. Think about that. Think about
conflict of interest."

"And what does this have to do with the Hulfingers?" I doodled wheels on my notepad, feeling hungry, knowing there wasn't any room service.

"Okay. HulCorp board members include a chairman of the Oklahoma Republican party, an ex-assistant director of the Federal Bureau of Prisons, a retired Navy general, and ex-honchos from the U.S. Attorney General's office, the INS, the CIA."

"So?"

"So these are people who shape policy. These are people who have dinner with the people who think the War on Drugs, while it's been an abject failure at having the slightest impact on drug use, is a wise policy that ought to be perpetrated."

"Perpetuated," I corrected, before realizing it was a joke.

Gustine snorted. "And it's not only prisons, guards and administrators—you have architects, construction companies, people selling razor wire and uniforms and Buck Rogers electronic bracelets. All making a buck from black gold. Then you have cotton picking."

I knew I was supposed to ask: "Cotton-picking?"

He told me about corporations hiring prisoners for twenty-seven cents an hour, in what he called cubicle fields. Selling newspaper subscriptions and making reservations and taking orders. He said their great-grandparents had worked different fields for the great-grandparents of the people who owned the corporations, and only been paid twenty-seven cents an hour less.

"What do corporations do to increase profits?" he said. "Cut costs. You've got inmates with no shoes, guards with no training. The health care is dead negligent—inmates with chronic illnesses being overlooked for years. Plus, shit, at Greenview Bay you had eleven million gone missing from the health-care contractor, and the auditor's got no idea where it went. That's how efficient they are. They might as well be in Iraq. Then there's 'picking jackets.' They accept only the most docile—"

"Jody Hulfinger," I said, because I was depressed enough already. Plus, it was making me feel old. All stuff I'd learned in college and forgotten about. Guess I really wasn't like Jody.

Without hesitation, as if it was part of the same thought, he said: "We met at a protest outside Greenview. She picked up some of our literature. Came to the office the next week. You know, we get a few white girls in here. Some of them don't have what you'd call entirely pure motives. But Jody, first day, starts talking about Michel Foucault."

"Discipline and Punish?" A text I'd been assigned in college. Other than the title, the only thing I remember about it is that it was beyond me.

"He said prison is determinant of the entire model of social control that characterizes industrialized societies."

"Not sure I follow." Apparently it was still over my head.

"Point is, that's what Jody comes in talking about. She'd talk the issues, too, but she didn't pretend to be something she wasn't. She made sure we knew her name—Jody HulCorp—up front. That's the kind of girl she is."

Everyone loved Jody Hulfinger. "When's the last time you saw her?"

"Three or four months now. She was a fixture in the office for six months, then poof."

"She that kind of girl, too?"

"No. No, I was surprised. There was no warning—one day she was on fire, the next I couldn't get her on the phone. Figured she had some personal life happening." He paused a second. "Or family problems."

I followed that up, but he meant nothing other than being a Hulfinger protesting HulCorp.

"She raise any money for you?"

"She cut us a check or two."

"Promise of more to come?"

"I assumed there would be, but we didn't squeeze her. Her energy was worth more than her checkbook." He paused, and I heard a smile in his voice as he said, "Well, maybe not *more*."

"Kind of poetic justice to have Hulfinger money paying for your activities."

"I'll take whatever justice I get."

"By any means necessary?"

"You know, Miss Ashbury, one thing about being in this business—I had to learn my rights. Happy to talk to you about Jody. But if you're trying to make it out the FTA was involved in her disappearing, I'm also happy to stop talking altogether."

Theresa Udall reminded Aaron of a woman he used to know. Nadine. A freckled and fresh-faced lawyer friend of his cousin Josh. He met her at a family event; wedding or funeral, Aaron couldn't remember. But he did remember she was quick and attractive, wearing her hair in a bun with ceramic chopsticks through it. He liked her immediately. But fleetingly.

Because, despite the allure of the chopsticks and the freckles,

she lost him when she mentioned—three times in one evening—
how good she was in bed.

"*Desperado*. Now there's a movie," Aaron said.

She hadn't liked it. "But I loved that sex scene. With Antonio
and Salma Hayek. They're getting rarer, sex scenes. In the eighties,
it was part of the formula. You don't see good movie sex anymore.
It's the new Victorianism. The thing is, I'm extremely good in bed,
and—"

He didn't hear the rest of her words over the rush of disbelief.
Had she really said *I'm extremely good in bed?* He tried pretending
he'd misheard, but she said it twice more before the evening was
through. Incredibly off-putting. Freckles and chopsticks are great,
but hearing her say how good she was in bed? Incredibly off-
putting.

Turned out to be true, as it happened. She was *extremely good*.
Still, he couldn't believe she'd said it.

Theresa Udall reminded Aaron of her. Theresa Udall was extremely fond of Theresa Udall. She was attractive, smart, dynamic.
She'd achieved impressive things. But life was a football game to
her, and guess who her favorite team was.

So he heard an awful lot about Theresa Udall. Took half the evening before he got her talking about what—who—he wanted. "So
your title is Investigator in Charge?" he said. "I thought Brigid was
in charge."

"She's an acting consultant. She used to be an IIC—we started
as investigators together."

"You must be close," he said.

"Like sisters. Spend half our time bickering, the other half making up." She smiled quite a pretty smile. "Doesn't get closer than that."

"Then she quit, huh?"

"Yeah."

"But she'd be an IIC if she stayed? I mean, you were promoted at the same time?"

"She got senior investigator before I did."

"Really?"

"A year earlier. But she cheated." She leaned closer. Her shirt gaped slightly, and it took some effort to keep his gaze on her face. "Have you seen the scars on her hands?"

"No," Aaron lied. "She has scars?"

"They're faded now. She got them four or five years ago. Outside Santa Barbara, one of those little beach communities along the 101. Conchita Flats or something. She's having lunch at this hole-in-the wall Mexican place she likes. Sees a gasoline tanker truck taking a right off the highway, over the railroad crossing. It gets three-quarters of the way over and stops— there's traffic backed up in the road ahead. Someone's car broken down."

"Oh, no," he said.

"Oh, yes. You see where this is going." She took a sip of wine. "Here comes the train, a twentysomething-car freight train. Like a scene from the *Perils of Penelope,* is how I always see it. The train hits the back end of the tanker. Driver's DOA, but gas is spilling everywhere. And there are eight cars behind the broken-down car.

"Less than a minute, they're engulfed in flames. Bridge runs into the fire, starts dragging people out. Clears two cars, starts on the third. Pulls this old man out, drags him ten yards.

"By now—well, you've got to see it—the flames are out of control. There's one more car in there. Plus this old guy's wife. Brigid looks at the fire and kinda shrugs, like 'here we go again'—"

"You were there?"

"No, this is on video. Couple of French tourists were antique shopping with their camcorder. You never heard about it? It was all over the news."

Aaron shook his head. "So she shrugs...?"

"My theory is, it's the shrug that did it. It was an eloquent shrug. It said, here goes nothing, and I don't think I'm gonna make it, but—" Theresa shrugged, maybe in unconscious imitation. "Anyway, she jogs back into the fire and gets the old guy's wife, along with second-degree burns on her hands and arms."

Aaron shook his head. How the hell do you make an impression on a woman like that? Coffee in bed might not work.

"She heaves the old lady next to her husband. Checks she's breathing and turns back—there's one more car. You can see on the videotape it's hopeless—they're dead already, it was billowing black smoke, the fire was just...awesome. Bridge wipes her face on her sleeve, turns and heads back toward it. Halfway there, she collapses. Smoke inhalation and shock. Saved her life."

"Jesus," he said. "One time I tried to rescue a raccoon."

"See? Cheating. Of course they're gonna promote her after that. Glory hog."

"Is that when her...problem with cars started?"

"You want to get me talking about Brigid, that's fine." She looked at him over her wineglass, evidently disappointed. "She could use a man like you, give her a holiday from herself. I don't mind, you feeding me dinner in exchange for picking my brain about her."

"What?" he said. "What? No, I thought dinner would be—"

"Happy to fill you in on what's public record. But you expect I'd betray her confidence, you're wrong." That was a tone he knew better than to argue with. "Dead wrong."

She sipped. He sipped. He filled their wineglasses.

"Then we'll talk about something else," he said. "You like movies?"

I came fully awake at five in the morning. I rolled over and flipped the lamp switch next to the bed.

"Eleven million," I said in a voice cracked from sleep. That's how much Sesame Gustine had mentioned had gone missing. I grabbed my bag from the chair and pulled the file from it. Leafed through until I found the photocopy.

11$11

Jody Hulfinger wrote in lowercase. The whole page was lowercase, as if she'd learned English on MySpace. That wasn't eleven dollar-sign eleven. It was *LL* dollar-sign eleven. Leanne Laclaire dollar sign eleven.

Eleven million dollars missing from Greenville Bay's medical contract. And Jody carrying around a note tying the missing money to a member of the HulCorp Board.

"Eleven million reasons," I said.

"It's not proof of anything." Van Huut slid the sheet of paper back across the conference-room table to me.

"I know it's not proof, Walter," I said. I was doing my *thing* this evening, and I didn't have the patience. "I'm not saying it's proof. I'm saying it's motive, and if we play it right, it'll lead to proof."

"It's not motive. It's a doodle."

I stared at him. I was asking for his help, because I'd calmed down enough to realize it'd make my life easier. He knew the primaries, he knew his business. Having him run interference for me—as Theresa might say—was the best way. And now that I was asking, he was giving me hassle?

"Okay," he said. "How would you follow up?"

"Assume Laclaire embezzled the money. Assume Jody found out. Assume Laclaire found out that Jody found out."

"How'd Jody find out?"

"Doesn't matter. From poking around the office, overhearing something on a phone. But if Laclaire thought Jody would reveal all—and she would have, just to give HulCorp some bad press, then—"

"Who's the body in the car?"

"Doesn't matter." I shrugged, declining to share my private theory. "Maybe Jody's guardian angel—Laclaire killed the wrong woman and Jody's alive somewhere, hiding out."

"You don't believe that."

"No. Could be a friend of Jody's who was going to help the kidnapping setup. Dressed just like her, driving her car, to provide a 'Jody-spotting' somewhere where Jody was not. It doesn't matter, not yet. But assume this—" I indicated the ll$11 "—is exactly what it looks like."

"Frankly, Ashbury, it looks exactly like a doodle." He pulled the sheet forward. "What's the rest of this? Trepca mines, baku-ceyhan. What's a broccoli rabe? Cashews, oranges, a picture of an aardvark and eleven dollars eleven."

"You don't think it's worth my follow-up?"

"Could I stop you?"

"You could slow me."

"An aardvark." He considered the scribbles. "Okay. How do you want to proceed?"

"I'll make some calls. The auditing firm—their name is in the report? And the accounting department at HulCorp."

"Sure. They'll share all their secrets. Then you want to hit the family again?"

"We'll start with Small. Ask about the missing money, the audit. Then Laclaire." Down in Massachusetts. "You can have one of your agents in Boston talk to her."

He said if it got that far, he'd be surprised. But he busied himself elsewhere while I made the calls, and an hour later—after I'd learned what little I could—he followed me outside. We stopped at his car. I'd driven more in the past three days than the previous year. And this evening I was doing my *thing*. One more trip to the Hulfinger summer camp wouldn't kill me. Probably. I felt his eyes on me.

"What?" I said.

"I called White," he said. "He'll be here in fifteen."

"White?"

"To drive you."

"What're you saying? How bad do you drive?"

"He's the only one you can ride with," he said. "Without getting that look in your eyes."

"Screw you."

"Fine," he said, evenly.

"Ah, screw you." I turned away. I got the impression he was smiling at the back of my head. "And, Walter?"

"What?"

"It's a three-legged horse."

"Sure," he said. "That makes more sense than an aardvark."

I stared out the passenger window of Aaron's car. Did Van Huut think I preferred Aaron's driving because I respected him? The opposite was true. I didn't care what he thought, so I could bear his company.

Aaron White. From Phillipa to Theresa.

At least he was smart enough not to say a single word. He'd rolled up in his Subaru. I'd opened the door, slid into the passenger side, buckled the belt, said thanks, and that had been that.

Until we'd turned down the Hulfingers' street, and a siren shrieked behind us. My heart turned to ice and shattered in my chest. I felt some words come out of my mouth, but didn't understand them.

"It's him," Aaron said. "It's just him."

Van Huut. Behind us. Aaron pulled over. Van Huut's door opened and closed, and he was at my window.

"Got a call," he said. "I'm needed in Boston."

"What?"

"Right now. Senator Morrisey is— Doesn't matter. You'll fax me a report?"

He was gone before I could answer.

Aaron figured Small had recovered about half his size. He wasn't shrunken, like yesterday, but he wasn't larger than life, either. He raised his head when they entered—Brigid and Aaron—and it was like a moose looking up from a watering hole. Wary, suspicious and powerful.

"One more round of questions, Mr. Hulfinger," Brigid said. "About some financial irregularities."

"Why?"

Brigid paused, looking as though she didn't know whether to take the question seriously. She cocked her head half-an-inch, her neck arched, and Aaron wanted to kiss her, right there on the nape.

Brigid sighed. "Most likely," she said, "to give me another dead end to explore, but it may lead to a motive."

"Want to know about the will, do you?"

She shook her head no.

Small didn't notice, or didn't care. "I've got three kids. Three natural kids. Had planned on splitting it between them, thirty-three apiece."

"But you worried that Jody would—"

"So I cut her out. Except for a modest trust fund."

"How modest?" Aaron asked. He'd always wondered.

"Aaron." Brigid's tone told him to shut up.

"A million," Small said, without taking his gaze from Brigid. "Point is, she was cut out of the money. But not out of HulCorp."

"I don't understand."

"Two of my kids were—are—were genuinely interested in HulCorp. TJ and Jody. Cate keeps up on the company because it's the goose, and she knows where golden eggs come from. If I leave control of the company to TJ and Cate, it'll be TJ's alone. Worst thing I could do for him is make it too easy."

He said it as if it meant something, but Aaron didn't know what.

"You want him to ease into the role," Brigid said. "Sharpen his claws on some in-house opposition."

A glint appeared in Small's eye. "You call 'em like you see 'em, Inspector. I left Jody a seat on the board to give her a voice. A loud voice. But never a controlling one. TJ and Cate can outvote her every time—and they will."

"What was that supposed to be? A lesson for Jody, teach her to compromise on her principles?"

"Nothing so charitable. I hope she learns to enjoy the work. Once I'm gone, maybe she'll find, she would've found—" A film of sadness washed over his eyes. "But it's true, compromise is—was—my backup plan."

"Who knows this?"

"TJ and Phillipa. Maybe Nile, if Phil told her. Maybe Jody, if Nile told her. I don't know." He looked at Aaron. "Had you heard?"

Aaron shook his head.

"I assume Cate would've told Aaron if she knew," Small told Brigid, and they exchanged a look that excluded Aaron.

"And if one of your children—if Jody predeceased you?" Brigid asked. "The stock would be divided between the other two?"

"You're thinking about TJ," he said. "You're wondering if this is a motive."

She gave him a bland look that was as good as an admission.

"If Jody's gone, his position doesn't change. Company would be divided in half, but I'd have the board act as a brake on him. Only thing that'd make a difference to TJ is if Cate died, too. With only one heir, there's no way he wouldn't have a controlling interest."

"Or she," Brigid said, too softly for Small to hear.

Aaron had a flash. He'd read enough detective novels to know the corpse is the killer half the time. So say Jody committed the crime…hmm…that's as far as he could go with it.

"I went over all this with Walter," Small was saying. "TJ's got a streak of me in him. Keeps his eye on the bottom line, he knows what's good for TJ—but he doesn't benefit from Jody's being gone. And he's savvy enough to know if Cate disappeared, too, he'd be sitting in the hot seat."

"The hot seat," Aaron said.

They looked at him.

"That's why you think your son didn't kill his sister?" he said. "Because he'd be sitting in the fucking hot seat?"

"Let me give you a word of advice, Aaron," Small said. "When you talk to someone, you speak their language. Understand? The inspector won't be impressed if I say TJ's too sweet to kill. Such a quiet boy. No. She'll be impressed if I show he has no motive. And he has no motive."

"Aaron will be leaving us," Brigid said.

"Doesn't matter," Small said. "We're done."

"Not yet." Brigid's voice didn't allow for disagreement.

That was the worst way to handle Small. Something sparked in his eyes, and he sat a little straighter—then subsided. As if he'd decided it wasn't worth it.

"Ask your questions, then." And, putting in a token objection to prove he wasn't cowed. "But Aaron stays."

Brigid shrugged. "It's about HulCorp. The eleven million missing from the health-care contractor."

"Accounting error."

"Bullshit."

A long pause.

"It was an accounting error."

"It was embezzled," Brigid said. "And I know who did it."

I obsessive-compulsively fiddled with my hangnail, letting the silence build in the room after dropping my "I know who did it" bombshell. It was a pity real life didn't come with commercial breaks. I needed the time to gauge the feeling in the room, before continuing with our soap opera.

Small was difficult to read. He looked concerned, curious and grief stricken. But maybe those were just the obvious sentiments, concealing other emotions, other motivations. Aaron White was easier: naked interest. In me and in what I was saying. In the title of the books in the bookcase. In the pastoral lake scene out the window. But mostly in me.

I was half flattered, half horrified. The truth is, Aaron White had surprised me. Yes, I'd found him oddly attractive for a while now. But I was also repelled by his two-dimensional-mutt act. Turned out he was more of a three-dimensional mutt. And not a bad investigator.

It shouldn't have come as such a surprise. He had a knack for people. Women, at least.

When we'd arrived he'd led me to Small's office, where we'd been met—well, where *I'd* been met—by waves of indifference and disdain. The indifference had been Small's; the disdain, Gayle Cornell's.

"Back again?" Cornell had said. "Have you any idea what you're doing, or do you simply play it by ear like an inebriate street musician?"

"I apologize for the intrusion," I said. All I needed was Cornell getting between me and Small. I addressed Small directly. "But I do have a few more questions for you, if you don't mind."

"And these are the last few questions?" Gayle said. "Or will you be back tomorrow with a few more? And a few more after that."

"I'll keep asking questions, Ms. Cornell, until I begin to understand the answers."

"If we have to wait upon your understanding, can we ever expect you to leave us alone?"

What sin had I committed, that I deserved this—today, of all days? "My concern is Jody, and my job is asking questions."

"Put it in writing. Stanwood has no reason to speak with you."

"Small." I appealed to Hulfinger, but he was staring vacantly out the window. The sunlight shimmered on the lake. Pine trees swayed in the breeze. He didn't turn at the sound of his name.

"Send a list, if you must," Gayle said, in a tone that suggested she'd file it in the garbage disposal. "But do stop badgering us."

"Beautiful day," Aaron said to Small, as if the weather wasn't the most trivial topic. "I never realized how beautiful Maine is. Cate and I went up to Acadia. Did she tell you? And around Castine and Blue Hill. I want to go to the County next. Hear it's stunning up there."

Small grunted.

Gayle turned to Aaron, something biting in her expression. But before she spoke, Aaron murmured something so softly it took me a moment to realize what he said: "This light brings out your Adam's apple, Gayle."

"Don't be juvenile," she snapped at him.

He smiled, a deeply insinuating smile. Gayle colored and I wondered what kind of history they had. Surely even Aaron couldn't have had sex with his girlfriend's father's girlfriend—especially if she was twice his age. Of course, she had those legs. Phillipa didn't have legs like that and he'd slept with her.

"Oh, I'm sorry. Did I start with name-calling for no reason?" His voice was mild and serpentine. "Are those Gucci?"

Gayle glanced at her feet. "Jimmy Choo."

Ah, I thought: *F* for fluster. I liked the way he'd stepped in and I suddenly yearned for the partner I'd never had.

"Look like Gucci. Ever been to the County, Gayle?"

"Have you heard the saying?" Gayle asked. "Fish and houseguests—both begin to stink after a week. How long have you been with us, now?"

"Not a quarter as long as you, Gayle."

"Get the shit out of my house," she said, before he finished saying her name.

He was equally quick. "We could all use a drink. Be a darling and get the Scotch. You do know where it's kept?"

"I don't like your tone, Aaron."

"No?" he said.

He shot a masculine look—amused superiority and a sort of bone-deep patronizing indulgence—toward Small. A look that contained a hundred years of "don't worry your pretty little head about it" and "isn't she cute when she's mad?"

My God. He was rewarded with a grin.

"Haven't turned teetotaler," Small roused himself to say. "Scotch sounds fine."

Gayle went still for a moment, like a bird of prey at the peak of its arc, deciding whether to dive toward the field mouse or float away on the breeze. She spun on a heel and left the room.

I ought to have been offended. But the look in Aaron's eye told me he knew exactly how offensive he'd been. As a favor to me. And it had worked. Gayle had left, and Small slowly emerged from his internal cell.

Aaron had leaned against the desk and fiddled with a paper-weight in the shape of a sailor knot or maybe it was a pretzel. He asked a couple stupidly innocuous questions about the lake and said he might do some fishing, and led Small into a pattern of answering questions. *Yes. No. Lobster. Dawn.* Then Aaron glanced at me. Passing the torch, Theresa would say.

Very smoothly done. As if we'd rehearsed.

And now I was exactly where I wanted to be. Small was talking. He'd opened up and I'd listened. Now it was his turn to listen.

"It was embezzled," I said. "Leanne Laclaire took eleven million dollars."

He shook his head, but I saw the worry in his eyes.

"You have no proof," he said. "Or you'd be speaking to her, not me."

"I spoke with Nesbitt-McGregor. The auditing firm."

"I know who they are."

"There's no proof. You're right about that. But let me tell you a story, Mr. Hulfinger. Leanne Laclaire stole eleven million dollars from HulCorp, from the health-care contractor."

"How?"

"If I knew that, there'd be proof. Nesbitt-McGregor suspects she used—what're they called?—inmate clerks, with or without their knowledge. She drained off the money, and—"

"Where'd it go, then?" Small said. "You think I didn't have her checked thirty ways from Wednesday when the money went missing?"

"She took it. It's gone. I have no idea where—doesn't matter."

Small snorted. "Eleven million dollars always matters. Didn't show up in Leanne's personal accounts, did it? Any offshore account, any financial instrument or bond. Fact is, there's not a single thing tying the money to Leanne, is there?"

"Let me finish. This is speculation—"

Small started to say something, but I stopped him with a gesture.

"Most of it is speculation. Laclaire embezzled the money. Your daughter found out. I don't know how. Possibly one of the inmate clerks is now with FTA. Possibly she found out on her own. She was seen by Gary Putnam at the office, maybe she was looking for information. It doesn't matter.

"She knew Laclaire took the money. What does she do? Run to you? No—that's not Jody, is it? She doesn't care about money. What she wants is to maximize the damage to HulCorp. Laclaire realizes Jody knows—maybe she sees Putnam's report saying she'd been using the gym. She waits for Jody—probably been watching her, knows she'd been driving to Sears Island—and picks a spot. The perfect spot for an accident. I don't know what she did to the car, not exactly, but—"

"Enough," Small said, resigned. "Enough."

The SVA that wasn't an SVA, the kidnapping that wasn't a kidnapping, the body that wasn't the victim—all wrapped around 11$11. I had found the one loose thread. No finer feeling. Except, maybe, thinking I wouldn't have to do my *thing* after all.

"Enough," Small said a third time. "There's no proof Leanne took that money. There will never be proof."

"I don't care about embezzlement. I care about traffic homicide."

"You're saying her motive for homicide was to keep the embezzlement quiet?"

"That's right. Leanne had to ensure Jody told no one. So she—"

"I knew."

"—set up a… What?"

"I knew. We knew."

"What?" I said. "What?"

"You will never find proof she took the money, because she didn't."

"It's gone. Eleven million dollars is gone."

"She transferred it from the health-care contractor to the public-relations firm. That's the sum total of what she did. Helped with Tylon-Ball, too. The congressional subcommittee. The money paid for a half-dozen expert witnesses and—"

"Wait—wait. You're telling me you knew she took the money?"

"Moved the money. Yes."

"Who told you?"

"She did. And two weeks later, TJ did."

I shook my head. What the hell was *this?*

"Leanne's a bit…enthusiastic," Small said. "The health-care contract was running under budget—due to her management, I should say. We got paid thirty-two million. We spent twenty-one. That's some surplus. Her options were to lose the money or divert it. She chose the latter."

"Sounds unethical."

"But not illegal. And the health-care company is a wholly owned subsidiary of HulCorp. She moved a couple zeros from one column to another. It was profit from her excellent management of the health care system. She transferred the funds. Once it was done, she came to me and said, oops, look what I did, you want me to undo it? Well, there's no way of undoing it without making a fuss with the accountants. She did it intentionally and covertly, but there's no way to prove it. I could fire her for incompetence and inviting undue scrutiny, or I could promote her for initiative. She earned herself a hefty bonus."

I didn't know what to say to that. Was the motive still there? Not if Laclaire had confessed all. I opened my mouth, and nothing came out.

Aaron stepped into the breach. "Who paid you the thirty-two?"

"The State."

"Don't they care you were missing eleven million? You hear about military overbilling getting investigated all the time. Profiteering."

"Five years ago, under their own management, they were paying thirty-seven. They paid us thirty-two. The state ain't good at much, but they can do simple math."

Okay, Bridge. Focus on the people. "And TJ?" I asked.

"TJ earned a bonus, too, even if he's not going to get one. He discovered the money was missing—and tracked it down—two weeks after it was gone. Came to me. We agreed it ought to be kept quiet."

"But if it did get out...?" Was keeping it quiet the motive?

Small shrugged. "Might lower the stock value. Might raise it. People get antsy when they hear about *any* investigative action in the market nowadays. Not a gamble I wanted to take, not right now. But it's never been a major worry, because it's profit, not theft."

Wonderful. The whole fucking house of cards. Laclaire hadn't embezzled. She'd transferred. She didn't kill to keep it quiet. She admitted it immediately.

I sat on the French-ticking couch. In four hours, I'd be doing my *thing,* and now I didn't have a single fucking clue.

"Eleven million dollars," Aaron said.

Small swiveled his head like he'd forgotten Aaron was there. "Hmm?"

"Eleven million dollars under budget. Eleven million dollars that went unspent in health care?"

"Leanne's good at her job," Small said with a slight smile. "Don't know that I'd fire her even if she *had* embezzled that money."

It pissed Aaron off. *He's not good with shades of gray.* Jody would've rammed that smile down his throat. Smug fucker—smug tone. Saying Leanne's very good at her job.

"So what wasn't it spent on? Medicine? Nurses? Drugs?" Aaron had read Jody's FTA brochures. "You know what kills more prisoners than violence and drugs? Asthma and tuberculosis."

"It's a prison," Small said. "Not a play school."

"*TB,* Small. People dying of that medieval shit and Leanne carves eleven million out of health care, and you wanna give her a fucking raise?"

"I was considering it. Listening to you, I've decided."

Aaron took a step toward Small. He raised his voice.

Jody did what she thought was right. She had a quality of goodness that was hard to explain—but unmistakable when you felt its warmth against your skin. And here was Small, scoffing at her. Scoffing at the naive goodness, the stupid reflexive decency and integrity and kindness that had somehow taken such deep root in his daughter.

Aaron knew that Small was grieving. Knew he was shattered beyond what Aaron could imagine, with his daughter gone and probably dead. But he had so little idea who she was. Who she had been. And so little respect. That's what bothered Aaron. So he raised his voice.

He liked to think Jody would have been proud.

So I was gone. Off the case. Yet again.

Van Huut stopped by with the news. Took me five minutes to realize what he was saying for all his waffling about new considerations coming to light. I was off the case. And it had to be because of Aaron.

"He wasn't out of bounds," I said. "Even if he was—he's not my responsibility."

"What? Who?"

"White."

"White?" Van Huut paused. "What did he do?"

So it wasn't Aaron. "Nothing Small hasn't seen a dozen times from Jody."

Only maybe not so physically imposing. It had surprised me. Aaron came across as a lounger, in a state of constant repose.

Aware, amused, graceful—but more sleek than powerful. Turned out he could get angry, too.

Small had been intimidated. Then relieved when Gayle Cornell had returned—minus any Scotch—and told Aaron his bags were on the front step. He'd said "okay" and left, and had been waiting calmly in his car for me when I followed ten minutes later.

"Ah," Van Huut said, after I explained. "So he's no longer staying at the house?"

"Do I care?"

"It's not about White, anyway. It's about Senator Liam Morrisey." Van Huut sat rigidly in the antique chair. "He heads up the Privatization and Special Projects Division of the Federal Bureau of Corrections."

"He knows Hulfinger?"

"Close personal friend. Introduced him to Governor Helt." Governor of Massachusetts. Left-wing Republican, or right-wing Democrat. I never could remember. "They're both on his reelection committee."

"And this has to do with me how exactly?"

"Not you. Everyone. The NTSB. The Maine State Police. Everyone but us."

"Question stands."

"Senator Morrisey's niece lives with him. His brother died, he took her in, and now she's missing."

"The niece is missing."

"Two missing women, both relations of men on Helt's reelection committee."

"How long?"

"Not quite two days," he said.

But he was holding something back. "What?"

"Well." He pursed his thin lips. "She has a history. She's gone missing before. Usually with a man. Three days, a week later, she shows up claiming she would've left a message, but the answering machine was broken."

"So what's the rest of it?"

"There've been threats against the Governor. And some concern at the Bureau that Jody's disappearance was tied into Helt. Someone trying to get leverage on Small to set up Helt. But there was no evidence."

"And now, with the niece gone, despite there's still no evidence…" Too suggestive to ignore.

"Exactly," he said. "A daughter and a niece disappearing within a month of each other, and both families on the Governor's reelection committee…"

"What're the threats?"

He shook his head.

"C'mon, Van Huut. What am I, gonna go to the press?"

"Forget it."

A lost battle—and I didn't care. "So the Bureau is taking over my investigation. Well, the Kidnap Team has done such good work already."

"The Kidnap Team sifted through three hundred tips. They did a backgrounder on everyone with a grudge against Jody and the Hulfingers and HulCorp—imagine how long a list that is. They investigated anyone who asked Jody the time in the past three years. They went over your evidence, and they covered the coast of Maine from Rockland to Bar Harbor. They've been doing the tedious work that closes cases."

"They find a friend of Jody's who might've dressed in her clothes and driven her car, to help lay a false trail?"

"Yeah. Nile. But she's alive."

"Still nothing on the identity of the deceased?"

He shot me a look—of course there wasn't. Well, I had my pet theory, but I wasn't about to expose it—and myself—to ridicule. Not without proof. "And the accident?" I asked.

"Operator error."

I looked at him.

"We have our reconstructionist on it," he said.

"He says operator error?"

"He read an article in *Police Technology Journal* couple years ago where one of the top THIs in the country estimated that in thirty-five to forty percent of nighttime crashes, exhaustion is a contributing factor. Falling asleep at the wheel."

I'd written that article, of course. "Maybe the author was full of shit."

"I don't doubt it. But our guy's leaning that way. Checking for medical impairment, but thinks it's probably due to nighttime visual acuity problem—"

"That's another way of saying he has no clue."

"Sometimes people crash for no reason, don't they?"

"No..."

"But?"

"Sometimes there's no way to track it back to anything but bad driving. But there's always a reason."

"That's what this was, then. Operator error."

"That's bullshit."

"Can you prove it?"

"Not yet."

"You're off the case."

Nope. I'd finish it. I'd do my *thing*. I'd walked away from a case once. Wasn't going to happen again. "Not until the paperwork goes through."

The Principal's Daughter shredded the paper into thin serrated strips. An obsessive behavior, and one she thought she'd mastered. It worried her. But she liked the sound it made, the ripping, done with her own hands.

She might have to use her own hands on the so-called investigator—discover *her* hidden seams. That worried her, too. But she would do it. If it meant protecting him.

The so-called inspector had been taken off the case. The FBI had removed her. And while the Principal's Daughter couldn't claim she'd initiated the FBI's decision, she had supported it. Quietly, blandly—she'd encouraged Ashbury's dismissal. He would be proud. If he'd known, he'd be proud. She'd basked in the warmth of the approval she knew he'd feel—until the second call came.

The call saying Ashbury had been removed—but still investigated.

The Principal's Daughter shredded another sheet of paper. Sitting in the silence of her living room. Heavy curtains drawn. Doors closed. She was afraid. But she'd do what she must.

She imagined Ashbury rigid in the driver's seat, trembling as panic constricted around her like a serpent squeezing the life out of its prey. They were alike, she and Ashbury. Both afraid, both pushing through it. Problem was, Ashbury wasn't frightened enough.

She would be.

Sears Island Causeway. Evening.

My *thing.*

A green 1985 VW Jetta was parked on the shoulder. Squat and hunched. Looked as though it was cringing in fear. Talk about projection.

I took the keys Trooper Cowan offered me. I knew I ought to thank him for locating a vehicle I could use, but I couldn't bring myself to say the words. He was a blur on the horizon. Only thing I really saw, front and center with razor clarity, was the car.

I walked around it, the way I'd walked around Jody Hulfinger's enshrouded red Jetta at the impound yard. Then, it'd been procedure, despite what Cowan might have thought. This time it was fear.

I opened the driver's-side door, sat and buckled myself in. I tried to get the key in the ignition, but my hand was shaking and I dropped it in the footwell. I bent over to get it, and wanted to stay that way, emergency crash position, head between my knees.

"You don't have to do this," Cowan said. "Ashbury...Brigid, no one thinks you have to—"

I sat up and popped the emergency brake and put my foot on the clutch. I got the key in the ignition—turned it before I could lose my nerve—and touched the accelerator.

The engine moaned.

My lungs constricted.

The car reeked of blood; the seat was sticky with it. I heard quiet panting baby breaths over the combustion of the engine. Wet and livid. I sat motionless until I could breathe without the air catching in my throat.

I checked the rearview mirror and the side mirror. Then turned my head to look out the rear-side window—the blind spot—and felt the skin of my neck prickle. It was dusk. The final light of day.

The causeway was taped off, but I checked for traffic. Then I checked again. I lightened up on the clutch, pressed the accelerator and pulled off the shoulder, into the right lane.

My *thing*.

The skid marks rode toward the shoulder, hit the gravel and turned into a furrow for twelve feet, then back onto the pavement. Thirty feet down, at the exit point, they left the road one last time. The car had impacted boulders, tree stumps, bushes and finally the bay.

I followed the skids going five miles an hour. Test skids and tire sleds were one thing used to determine minimum speed. My *thing* was something else. The opposite of science.

I drove over the skids, drifting right, five miles an hour. I went onto the gravel and back onto the pavement. Another thirty feet, and I pulled to the exit point and turned the car off. My blouse was sticking under my arms. My face ached from grinding my teeth, my jaw clenched into a knot of muscle.

I'd learned exactly nothing, except that I could do this and live. I could do this. I checked the road. Checked it again. Pulled a three-point turn and went back to the starting point.

I did it again. Five miles an hour.

And again.

Again.

Ten miles an hour.

Again.

The seventh time, I lost myself.

The Jetta steered itself to the right, its tires sought the furrows without my direction. The steering wheel jerked, pulled my hands along with it, the tires gripped the asphalt. The accelerator lowered, the car sped—fifteen miles an hour—the wheel lurched left, then right. The car shuddered, slid to the right, toward the exit point.

It slowed, it stopped. I sat in the motionless car and my imagination—the double-edged blade—continued onward.

The glass shattered next to her ear. Her jawbone impacted so violently it snapped off. The car on two wheels, then none, flipping and flipping again. The interior battering her—jagged unyielding metal snapping her bones and rending her flesh. The motion, the sounds, the pain...

I sat in the driver's seat. Silent and still.

I was beginning to understand.

I drove it again.

"The Sunflower Room won't work," Aaron told the innkeeper. It was in a separate building, which would defeat the purpose.

"Hmm?" the innkeeper said.

"I'm allergic to sunflowers."

"Oh, that's just the name. There aren't any actual—"

"Do you have anything in, for example—" Aaron couldn't believe he was going to say this "—a sea-captain motif?"

"There's the Captain Armitage Room." The innkeeper looked Aaron over, and his mouth turned slightly down. Aaron's face was still pulped from its encounter with the Hulfinger kitchen. "It's a suite," the innkeeper said. "A bit more expensive…"

"Captain Armitage would be perfect." It was the only room he wanted. Next door to the Lilac Room. He slid his credit card across the counter. "My middle name is Armitage."

The innkeeper glanced at the card. Aaron's middle name was not Armitage. But the innkeeper ran his card through the machine, and it said Aaron was okay. He gave him a registration slip, a key card and his welcoming spiel.

"And breakfast?" Aaron asked when he finished. "You serve Aunt Jemima?"

"We offer real maple syrup—"

The front door opened, letting in a cool breeze. Aaron turned, and there was Brigid. She stumbled inside, holding her arms in front of her as if she was warding off a blow. Her skin was translucent, her eyes red.

A man was behind her, in a State Policeman uniform. He was an older guy, heavyset, with a creased face and a concerned expression. "Inspector," he said. "Ashbury."

Brigid lurched through the lobby. Aaron took a step forward, and the cop glanced at him. They exchanged some kind of look; Aaron didn't know what the cop saw in his eyes, but after a pause he stepped back and let Aaron follow Brigid alone.

He followed her down the hall, ten feet behind her. She fumbled at her bag, her hands shaking so hard she couldn't find the clasp.

"Brigid," he said, afraid she didn't know he was there, and that he'd frighten her. Afraid she *did* know, and that he'd frighten her.

She shoved her bag at him without turning her head. He unclasped it, found the key card. Unlocked the door and opened it. She brushed past him, put her hand on the knob, and—finally— showed him her face. She was ravaged. Exposed. Her fears, her frailties—naked on her face.

He tried to offer some comforting words, knowing better than to ask her what happened. She shook her head, suddenly looking very small, like a young girl. He wanted to touch her, cradle her in his arms. She shook her head again, and closed the door. The words *The Lilac Room* were written in lavender script on the outside of the door.

He looked at them for a long time. He took a breath. Okay. When did this happen?

He'd fallen in love.

I stumbled into the bathroom and splashed water on my face. I didn't bother checking the mirror. I'd seen enough for one night.

The Jetta had been driving thirty-five miles an hour. Another vehicle had swerved toward it from the left—but hadn't hit it. The driver of the Jetta had veered right to avoid collision. She'd gone off the road, into the gravel, but there had been no contact.

I placed my open palm against the mirror, feeling the cool damp surface. No contact. It reminded me of a hesitation mark on a suicide's wrist. The first attempt hadn't been decisive. The Jetta had regained the road, the driver probably faint with relief. An accident avoided. An injury unsustained.

Then the impact.

This time, the other vehicle hadn't hesitated. It smashed to the right, gouged down the length of the Jetta, sheared through the window, shattered the driver's face. Forced the car to the right— the two vehicles locked together, briefly—tossed it off the road like a cat flinging a broken-necked mouse to the side. The car rolled, hitting a boulder and tree stump and grass and water, over and over until the driver—still alive, her heart beating faintly under broken skin—sank beneath the suffocating sea.

And the second vehicle had done it without leaving a trace. No paint transfer. No identifiable debris or metal imprint.

I removed my hand from the mirror and watched my palm print disappear.

The traces were there.

The Principal's Daughter's hand shook in the warmth of her bag. She gripped the rubberized handle of the stun baton so hard her forearm hurt. The baton delivered five hundred thousand volts, both at the two-pronged tip and anywhere along the glossy top half. A half-million volts—nonlethal, but punishing enough that Amnesty International called it cruel and unusual.

She was shivering. She breathed in the darkness, and it calmed her. Ashbury had returned to the Inn an hour after dark, the Trooper following behind her like an anxious nursemaid.

The so-called inspector was brittle and damaged. Good.

The Principal's Daughter had expected the Pierce House Inn would have antique iron keys—distressed à la Martha Stewart. But, as she discovered on a preliminary drive-by, they used plastic key cards. Programmable, disposable key cards. Manufactured by Trexar.

More than a coincidence; it was a sign. She had access to a Trexar key coder and now she had a card that would open any Trexar lock on the planet. Getting into Ashbury's room unseen didn't worry her. But getting her out of it…her fingers fidgeted on the baton handle.

It was time. Darkness had fallen. Ashbury was alone. The Principal's Daughter had waited three hours, before she'd finally placed the call and heard the report: the inspector had made certain claims. She'd assured the State Trooper that she understood. All Ashbury lacked was proof.

Proof would not be forthcoming.

The Lilac Room was on the ground floor, the last room at the end of a short hallway. The Principal's Daughter could slip in and out in five minutes. But how to move the body? Dragging one hundred forty pounds any distance would be unwise. She'd have to use the fenced, private garden attached to Ashbury's room.

She backed the van to the gate, kept the engine running and checked the contents. She was well prepared. She could do this. She would do it for *him*.

She sat for a long moment, remembering the footfalls outside her bedroom door. Pausing, then walking past. She'd never asked, she'd never acted. And he was gone.

It would not happen again. She clamped down on the fear, stepped outside and closed the van door silently. She opened the gate and slipped into the patio, finding the corner where the shadow was thickest.

She listened. Nothing but distant traffic.

It would be louder, soon.

The traces were there. I just had to find them.

Sometimes a tremendous impact left only the slightest trace. But always a trace. And I would find it. The hardest work was over— it was all downhill, now. I knew what happened. I had only to discover how. What vehicle could have done that? Which marks didn't fit—and why?

I turned the bedside light off and pulled up the comforter. I expected to be trembling with the aftershocks. But I wasn't. I'd sleep well tonight.

I'd felt my own impact in a way tonight, and it had left its traces, too. Standing outside my door, Aaron had taken my bag from my hand as if it was the most natural thing. I'd turned to him, lifted my face—wanting him to see what it cost me. The hallway, the walls and carpet, had gone shadowy and distant. All I saw was Aaron; and the tiny, perfect reflection of myself in his eyes.

I saw something else, too. An offer. I wasn't the first woman to see it. Not this week. Probably not this afternoon. But it was an offer, transparently genuine, and it pleased me. I'd never been one of those girls who crushes on the guy that everyone else likes. I couldn't care less about George Clooney. But I was warming to Aaron.

I'd shaken my head no, refused the offer, and closed the door on him—both literally and figuratively. That had pleased me, too.

I'd splashed water on my face in the bathroom, mulling over the case. A couple hours with the reports, and I'd understand. I yawned and settled under the covers. It'd have to wait till morning. I rolled over and waited for sleep.

A minute later I sat up, switched the light on, and pulled the reports into bed with me—I was exhausted, but couldn't sleep without knowing.

An hour later, I still didn't understand. The second vehicle was a truck, I knew that. Probably the source of skid three—the under-deflected marks, the underloaded truck with the skip skids. The marks that looked like a dotted line. But what truck could crush a car and leave no traces?

I turned the light off again. There was always a trace; I saw Aaron's eyes when I closed my own.

A draft woke me. I rolled over and opened a sleepy eye.

There was a shadow by the bed. Looked like a person, standing over me, draped in darkness.

It was just the curtain blowing in the wind.

No, a person. I could feel the presence, almost hear the breathing.

I knew I should be frightened. But I was groggy and half-dreaming. I felt a grin curling at my lips. Aaron White. The bed was large and warm. It was late. I was...I wasn't quite myself. So, maybe I'd been regretting the offer I'd refused. It had been a long time. A long time since I'd even been held.

I pulled myself up in bed, this time not bothering to check my nightgown. I didn't even care about my mussed hair and sleep-blurred face. Aaron took a step forward.

Only it wasn't Aaron.

It moved wrong, smelled wrong, its face was a smear of garish colors. It swung a bat—hitting me in the side and a light sparked and a current burned like needles through my skin. There was a burst of pain and I went numb. I tried to move and couldn't. Tried to claw away, but it was everywhere, a fist of pain squeezing the muscles in my back and neck and legs; my lungs felt dead, my tongue thickened in my mouth as I choked and—

There was a lobster trap hanging over Aaron's bed painted yellow and red. It caught the light of the bedside lamp and cast grids of shadow across the ceiling. He thought it was intended as self-mocking camp, like the signs on the road advertising "lobstah."

He tossed a pillow at it, and it spun. The shadows veered crazily around the room.

The suite was nautical-themed, but with the exception of the lobster trap was more like a high-end yacht than a set from *Pirates of the Caribbean*. The bedroom was large and light, the sitting room larger and lighter, and the bathroom had a claw-foot tub.

After memorizing the outside of Brigid's door, Aaron had grabbed his bags, settled into the suite and soaked himself in a painfully hot bath.

She was a contrary woman. Contrary and damaged. Magnificent and contrary and damaged. Magnificent and contrary and damaged and—ah, fuck it. Aaron was no poet. He liked her, is all. Wanted to be with her, watch her work, comfort her, protect her, laugh with her and…love her, maybe. If she'd let him.

Her room was right next door. He imagined he could feel her body through the wall. He wanted to touch her, run a finger down her neck and watch the goose bumps rise. He wanted her head on his chest and her red-brown hair tickling his nose, her—

He heard something from her room.

A thump.

He stood. Stared at the common wall. Would it be too much to knock on her door? What would he say? *Thought I heard something. Are you okay? Having a hard time sleeping? I want your hair fanned out on my chest, tickling my nose.*

Her hair would smell of rosemary and mint.

* * *

"I can do this," the Principal's Daughter had whispered, and Ashbury had woken.

She'd rolled to her side, her face bruised with sleep, and she'd gazed at the Principal's Daughter with unfocused eyes. Her lips parted and she'd made a noise deep in her throat; almost a growl, but more pleased than predatory.

Then her eyes had widened, and the Principal's Daughter had swung. The stun baton made contact, sparked in the darkness— Ashbury jerked, choked and was still. She hit her again, and the inspector's limbs twitched. She gagged her, flopped her onto her stomach and bound her hands with plastic cuffs.

She bent at the knees and lifted Ashbury into a fireman's carry. But Ashbury—even after five hundred thousand volts delivered twice—scissored her legs and smashed her forehead into the small of the Principal's Daughter's back.

It spun her off balance—there was a panicked moment: *what if I fail him?*—and she smacked the bedside table, sending Ashbury's bag clattering across the room. She dumped the inspector's semi-conscious body hard onto the rug and froze, Taser ready.

Listened. How loud had that been?

Not very. Not much louder than the inspector's moans muffled by the gag. Not much louder than her bound fingers scrabbling against the rug beneath her. Which the Principal's Daughter could barely hear over the terrified beating of her heart.

"What was that?" She made her voice a harsh whisper. She showed Ashbury the baton. Saw fear, and liked it. She was in control. She would not fail him. "Stay away from him. You stay away."

Next: get the body to the van. She checked the gag was secure, and pinched Ashbury's nose closed. "Airway, breathing, circulation. That's how easy it is. Do you want to breathe? Are you willing to beg?"

She waited. Ashbury's oxygen-deprived body would soon send an unendurable message to her brain.

Aaron had only heard the one thump, but from that thump he'd developed a theory: she was going for a moonlit stroll. Maybe a cup of Swiss Miss. Maybe he could join her.

He pulled on a pair of jeans and a T-shirt—considered a linen button-down, but even he was not that ridiculous—and padded into the hallway. The hardwood floor was cool on his feet. He paused outside The Lilac Room. What he needed was an excuse. Something about the investigation. Or he could bring her something sweet, a postmidnight snack.

He continued down the hallway. A proper movie moment would mean he came upon her all unawares, as she was picking the petals off a daisy. Maybe he wasn't expecting it'd actually happen, but you had to give these things a chance.

He checked the lobby for her, the breakfast room and the study. All were empty. He went outside where a brisk wind blew salt air in from the water. There were stars in the sky. Brigid was not silhouetted against the full moon, her summery skirt fluttering in the wind.

What a surprise. He walked down the path that led to his private garden, and hers. Her fence door was unlatched. An invitation?

He put his hand on the unlatched fence. He took a step inside.

Sure it was an invitation. It couldn't just be an open gate. What was he doing? Stalking her? An unlatched gate and he thought it was an invitation? He shook his head. Started backing away when he saw a faint light flash through the window. As if Brigid had switched on a lamp and the bulb had blown.

He backpedaled from the garden, suddenly worried she'd catch him lurking. College-boy games would not impress her. He didn't know what would, but his face in the window in the middle of the night was not it.

He went back inside and sat in the plush settee in the lobby. Alone in the middle of the night.

It was an orange traffic barrel. A fifty-five-gallon safety traffic barrel made of low-density polyethylene, with stripes of reflective white and orange and six-inch high-performance reflective sheeting.

I stifled a sob. Low-density polyethylene. My face was on fire, my hands, my knees, the tendons in my ankles, my twisted neck— encased in a suffocating plastic shell.

I knew exactly where I was. The Manual on Uniform Fucking Traffic Control Devices. I'd been a consultant. I could still recite the test procedures:

Four plastic barrels or drums with recommended ballast shall be hit by a standard-size sedan at a bumper height of approximately eighteen inches while traveling at a speed of fifty-three to fifty-seven mph. Each barrel or drum is to be impacted ten times, then reshaped and stacked; checked for deformation and distress.

The woman in the ski mask had waited until I was frantic for air, then released my nose—and shocked me again with the baton. I'd been led outside and shoved into the back of a van, unable to resist, only aware of the necessity of keeping my left hand clenched. Then Ski Mask had said in a deadly toneless whisper— "Inside the barrel."

My hands had been tied, my vision blurred—my mind unable to make sense of the nightmare, and my muscles unable to respond.

"I won't tell you again," Ski Mask had said.

I stepped clumsily in and fell heavily against the side of the van. I knocked my face against the metal rib and almost dropped the nail file I was clutching desperately in my left hand. I was suddenly afraid I'd start to cry. A normal reaction, I know. But not for me.

"Kneel."

Kneel? I might as well dig my own grave. I wouldn't kneel. Last time I ended on the floor I'd lifted the nail file, but I'd paid too high a price.

I stared at Ski Mask. The mask itself was kaleidoscopic; bizarre cartoon characters romping from the forehead to the chin. Made it that much harder to pick out features, and the darkness and fear obscured my vision further. I still looked hard. Who was she? Was she familiar? Was she—

Ski Mask didn't like the attention. The baton came up, and I couldn't keep from flinching.

"Kneel."

I shook my head. My fingers were numb from the handcuffs. I forced my fist closed. Get a grip, Brigid. Don't drop the fucking nail file. It's the only—

Ski Mask swung the stun baton in a casual arc toward my head, and in the instant before I lost consciousness, I felt my hand twitch and the nail file slip from my fingers.

Darkness.

An engine combusting. The stench of plastic; polyethylene. Pain in my knees, my ankles, my neck. Dull pain, becoming sharper. My body throbbing in time with my heart; the van shuddering around me.

I was paralyzed, stuffed in the barrel in a crouched position. My knees were up around my shoulders, my neck torqued under the lid. The gag was gone and I massaged my ankle with my hand and realized my wrists were unbound. But I was jammed in so tightly I couldn't move my hands more than six inches. I tugged, wrenching my arms upward. If I could pop the lid, maybe I could straighten my legs, stand, escape...

No.

Even if I could move my arms, I wouldn't be able to stand, not with my knees wrapped around my ears, trapped in this van driven by a madman, a madwoman, the road beneath us choppy and unstable, the barrel sliding across the van floor, the van careening eighty miles-an-hour off the road, me pinballing from one wall to the other, the low-fucking-density plastic retaining its shape as I was battered to a pulp inside, blood weeping from my eyes and nose and—

The motion stopped.

I had to get out. I had to get out. I started to pant. Forced myself to take a deep breath—and released it with one explosive push, straining upward. I failed.

A door opened in the silence. The sound of someone moving toward me.

"A dark night. A deserted stretch." Ski Mask's toneless whisper. "A line of orange barrels. One is closer to the traffic than the others. Imagine the cars speeding past."

Then my world spun—the barrel being shifted toward the open door of the van. And shoved off the edge.

It was only a three-foot drop. The impact tore a short scream from my throat. I was shivering, panting with fear. The barrel rolled again. Crunched across asphalt. Then stopped.

Imagine the cars speeding past.

The Doppler of an engine whined past; not too close, on the other side of whatever road I was on. Its headlight illuminated my world with an orange glow, then darkness returned.

"You're at the edge of a long curve," the whisper said. "Visibility is poor. Nighttime. I removed the reflective strips from the barrel. You are four feet from the path of traffic. Fifty-five-mile zone. Is there something you want to say?"

"Please," I said. I couldn't stop myself. "Please, no. Please."

I begged until my throat was too dry to speak.

Then realized I was alone.

"Mr. White?"

Someone was standing on his neck—that was the first thing Aaron noticed. The second was that the woman saying "Mr. White" sounded utterly polite—so he couldn't imagine who she was.

He opened his eyes. The lobby of the Pierce House Inn. He'd fallen asleep on the settee. A woman was hovering over him, a stocky brunette in her fifties with a pleasant face and a smoker's voice. Her name tag said Betty. She worked behind the counter— he'd met her when he brought the doughnuts for Brigid.

"Fell asleep in the chair," he said, and asked what time it was.

Five-fifteen.

"In the morning?"

In the morning.

He slumped back to his room. Showered and shaved and figured he'd infest the dining room from six-thirty to nine, which is when they served breakfast, and eventually Brigid would arrive.

He looked at his watch. It was five thirty-one. He lay back on the bed, willing time to pass. That lobster trap was heinous. He turned the TV on, then off. He checked the sitting room. Still there. The bedroom. Ditto.

He stared at the wall for an hour, checked his watch again. Five-forty.

"Oh, screw it." She liked chocolate doughnuts. Breakfast in bed, again—second time's a charm.

Light came as a dim orange glow, with the faint roar of an engine. Brighter and brighter until I was bathed in orange—the roar earsplitting and accelerating toward me.

Exhaust fumes filled the barrel. Exhaust clung to my hair, burning my eyes and nose. I couldn't stop trembling. The night was cool, and I was burning up....

There was the rumble of a truck, an 18-wheeler. It whipped past, the barrel swaying in its brutal wake of air....

Then there was quiet. Absolute darkness and quiet. Then a whine of sound. A line of cars. Light then dark, hissing then howling. Each one closer, pounding the barrel with a hammer of air, a strobe of orange light; I seized. My body clenched, became stone, rigid cords of frozen muscle. The light dimmed, and continued dimming.

Light again. Conscious again. I didn't know how long I'd been out. Ten seconds? An hour? The glow intensified, and I looked down at myself. My nightgown was slick with sweat.

The light was orange—except for a crescent of white, a crack at the base of the barrel. It must've snapped when I'd been dropped off the edge of the van. Or it was an old barrel, distressed and cannibalized from a construction site.

The crescent of light let in rays of hope.

I could reach it with my right hand. I felt the sharp serrated edge of it, measured its length. Three inches. I clawed at it, until my fingers bled, conscious of nothing but my two fingers trying to widen the crack.

Cars passed. Light. Darkness.

I dug at the jagged opening. Then twisted my head and looked down. The crescent hadn't widened. Not a quarter of an inch. I went limp in defeat, and something moved beneath my fingers. The nail file! I scratched at it. Hooked it with my pinkie, drew it into my hand and eased it through the crack in the barrel, the crescent tear.

Ring the bells that still will ring. Forget your perfect offering. There is a crack in everything. It's how the light gets in.

Don't drop it. Don't drop it outside, onto the deadly distant asphalt. I sawed at the plastic, the low-density polyethylene. There was a seam of white running up the barrel, a bent and weakened suture.

I sawed with the nail file. My hand lubricated it with blood. A car passed; another. My forearm cramped. I'd widened the crack two inches. I felt nothing. I was nothing but a hand sawing steadily with a file. A car, a truck, the spastic rumble of an untuned RV—

I dropped the file.

* * *

The Principal's Daughter stepped silently into her dark study. She tapped the space bar on her computer, and monitor light bathed the room.

It was done. She'd done it.

She felt faint with relief. She even had an alibi—not that it would come to that. But she had one, simple and flawed and believable. An elegant little program that surfed the Net for her, a program she'd even coded to post a short message on a mailing list during her absence. Not proof, but it would strongly suggest she'd been here during the inspector's sad ordeal.

She'd taken pains. The so-called inspector would survive, or not survive. If she survived, she'd be found wandering the highway, babbling in terror. The police would pick her up. A report would be filed. Her reputation—what was left of it—would be destroyed.

But she would not survive. She would be found—in a day or a week or a month—crushed inside a discarded traffic barrel. No cuffs, so it wouldn't look as if she'd been forced.

Her psychological evaluation would be pulled. All would become clear. Post-traumatic stress disorder—suicide, or madness. Proximate cause; massive trauma due to high-speed vehicular impact.

The barrel walls were slick with condensation. My hair was sticking to my face. It itched. It itched, and I could not scratch it. I raged against the cramped plastic prison, twitching violently and my body set the barrel rocking. One edge, then the other…teetering slowly forward toward the dead zone when something slid against my hand.

The file—it had dropped inside the barrel. I sobbed in relief. Inserted it into the crescent-shaped scar and sawed.

And sawed. Until, finally, I could shove my fingers through the crack. One inch, then another. My hand went out. Then my forearm. I shoved with my shoulder; the crack gaped—the barrel split, the lid popped.

I stood, swayed, almost fell and grabbed the sides of the barrel for support. My knees were lacerated, my neck shattered. My left hand clutched the barrel, my right was bloody and useless. I breathed cold highway air.

I was alive.

It was dawn and I was still alive. There was a glow over the horizon. A glow on the back of my arms. Headlights. I turned, very slowly.

The barrel was at the edge of the shoulder of a two-lane highway. There were a dozen other barrels. I recognized the road; Route One, a half mile from the Inn. A mile or two from the bridge spanning the bay. A picturesque view of Belfast Harbor. Fishing boats bobbing. Old colonial houses on the shore. The rising sun illuminating the clouds with gold.

The headlights were approaching at sixty miles an hour. It was a logging truck, a towering metal juggernaut. Its grill loomed above me; a thousand tons of logs stacked horizontally on its bed, confined by huge metal stakes that pierced the sky.

I was dead.

The bakery was in a white Victorian off the side of the road, maybe two hundred yards from the Inn. Aaron cut across the front lawn. A skinny guy with a weedy beard came through the door, a coffee cup in his hand. Aaron saw something in his face and turned.

Three women stood at the base of the driveway. Two were Maine matron types, wearing matching Lands' End outfits. They were sort of fluttering around the third woman, who was walking past as if they didn't exist, wearing what looked like a slip or gauzy white gown.

In the moment before he recognized her, he thought: *Ophelia.* Tragic, mad Ophelia.

He had no memory of approaching her. She was far, then she was near. She was holding her bloody right hand to her chest, clenched around a sliver of metal. She was breathing in short gasps. Her eyes were the mindless rolling eyes of a panicked horse. She started past him. He said something. He laid a hand on her shoulder. She flinched.

He said, "Brigid."

She stopped, and he said her name again. She turned her expressionless face to him.

Aaron gathered her into his arms and took her back to his room at the Inn. He led her to the bathroom, started the shower running hot and pointed the nozzle toward the far wall. He lifted her ruined nightgown over her head and dropped it on the floor. She was a mannequin, her skin too-cold and too-white, her face inhumanly calm.

He offered his hand. The motion drew her eyes. She stared at his hand, then gave him hers. It was cool and small. He guided her toward the shower, and she stepped in, as compliant as a child.

He tried to pry a bit of metal—a twisted nail file—from her fist. She shook her head.

He'd told her she had to go to the hospital. She'd said no, word-lessly, with the hunch of her shoulders and the set of her jaw. He'd told her twice more, and she'd stared past him, her eyes reflecting no light. Maybe he should've taken her anyway. Or called 9-1-1. He chose to trust her instead. There was something about her, even in this state.

Her hair was matted. Blood streaked from her right breast to her hip, smudged down her flank and encrusted at her knee. She stank of fear, of desperation. A smell he associated with dog ken-nels, never a woman.

Her eyes had gone from panicked to numb. He hoped it was a good sign.

He aimed the spray of water at her. Rubbed her down with a washcloth. Washed her hair. Wiped shampoo out of her gold-flecked eyes. Checked her for injuries—she was bruised and scraped, nothing more that he could see. He cleaned the cuts on her hand, and the water soon ran clear. He tried once again for the nail file, and once again was rebuffed.

He wrapped her in a towel. Gently dried her hair, and she sub-mitted. Led her to the bedroom, and put her to bed. Tucked the comforter up to her neck. He didn't kiss her on the forehead.

He sat in the chair next to her, and waited.

Brigid woke at a quarter of two. Sat up abruptly, the comforter falling to her waist, and stared terrified around the room. Her gaze found Aaron. Her expression changed from fear to blankness.

She lay back down and pulled the covers to her chin, and stared at the ceiling. Twenty minutes later, she said: "Get rid of that fuck-ing thing."

"What?" he said. "Brigid?"

"Get rid of it."

She was babbling. Aaron knew he should've called 9-1-1—then he understood.

He stepped onto the bed, careful to avoid her legs, and grabbed the thick twine that held the yellow-and-red lobster cage suspended. He yanked the hook from the ceiling. A thin dust of plaster drifted down and the trap came free in his hand. He hopped off the bed and tossed the trap on the floor next to the dresser.

He pulled the chair closer to the bed. "Brigid," he said softly.

She was asleep.

A day passed and they didn't leave the room.

"I know what killed her," Brigid said, when she woke for the fourth time. "That great behemoth fucking log truck."

"What?" Aaron asked, still drowsy. "What?"

"The log truck, stacked with wood. Except not a big rig. The strike point was too low. Jody Hulfinger, Aaron."

He thought she was feverish. He reached toward her forehead.

"No," she said, meaning his hand. "The log truck, Aaron. Keep up."

"Um…" he said.

"Get my bag."

He'd jumped the fence between their garden patios yesterday to get her stuff, and found her outside door unlocked. In her room, rosemary mint was only the beginning. She had a complete collection of cosmetics, mostly Aveda and Chanel. No perfume—he'd been right about that—but there was a light scent in the room.

Cucumber & Melon body lotion; he had a friend who used to wear it. Avon, he thought. He hadn't noticed it on Brigid. He'd wondered, a little lecherously, where it got applied. He'd opened her drawers, managing not to paw through her underthings. He'd packed them. That's all.

He got her bag from the sitting room, put it on the bed next to the lump that was her knees.

"Get out," she said.

He got out.

From the other room, seven minutes later: "Aaron."

He got back in. Looked as though she was fully dressed, though she was still in bed, obscured by the comforter.

"I need you to make some calls."

"May I speak with Dr. MacRoule?" he said.

"Speaking."

"This is Aaron White. I'm calling on behalf of Brigid Ashbury."

"Are you?" he said, as if he didn't believe Aaron.

"Yes, I'm working as her assistant on the—"

"I *do* read the reports," he said. "Aaron White, *as in* 'the suspect apprehended at Cumberland and remanded into custody in Portland.'"

"No, I'm the good twin. Aaron White the suspect has a black mustache—that's how you can tell us apart."

"Ah." He sighed. "Is she there?"

Aaron held the phone toward her. She roused herself sufficiently to explain to the doctor that Aaron was empowered to speak for her. She didn't use quite those words.

He got back on the phone, and MacRoule was sighing again.

"Yes, sir." Aaron said. Because he didn't know what else to say. Seemed to liven the doctor up, though.

"I'm not a sir, I'm a doctor, and you can tell Ms. Ashbury—"

"The reason I'm calling—"

"I know why you're calling, and you can tell her the latest sample was as unrelated to Catherine Hulfinger as the first had been."

"Okay," he said.

"Does she want to visit the lab and run the tests herself? I'd be happy to explain Southern blotting in more detail."

"Well," he said.

"The body in the car is not related to Hulfinger. This new mystery evidence is not related to Hulfinger. And, you will no doubt be surprised to hear, Mr. White, you yourself are not related to the Hulfingers."

"What?" he said. She'd checked his DNA to see if he was a Hulfinger?

"You are not the long-lost son, separated at birth—and I presume the same can be said of your mustachioed twin."

"Oh," he said.

"And tell Ms. Ashbury she'll have no more information from me until she drops by the lab. I'm quite eager to meet her."

"Are you?" Aaron said, as if he didn't believe him.

The doctor hung up.

I lay in bed thinking about the case. The log truck. The DNA. The temper and the sense of ownership. The absent alibi. It all fit.

Except the woman. Ski Mask.

I shivered and pulled the comforter more tightly around myself. The kaleidoscopic ski mask and the lifeless whisper and brutal dark slits where the eyes should have been. It had been coming back in flashes:

"Do you want to breathe?"

The fetid exudation of polyethylene, the deadening black-orange strobe.

The log truck, metal spikes impaling the sky, bearing down with the stench of exhaust and fresh-cut pine, and smacking me brutally with its wind as it passed eighteen inches from my face.

No. Ski Mask fit, too—*"stay away from him."* She fit. I shivered again, tried to cover it by grabbing the glass of water Aaron had left on the bedside table. But he noticed the shiver. Of course he did. He noticed everything.

"Brigid?" he said in his soft voice. Easy as his smile.

I snapped at him. I'd been snapping all morning.

He turned blandly away. He would not be ruffled. He returned every discourtesy with kindness, and when I attacked him for patronizing me, he effaced himself so completely I was left wrestling with myself. I hated him for it, and the anger was all that kept the flashes of memory from overwhelming me.

A bead of condensation dripped from my glass of water onto the hollow of my throat. I wiped it off, disgusted. I should leave. I should tell him to leave. I needed to go back to my own room. My own cabin, my juncos and the smell of Santa Barbara chaparral. Not yet, not yet…

Here I was warm. I was safe. Aaron would make my calls, and I would think. Think, and try to catch glimpses of myself, reflected in his eyes. Because that is who I yearned to be again.

* * *

"Who's next?" He still had the phone in his hand, and Brigid still had her address book open, propped on her chest, but she'd gone elsewhere. "Brigid?"

She startled. Turned her head obliquely, and Aaron could see her struggling against something. She had a kind of endless tenacious endurance that awed him. She faced it and faced it and faced it, until she finally faced it down.

But what she needed from Aaron—or at least what she was willing to accept—wasn't his admiration. So he just said: "You have more people you want me to call?"

She was silent for maybe two minutes.

"The sample was not related to Cate," she repeated.

"That's what the doctor said," Aaron said. "But why have me checked? Of course I'm not related to Cate and Jody. That's too Caligula, even for me."

"And the body wasn't related to her, either. The body in the car."

He nodded.

"So can it be two of them? Two unrelated..." She shook her head, retreated into herself. She wasn't thinking about the case.

"Tell me," he said.

She drew the comforter closer. "She was wearing a ski mask."

"And?"

"Not yet."

He murmured something meant to be comforting.

"Not yet, Aaron."

He nodded. "You have more calls?"

"No. Okay," she said, after a dense silence. "Van Huut, next. Then Ralph or Theresa. Then we'll see about San Francisco."

"San Francisco?"

"We'll have someone search the news archives, police records. Maybe Van Huut will give us a contact. Maybe..." Her tone slipped, went sideways.

Aaron took her hand. He ran a finger along one of the smooth scars on the back of her wrist. He'd wanted to examine them in the light, to see how far they extended up her sleeve. He'd seen.

"What'd she do to you?" he asked.

I told him. I told him everything. Even about Jon and Satchel. I babbled and clung to him, and couldn't even find it in myself to feel humiliated for revealing my incoherence and my need.

"There is a crack in everything—" I said, and choked.

"It's how the light gets in," he said.

I wept. I let him see me weep and I let him comfort me.

Brigid stood without a word, and walked to the bathroom. Closed the door behind her with a firm, soft click, and Aaron thought: that door was open, and now it is closed.

A moment later, he heard the sound of water running. He listened to it—deep in incoherent thought—until the phone rang in his hand.

"Hello," he said.

"So, Aaron." It was Cate. "Are you gone for good?"

"You mean 'for good' or 'for good riddance'?"

"I mean, Aaron, are you not coming back?"

"Gayle showed me the front door. You got my note?"

"I got your note. It said you'd call." But she wasn't angry. Which meant...

"I'm sorry, Catie. I should have called. I'm sorry." The goodbye smile, the goodbye call. "Umm, do you want to do this in person?"

"Do we have to do it at all? Can't we just skip it?"

He smiled. He'd miss her. "Consider it skipped."

"What happened? It's not like you."

"Things got a little crazy."

"You're with her, aren't you?"

"Her?"

"Walter's been looking for her—she missed her plane yesterday."

"Walter seems nice."

"Oh, shut up, Aaron," she said. Then, "He does, doesn't he?"

"How long has he been in love with you?"

She let Aaron hear silence for a minute. "Ten years, he says."

"Believe him. He's a smart man."

"And you're not?"

He told her a little about Brigid. More than a little. Saying goodbye had that effect on him. "And she still doesn't have much appetite," he said. "This morning, she woke up mumbling about logging trucks. She says she wants to go back to the island this afternoon, and she can barely— Do you think I should make her see a doctor?"

"You should've made her see a doctor ten minutes after you found her."

"What, I should've dragged her by her hair?"

"You have other charms, Aaron," she said, laughing at him.

"Half the time she looks ready to feed me my liver. I'm not about to—" He heard something on the line. "Where are you?"

"Nile's house."

He heard something else. "Nile?" he asked. "Phillipa?"

"What?" Cate said.

There was a breath, and then a click.

"What?" Cate said. "What was that?"

"Someone was on the extension."

There was another click.

"I'm sorry," Nile said. "I picked up and...sorry."

Nile got off the line. Cate and Aaron spoke for another five minutes. Then she said, "Hey, and, Aaron?"

Here it came:

"Thanks."

Brigid stepped out of the bathroom, dressed in a suit Aaron had seen before, her face made-up and composed. She headed for the bed, then swerved and sat across from him at the table. She flipped through her address book, and gave him the number.

Six minutes and three transfers later, Aaron heard a familiar voice through a bad connection in Boston. Van Huut must be on his cell phone.

"Special Agent Van Huut," he answered.

"Ordinary Citizen White," Aaron said.

"Jesus H. How'd you get this number?"

"Good afternoon to you, too. I'm calling on behalf of Brigid. Playing secretary."

Brigid grimaced at the expression.

Van Huut must've heard something in Aaron's voice. "Did her *thing* go that badly?"

"Sure," he said. Her *thing?* "Pretty much."

"What'd she learn?"

He mouthed the question to Brigid. *What did you learn from your thing?* She shook her head.

"She's still organizing her thoughts."

"Ought to organize her travel plans instead. She missed her plane. I just got off the phone with Ralph Nicencio. NTSB. You know about him?"

"Ralph and Theresa," he said. He'd forgotten what NTSB stood for. "You know someone in the San Francisco area for some quick and dirty research?"

He asked why.

"For Brigid."

He asked why again. Aaron looked at Brigid. She shook her head.

"You know she's going to solve this," Aaron said.

Van Huut grumbled, then rooted around in his memory and gave a name and number. Said it was a onetime-only. Said not to make him regret it. Continued in that vein for five minutes.

"She also wants to know," Aaron interrupted, "how the Morrisey thing is going."

"—if it gets back to me that… The Morrisey thing? Listen, a research contact in San Francisco is one thing, because it's not here. Tell her the niece resurfaced. But given the threats and the Helt connection, this is a federal matter. Tell her the paperwork has gone through. Tell her she's officially out of it, and has been for twenty-four hours."

"Walter says you're out of it," Aaron told her. He tried to make it sound like an insult—*you're out of it*—to see if she'd grin. She didn't.

"It was a log truck," she said. "Tell him that."

Aaron told him.

"I'll forward the opinion," he said. "But tell her...tell her she is no longer even an accident reconstruction consultant, NTSB, seconded to the FBI. And White?"

"Yeah?"

"Tell her to take care," he said, and didn't bother hiding the concern in his voice.

Sheesh. Just when you'd decided not to like someone. Aaron told him he'd pass on the message, and so on, and they hung up the best of friends.

I could hear someone knocking on a door somewhere. It started when Aaron was talking to Van Huut, and hadn't stopped. It was faint but annoying, like a mosquito buzzing around your head at night.

"Is that your door?" Aaron asked. Then glanced over and saw my icy glare. "What?"

"You can't trade Cate like she's a baseball card," I said.

"What?" he said. "What?"

"You know what."

"What did I say? That I'm not staying at the Hulfingers'?"

"I heard what you said, and I know what you meant."

He shrugged. "Van Huut's the kind of guy who'd feel he was poaching. He'd never make a move until officially notified the No Trespassing signs were gone."

"Unlike you."

The knocking stopped for a moment. Then started again.

"Yeah, unlike me. I figure every woman's her own territory. She can decide how to treat poachers without my help."

"How liberated of you."

"Why don't you just say it, Brigid?"

The knocking continued, louder. It was aiding my annoyance with Aaron. "You can pretend all you want that what you feel is respect, but—" My glare left him, and focused through the wall at the knocking. "Would you shut that up?"

Obviously seeing an easy out to my lecture, he quickly popped his head out the door and popped it back in.

"State Trooper," he told her. "Outside your room."

"Cowan? Older guy with a beer gut?"

Aaron shook his head. "Young guy, perfect skin."

"A local. Pomerleau. Go talk to him."

"I should invite him in?"

I gave him the look. Human contact was out of the question. Aaron was some kind of necessary evil, but I wouldn't consider seeing anyone else, speaking with anyone else.

"Well, what am I supposed to say? You're gonna have to—"

"Give me time, Aaron."

"I'll tell him about the barrel and—"

"No."

"You've got to tell the poli—"

"No."

"That woman—"

"I can't—take the circus. Okay?"

"Okay."

In the hall, Aaron introduced himself to Pomerleau and told him Brigid was in his room. The trooper looked Aaron over and seemed deeply unimpressed. He was getting that a lot from people who liked and respected Brigid. He wasn't sure he could blame them.

"We had some reports," Pomerleau said. "A woman meeting her description, on Route One."

"Have you spoken with Cowan?" Aaron asked. Because what the hell was he supposed to say?

"Trooper Cowan?"

"With the beer gut. He knows all about it. He drove her back. You know. From her *thing.*"

Pomerleau nodded as if that made sense. "Can I poke my head in?"

"She's in the bath."

He didn't believe it, but what was he going to do?

"Give her a message," he said. "I made those calls. Iqbal is happily married—to all appearances. Laclaire's happily single—same. Putnam's wife died ten years ago, he's single-dadding it with three teenage daughters." Pomerleau shook his head at the enormity of it. "Couldn't find any connection between them before HulCorp, except through Hulfinger, who knew them all. Gayle Cornell's apparently not guilty of anything more than being attracted to men with health problems. Oh, and she and Phillipa Lockwood go way back. Lockwood introduced Cornell to Hulfinger."

"While they were married?"

He nodded.

"Is Gayle why they divorced?"

"Not as far as I can tell. They didn't become romantic until two years after."

He ran down more background information; apparently Brigid had asked him to determine if there was a preexisting relationship between any two people that Jody had been in contact with in the weeks before her disappearance. Took him five minutes to get to the bottom line: other than Gayle and Phillipa, there were none.

Aaron thanked him and told him he'd pass on the information.

Pomerleau said *Ayuh* and took his complexion and left.

Aaron went back to the room and gave Brigid the summary. She was unsatisfied with his report and plagued him with questions.

He answered as best he could, finishing with, "Maybe next time I'll take a recorder with me."

She nodded vaguely as she stared out the window for a minute. When she turned back, he thought she was going to start arguing, but there was a *Mona Lisa* smile on her face.

"Young guy with perfect skin?" she said. Laughing at him a little. He liked it.

"Peaches and cream," he said. "What's this *thing* of yours?"

The Principal's Daughter put the brown bag on the center of her desk. Took off her shoes, scuffed her stocking feet on the carpet, and let herself enjoy the anticipation.

Yesterday, she ate yogurt and a bran muffin for breakfast, an undressed garden salad for lunch and a Lean Cuisine for dinner. Yesterday had been typical: *he* preferred skinny women, so she would stay one.

But today she was celebrating. Rewarding herself—she'd done it. She'd been terrified, burning through adrenaline, but she'd done it. Now anything was possible.

She reached into the bag. A quart of two-percent milk, and a package of Oreos. She filled her coffee mug with milk and dunked. Bliss. She'd have six of them now, in celebration. Two every night this week, for dessert. Then back on the diet.

She dunked another. Should she call him? No—no, she wouldn't pester him. And he probably had no news. As far as she knew, the so-called inspector's ordeal had not yet been discovered. But perhaps she should find out. She had the name of a woman who worked with one of the national crime databases. A woman who had access. Access and four sons, two of whom were tagged in the Principal's Daughter's records.

She reached for the phone, then stopped herself. She must take pains. No reason to expose herself. The news would come. She dunked another Oreo, and the phone rang under her hand. It was *him*. She heard his voice and felt herself respond. Since the day they met, she'd wanted to feel his weight—his gravity, his intensity—crushing her from above. Smothering her, blotting her out.

He spoke as if he suspected nothing. He'd called for a trivial matter, he said, as if any matter spoken in his voice could be trivial.

"And the investigation into Jody's disappearance?" she asked, when he was finished.

It was continuing. Under the sole direction of the FBI. Without the inspector. Driver error, he understood, would be the determination.

"Driver error," she said. "And the dead woman's identity?"

Remained unknown.

But do *you* know? Do you know? Where is Jody, and who is the woman in her place? Do you think it a coincidence Ashbury was removed, was disabled? That driver error would be the official cause? Won't you see what I've done for you? Won't you tell me I did well?

"Strange it took them so long to determine driver error," she said.

The FBI made the determination, he said. They were professionals—the consultant was not.

"Must be back in California by now, enjoying her fees." She said it because she needed information, but she cringed at how obvious it sounded.

Ashbury missed her flight, he said. There had been some concern.

"Oh?" Still in the barrel. "Some concern?"

Apparently, he said, Ashbury had holed up in her hotel room. She was phobic. But tenacious—he had to admire that. Even off the case, she was still pursuing leads. Admirable.

"Admirable," she said. Still pursuing leads? Off the case and out of the barrel and still pursuing leads? And he'd praised her; he *admired* her.

Shattering the bitch inspector with fear hadn't worked. It hadn't worked, and he had praised her, and the Principal's Daughter would not lose another man. She would not lose him. She would draw a razor edge across the inspector's throat before she lost him again.

Leave, Aaron. Leave.

I needed to be alone. I knew how much he'd helped. I'd still be comatose if it weren't for him. I knew my capacity for fear—how easily I could lose myself in the labyrinth, and that Aaron had led me out. But this first time, I needed to be alone.

After explaining my *thing,* I'd had him call Ralph to arrange a new flight and explain a few matters. They seemed to hit it off, Ralph and Aaron. Probably at my expense.

Aaron had hung up and turned to me. "You know Theresa filed a report on me?"

"I'm not surprised."

"Probably said I was a fair enough backcourt player but I fall apart under the pressure of a strong defense."

"Jesus." I stared at him; his easy smile, his easy voice. What was he saying? That he'd had sex with Theresa?

"That's not what I— Brigid. That's not what I meant. I meant she's protective of you. I pressured her for information, she wouldn't give it up. And you know how she talks." He changed his voice. "Watch for the quarterback rush. Call in a pinch hitter. Et-sports metaphor-cetera."

"You sound like Ralph."

"I like the phrase. The construction. What would you call that? Et-grammar lesson-cetera?"

"You have the number for the San Francisco woman?" I'd gestured for the phone as if I'd been on it all morning. As if chatting—interacting with anyone other than Aaron—was the easiest thing.

I could make a phone call. I could talk on the phone now. It was no problem. It was nothing, talking on the phone. This was a fear I wouldn't allow to take root. Because if I became a total agoraphobic I'd need the phone. I'd need some human contact other than the Internet. But I couldn't do it in front of him. I needed to be alone. Just this first time. Just in case.

So leave, Aaron. Don't make me ask.

"I'll be outside." He put the phone in my hand, and went into the garden.

Fifty minutes later, I hung up. Van Huut's San Francisco contact had done some initial research while I waited. She said there was a slight hint of impropriety—not even impropriety, more an irregularity—attached to the birthing center. Said she'd keep digging if Van Huut okayed it.

I told her he already had. A lie, but for a good cause. The San Francisco woman would give me the motive. Well, she'd give me evidence—I knew the motive already. And I thought I knew the means.

Still, I wasn't going to make another mistake like with the embezzling. No. I had to see for myself. Which meant back to the site, to find the proof. I knew where to look. It was the ninth inning, as Theresa might say, two outs and two strikes…only thing was, I didn't know if I could make it to the plate.

I opened the door to the garden. The fresh air and sunlight took me by surprise. I almost stepped back inside. Instead, I took a breath of roses, and watched Aaron.

He was sprawled in a dark green metal patio chair. A sketchbook balanced in the crook of his left arm. A charcoal pencil in his right hand. Drawing with quick, sure gestures, staring at the fence in front of him.

I looked over his shoulder. "That's supposed to be the fence?"

"I'm not that bad," he said. "It's an old tree trunk behind the Hulfinger's. Note the expressive shading, the interplay of light and dark—"

"It has hips, Aaron. And a crotch."

"Trees have crotches, Dr. Rorschach." He looked at it, cocked his head. "That's roots. And bark."

"Not that." I pointed. "Here. And here."

"Oh," he said. "Well. If you have a filthy mind..."

I smiled at him. I didn't know why. And it felt strange, smiling at him. I tried it again. A little less strange. "Are you ready to go?"

"The causeway?"

My grin faded. Yeah, the causeway.

By the time they crossed the railroad tracks, all the color had seeped from Brigid's face. Aaron couldn't guess the strength it took for her to continue. They continued past a ramshackle old house and the Sears Island sign and Aaron watched Brigid duck under the Crime Scene tape without hesitating.

"They wouldn't let *me* tape off the island," she said, her voice sounding okay. "FBI has it for two days and the place is hermetically sealed."

He hadn't been to Sears Island before. Not much there. Beautiful, but not spectacular like Acadia. A simple, small island left to nature. The wind picked up, and some seagulls cried. Across the water to the left was what looked like a lighthouse—to the right an industrial complex.

Brigid looked at neither. Brigid looked straight down. She stopped at a skid mark before following it with the concentration of a tightrope walker. Then she stepped off the road. Considered. Knelt. Stood. Took another five steps and considered again.

She pointed to a patch of grass. "That's it."

"That's what?"

"What does it look like?"

"Grass."

She walked back twenty feet, talking him through it. "Jody's car went off the road the second and final time here. You can see the tire marks. It's a forty-five-mile zone, but she was going slower. Minimum speed works out to thirty-two. Here. The car flipped to the right side. Slid. Until it impacted that—" She pointed to a boulder. "It cartwheeled, like this, and ended up on its roof in the water."

"Okay. But that doesn't answer the question—why?"

"Had to have been run off the road—except there's no paint transfer. And you can't have that kind of impact between two vehicles without transfer. It's impossible."

"So?"

"So there was damage on the car's left side. Traces of wood. From a tree stump. That's what I figured. From when it flipped, and slid on this tree trunk—" she pointed to the patch of grass, where a tree trunk was not "—right here."

"No tree trunk, so…" It took Aaron a couple seconds. "Traces of wood. The log truck."

"The log truck. Someone driving a log truck killed Jody Hulfinger, and only one person—"

"So she's dead. Jody's dead."

"She died right here, Aaron. That was her in the car."

"The DNA tests. You're saying the tests were wrong?"

"They were right. But what did they show? They showed that—" An air horn blew on Route One, and Brigid stumbled, like someone kicked in the back of the knee. Her eyes went vague. "And, um, they showed that…"

"Let's go for a walk in the woods," he said. In the woods and away from the road.

He led her onto the island. They passed a stone fence, stepped off the road onto a side trail. After twenty minutes of walking down the wooded paths, her eyes looked like hers again.

"Okay," he said. "The log truck."

"I pass your inspection?"

"Barely."

"Who drives a log truck?"

"Loggers," Aaron said. Because he was sharp that way.

"TJ," she said. "You mentioned it yourself. In the interview with Agent Dellgarda."

"Yeah, but—you heard Small. There's no motive. And a thousand other people drive log trucks, too. I mean, maybe not the 18-wheelers, but—"

"It wasn't a big rig. And it was underloaded—hence the over-deflected tire marks—"

He said, "Overdeflected?" but Brigid ignored him.

"—because it wasn't stacked to maximize the load, but to knock another vehicle off the road."

"There's no motive. He's still got to share the company with Cate, he doesn't have controlling interest or whatever, so Jody's death doesn't do him any good."

"How'd he react when he thought you'd slept with Nile? He's a bit overprotective—and he cares more for HulCorp than Nile. And think about the DNA."

"I'm thinking, but..." He wasn't getting very far.

"The body in the car was positively identified as Jody. Then it was unidentified, based on DNA comparison with Cate. I figured Jody was working with a friend to confuse her trail. But no one fit. Because it *was* Jody. The reason the DNA test said she's not related to Cate is because she's not."

"Jody and Cate aren't related?"

She nodded.

"They're twins, Brigid."

"That's another thing. That too-convenient story TJ told. It was in Van Huut's report, and it sounded too…convenient. The woman in San Francisco said there's no hard information on Sunrise Birthing Center, but it wouldn't be the first time a woman took home a baby not her own at a hippie maternity ward in the seventies. They even had a phrase for it."

"A phrase?" Aaron was absorbing maybe half of what she was saying.

"Yeah, an underpriviledged infant—or abandoned, or the mother died during childbirth. They'd give the baby away, to a middle or upper-middle class family. A share-the-wealth thing. Called them 'delivery-room adoptions.' A woman like Maureen Hulfinger, giving away her fur coat…"

It was too much to believe. "You're saying Jody wasn't Small's kid. Okay, say she wasn't, but—"

"Not Jody. Cate. The body in the car—Jody—was matched against Cate. They were not related. The blood on your shirt— the Hugo Boss?—I sent it in. TJ is also not related. To Cate. That's what MacRoule was telling you."

"Wait, wait. The blood on my shirt. My blood?"

"It was TJ's, from when you cracked his mouth open. I had

MacRoule check TJ's DNA against the body in the car. He's related. But the body in the car was not related to Cate—who we were using as the Hulfinger baseline."

"So TJ and Jody are siblings, but not Cate."

"Cate's not related to either of them."

"And you're saying only TJ knew?"

"Well, Maureen Hulfinger must've, but I doubt she told Small."

"Shit," I said. "The bobcat cub. And TJ killed Jody, his real sister."

"Because he can disinherit Cate by showing she's not Small's natural daughter."

"And the woman? Ski mask?"

"Nile." Her voice darkened. "She said, don't mess with my man. TJ's her man. I can't prove it, but I— What?"

She'd seen the look on Aaron's face. "I was on the phone with Cate. When you were in the bathroom. I might've mentioned coming back to the island this afternoon."

She stopped. Utterly still.

"Nile was on the extension," he said.

She spun toward him. At first he thought she slapped him. But it was chunks of wood spraying from the tree trunk next to him, stinging his face.

The *crack* of a gunshot came a moment later. If Bridge hadn't spun, she'd have taken the bullet in the back of her neck.

He stared vacantly at the tree trunk. Birch tree. White curling bark. Bullet hole. Dark cavity of pulped wood.

"Um," he said.

Brigid shoved him. He stumbled, half fell. *Crack.*

She grabbed his hand, hissed something. Yanked him toward

her, started running, dragging him behind her. Sharp-edged leaves flailed at his face, thorns jabbed his hands.

Brigid pulled him through piles of leaves that concealed half-buried ankle-twisting stones. Around the stone-pit foundation of a long-demolished house. *Crack.* They stumbled, they ran. It was the conveyor-belt nightmare, where as fast as you run, you cannot get away. And they were heading toward the center of the island—away from the road.

They weren't running; the shooter was herding them.

Thirty seconds later, Brigid pulled Aaron around a stand of birch. She was calmer than he'd seen her in days. A professional calm, hyperaware and unthinkingly competent.

"He shot at us," Aaron said. "He's shooting at us—if you didn't turn your head—"

"Aaron!" she said.

He took a breath. *If she hadn't turned her head…* He rested an unsteady hand on a tree. "If you hadn't—"

"Aaron. I'm okay. Let me see your shoulder."

"What?"

"Your shoulder."

And, sure enough, there was this perfect made-for-TV streak of red on his sleeve. A shot-in-the-shoulder-but-it's-just-a-scratch bullet wound. Completely painless, and absolutely manful.

"Oh, that," he said. Manfully. "It's nothing. Just a scratch."

He almost fainted.

She put a hand on his shoulder to steady him. Peeled back the ripped cloth of his shirt. "It *is* a scratch. You must've run into a branch."

Crack.

"Thirty-thirty," she said. "He's between us and the road. You're shivering."

"I'm okay." And he was. It was shock, maybe, but he felt calm and warm, and there was something unfurling in him that felt entirely comfortable. It might have been rage.

"I know you are, honey. Listen to me. We're gonna get out of here. Just do what I say. We have to split up."

Aaron shook his head. "How about we stick together?"

"We split up. Each loop around, back toward the causeway."

So one of them would make it. That's what she was saying.

"I don't like this plan." Brigid had called him *honey*.

"Circle around. Do you understand? Head that way, and make a big loop, and stay in the woods—it'll keep you from running in a straight line. Understand?"

"Kiss me for good luck?"

She leaned in close, put her hands on his chest—and shoved.

He was off running.

He was unflappable, I decided. With his easy smile and his easy grace.

I saw the decision in his eyes; he would cede control to me. Aaron assumed I'd be better at this, and would do as I said even as he tried to show his confidence with attempts at humor. It was reflexive, a part of him automatically aware of the path of least resistance. Unflappable, and graceful. He had a better chance of surviving this than I did.

I glanced back at him. In the distance, there was a flash of movement. Aaron loping through the woods as if he was born to it.

He was a civilian. I was no longer a cop—but I might as well have been. Like riding a bicycle, you never forget. Of course, I hadn't ridden a bike in a long time.

We'd passed an old stone foundation, with a newer drainage pipe running along it. A place to hide, a place to lure TJ in close. I took off my suit jacket—the black T-shirt I wore underneath would be better. I bunched the jacket in my hand, and kept low, my eyes to the ground—looking for obstructions, looking for a stick—and broke cover.

Aaron would circle toward the road.

I'd circle toward TJ.

Aaron ran. Tried not to think. Over the hump of roots caused by a fallen tree. Into a thicket of bushes—shoving blindly through. Out the other side, and to the easy-running woods, the trees having suffocated undergrowth.

Crack.

He ran. Slowed. Jogged. Stopped.

Panted. *Fuck.*

That was distant. That *crack* was faraway. Back where Brigid had headed.

Fuck.

He shrugged. Aiming for the shrug he imagined Brigid had made when she'd headed back into the gas-fueled flames.

He turned around and ran.

He'd fired once, when I had darted to the left, to the beach. A warning shot.

I'd swung behind a tree, headed back toward the center of the island. If I couldn't gain some distance, it was all over. I burst out of the underbrush, and was standing on a trail.

I was disoriented, but thought I recalled where the stone foundation was. I sprinted down a path, past a clearing and raspberry bushes, up and to the right. I got there ten seconds before TJ made the trail. Through the trees and over the drainage pipe. There it was: the foundation.

"Aaron's already back at the road," I shouted to TJ. I tossed my bunched-up jacket into the pipe and scuffed the dirt at its entrance. Please, let him see it and be distracted.

I needed five more seconds. I needed him distracted; I'd taken him once, in the kitchen. But now, in the shape I was in—weaker than I could ever remember being—with him already on the hunt. I wouldn't be so lucky again. Not unless he was distracted.

"Aaron's the one who killed you," TJ said.

"Nobody's gonna buy that."

"He was out here with you. Couple thirty-thirty cartridges in the zipper pocket of his bag. You've been shacked up together the past couple days." His voice coming closer. "And I'm having a picnic as we speak."

A picnic. "Nile?" I shouted.

He was forty feet from the old foundation.

"She's very obliging," he said. "Though I'm afraid even her powers of self-delusion are beginning to show strain."

Thirty feet away. Twenty.

Aaron was behind an oak tree. Fifty feet away. And he'd discovered the flaw in his plan. He had a softball-size rock in his hand. TJ had a rifle.

So he watched unbreathing as TJ approached the foundation where Brigid was hiding. Watched at he stopped at the edge of a corrugated metal pipe, maybe three feet in diameter. TJ glanced at it for the briefest fraction, then laughed.

"Never shot a person before." TJ's voice was conversational. "Bagged my share of deer, though. And you left tracks."

He walked past the pipe. His back—all Aaron could see—was mottled by the shade of a thousand swaying leaves as he approached. Fifteen feet. Ten. Five. And—

The clamor of something smashing through the woods. Frantic ungainly motion. TJ heard it first, and spun.

Aaron followed his gaze.

How Brigid got out of the foundation and twenty yards away—and why she was running straight toward TJ—he didn't know. He wanted to scream *turn around, turn around*. She was barely visible through the trees—glimpses of a skirt, the sounds of twigs snapping, saying no-no-stop-TJ-no.

In one motion TJ raised the rifle to his shoulder, tracked her movement.

Crack.

She jerked, the bullet taking her in the middle of the chest and shoving her shoulders backward, but her momentum carried her and she slid, her legs splaying in front, into the low-hanging branches of a pine, and Aaron's heart stopped beating. Then he stepped from behind the tree and started toward TJ with the rock in his hand like an amulet, and he didn't even bother hiding himself, but it was three seconds—a lifetime—before TJ noticed him. He was staring at Brigid's lifeless body, his mouth moving but no words coming, and Aaron had halved the distance between them, and he halved it again before the rifle swung up, its dead black eye fixing him. Aaron was ten feet away with a fucking rock and a bottomless anger and all TJ had was a rifle pointed at his stomach and he took another step and—

Brigid came from behind the tree, swinging a branch at the side of TJ's head. Something flew out of his mouth—spit or teeth— and he dropped, and she hit him again, then took the rifle and glanced at Aaron, her eyes red and frantic, but her voice mild as she said: "Check Nile."

Nile. Nile. Thank God.

"I thought—" he said. "I thought it was you—"

"So did he," she said. "Quickly. Go!"

Aaron checked her. Nile was dead. There was no dignity in it.

The Principal's Daughter would take a razor's edge across Ashbury's pliant pale throat. A simple, irreparable motion. *He* was still speaking on the phone, his voice still reverberating. Talking now about the diverted funds.

"Oh?" she said.

Ashbury had found out. Doesn't matter, though—he'd never worried about fallout. Page seventeen financial news. Simply wanted to give her a heads-up.

He'd never worried? But if he hadn't worried, why had he acted?

What if he hadn't? What if—what if she was protecting a man who didn't need protection. Loving a man who didn't need love. A man whose footfalls would always recede, never approach.

"But then—but then," she said, and her voice cracked, and she started again, "But then, don't you—"

Hold a moment, he said. Call on the other line.

He was back in twenty seconds. "It's TJ." His voice was weak, and it pained her to hear it. "He's shot Nile. Brigid Ashbury apprehended him into custody."

"TJ," she said. The so-called inspector had trapped, not the man she loved, but his son. Not Small, but TJ. Not Small, who had her father's hands, her father's eyes—Small, who would not walk away, whose footsteps would not recede, reject, refuse.

Weeks ago, she'd told Small about her transfer of funds—she'd confessed—she'd stood silently before him awaiting condemnation, or love. She'd received neither. But then Jody, who'd discovered what she'd done, had disappeared. She thought he'd removed his own daughter to protect her. Chosen her over his daughter, *as* his daughter...

She reached for another Oreo. The package was empty. She sat at her desk and felt herself recede. The lights flickered, dimmed. Small's weak voice hurt her. Ashbury had done this. The bitch inspector.

She would take pains.

It was three hours before the police finished questioning Aaron, and he sat for one more on a bench in the station's corridor, waiting for Brigid.

The waiting room outside the detectives' office was full. Apparently TJ's arrest—and Nile's murder—had sparked a new round of interviews. In less-friendly surroundings than the summer camp. Gayle Cornell stood with Small and two men who looked like lawyers. Cate was sitting in an orange plastic chair by herself; she caught Aaron's eye and turned away. He wondered where Van Huut was.

Iqbal, Laclaire and Putnam were all there. Three hours from Boston, too—then Aaron remembered they'd already been in Maine. Were they here to show support for TJ or curry favor with Small? Or engage in damage control.

Phillipa was not there. Poor plummy Phillipa. He was relieved by her absence. What would he tell her? That Nile's vague green eyes had been vaguer in death? That she'd been so in love with TJ she'd tried to kill Brigid to keep her from discovering the truth about him? That her little girl had hidden her malice with a ski mask?

He passed the HulCorp Three with a nod.

Then stopped short. He turned. *Holy shit*. Time stopped, then kicked back in.

"Gary Putnam," Aaron said. "DOS. John Iqbal, CEO, and Leanne Laclaire—COO, wasn't it? No, that's right." He stepped into their personal space. "TJ's the COO. You're the CFO. I'm SOL, remember?"

He breathed in deeply. *Holy. Shit.*

Gary Putnam—two or three inches shorter than Aaron—managed to loom over him. "We're having a private conversation."

Aaron took a step back, but only one. "What about?" he asked. But before Putnam could respond, Aaron realized what he had to do. "Gayle," he called too loudly across the room. "Be a dear and give me some tranquilizers."

She pretended she didn't hear.

"The sleeping pills, Gayle—the Zopi-whatever. For Brigid. I'm putting her up in my room. No need to be jealous, I'm sleeping on the couch in the sitting room. Have you seen her? She needs the tranquility."

"They're prescription," she said.

Took five loud minutes to wheedle three pills from her.

She finally gave in to shut him up. Fair enough. At least Brigid hadn't seen that display. He turned, and—of course—Brigid was standing motionless next to the wall. By the look in her eye, she'd been there quite some time.

"Stay in your own room tonight," Aaron told Brigid when they got back to the Inn.

She stared at him.

"Stay in your own room. I have a—an appointment. I'm expecting a guest. Later." He leered a little. "You know."

"Liar," she said.

"I'm not lying."

She measured his tone. Heard it was the truth. A smolder sparked somewhere behind her eyes, and he relaxed. If she could smolder, she'd be okay.

She opened the drawers, shoved clothes into her bag. He offered to help; she told him to fuck off without saying a word. He went into the bathroom. Opened each of her bottles, and sniffed. Nothing. A little late to check, anyway.

"You have anything that smells like cucumber and melon?" he asked, when she appeared behind him. "Body lotion, maybe?"

She didn't say anything as she grabbed her cosmetics from him. He took it as a no. He went into the garden and locked the fence. Then came back inside, and locked the outside door. Brigid's lightless eyes tracked him as he rattled the knob.

"Can't be too careful," he said. He wanted to tell her, but was afraid. Nile was not Ski Mask. Leanne Laclaire was. And Aaron had to catch her at it. "See you tomorrow morning?"

She left. He went out to his car, got the crowbar from the trunk. Back in the room, he locked the door. It made a satisfying click.

His plan was simple. Ski Mask now expected Brigid alone in his bed. Asleep, drugged on pills. She'd expect him in the sitting room and would enter through the garden like the first time.

He fluffed a few pillows on the couch and a few more on the bed. When he covered them with a quilt, they looked convincing enough. He turned the radio on low, to hide the absence of breathing.

Aaron stood in the shadow of the half-opened closet door, waiting, like a child playing hide-and-go-seek—a child with a death grip on a crowbar.

Leanne Laclaire breathed in the darkness outside the Inn. It filled her lungs.

Aaron White was transparent—it came from watching too much TV. What an idiot, announcing he'd be in the sitting room, and that the bitch inspector would be unconscious from sleeping pills. Too much TV, and in his ignorance he'd decided to set a trap. Like a mouse trapping a cat. She would not disappoint.

She had watched. There was no surveillance. Not in the Inn, not outside it. White was in his room. The inspector in hers. Waiting in the darkness and—

She was struck by a surge of vertigo. She was outside, Ashbury was in. The footfalls in the dark—the footfalls came from her own feet. She was her father, the bitch inspector was her. Waiting in the dark for a visit. A visit that never came. Small Hulfinger had never come, either. Despite everything she felt, everything she did, he hadn't understood—and the visit had never come.

She waited for absolute stillness, then stole through the side door into the hallway—not the fenced patio. She turned off the hall light and slid her Trexar card in the slot under the words *Captain Armitage.*

Opened the door and slipped in. Darkness. The radio played softly. A pile of pillows was on the couch. She felt the absence of life in the room.

Her eyes adjusted. She crouched at the open bedroom door and listened.

Nothing. Then, she heard something faintly, behind the closet door.

She let the darkness speak to her.

How popular is Cucumber & Melon body lotion?

It could be coincidence. Could be Nile happened to wear the same fragrance as Leanne Laclaire.

Aaron had two friends—Jacqui and Margaret—who wore the same perfume. Obsession. He'd open the door and see Margaret, but smell Jacqui. Or vice versa. He finally bought Margaret a bottle of Rush—from Gucci. She loved Gucci. But it turned out to be exactly the wrong thing to do, because—

But that's not the point. The point was, maybe it wasn't even Cucumber & Melon he'd smelled. That police station wasn't the least fragrant place he'd ever been. Maybe it was—

The closet door smashed him in the forehead and he heard something rip—the door tearing from a hinge—and he stumbled backward and a silent serpentine shape rose from a pool of blackness and whipped toward him and his right shoulder was livid with pain and he heard the crowbar drop and he fell and was struck again and again and he scrambled breathless backward until he hit something hard.

Ski Mask was a lot scarier than he expected. She whispered something he couldn't understand, and goose bumps rose on his arms.

"What perfume is that?" he asked, and tried to kick her legs from under her.

She wasn't there.

His shin smacked the closet door and he yelled *shit!* and half rolled. His kidney exploded in pain and he gasped and felt something in his left knee buckle and he tried to stand but couldn't.

"You have to take pains," she whispered. She leaned closer, and he nearly pissed himself. "Are you afraid of the dark?"

Something in her hand flickered light—*muzzle flash, a silenced gun, he was shot, he was dead*—and a shock ripped through him.

I couldn't believe he was expecting a guest. Aaron White was expecting a midnight caller, even after...after everything. Probably had his eye on Betty, the middle-aged chain-smoker who worked behind the desk. Or he planned one last romp with size-4 Cate Hulfinger. He'd tell himself he was comforting her.

I tugged my hair back into a braid. Forget it. Forget him. I was headed home to the cabin and the juncos. I was finally gone.

Except for wrapping up the paperwork, answering several hundred more questions. But even that was mostly over. And after hours of being debriefed by the cops, my conversation with Ralph had been blessedly short.

"Brigid Ashbury," he'd said when he reached me at the Inn. "How are you?"

"I'm okay."

"C'mon, Ashbury."

"Tired. Bruised. Getting better, I think."

"You think?"

"My hand is cut up."

"You've got medical in your contract. How about your head?"

"My head's fine." Except for the ringing in my ears, but I figured that was exhaustion.

"I mean, the contents thereof. Post-traumatic stress syndrome. Dr. Kugelmeyer. Et-psychological-cetera." He pitched his voice a little lower, letting her know he was serious. "You need anything, Brigid, you tell me. You got that?"

I said I was okay. He didn't believe me. I said it again. He still didn't believe me.

"You want the verbal report?" I asked, to change the subject.

"Tell me, then," he said. "I got a prelim report on my desk looks like it was written by the Brothers Grimm."

"Bottom line, TJ Hulfinger doesn't like to share his toys. He put in his time at HulCorp, he figured he deserved to take home the gold." Jesus. I sounded like Theresa. "He's jealous of Jody—one thing he and Small agree on is that she was his favorite—and he knows she wants to take the company down. His company down. He's borderline personality anyway, and two things sent him over the top. First, thanks to Nile, hearing Jody was planning to kidnap herself to screw the company."

"Told you she was a firebrand," Ralph said. "And the second thing is what? That she was going to go to the press with the news of the eleven million missing from health services?"

"Yeah. Now, TJ knows one thing nobody else does. Least not since Maureen Hulfinger died."

"Cate isn't Small's daughter."

"He'd have to be an idiot to think he can kill both sisters to inherit the company. And the death of one sister doesn't do him any good—it's why his motive never looked convincing. But he kills one sister—his only biological sister—and makes it look like an accident. Then five or ten years from now—maybe he waits until Small dies, so he can't write Cate back into the will—he arranges for it to become known that Cate isn't Small's biological child."

"And he scoops up HulCorp. Tidy enough, I suppose—if you've got the patience for it. Have to say, I expected Small Hulfinger to be involved."

"Well, he is, if you factor him into TJ's inherited personality. Entitlement issues, plus being a deeply creepy human being. Biggest question is, what did Nile see in him?"

"Tell me about her, then."

"I—" I couldn't bring myself to tell him about the orange barrel. "I'm dead on my feet. We'll talk later." I had the phone almost to the cradle, but brought it back to my mouth. "And Ralph?"

"Hmm?"

I didn't know what I wanted to say. That I'd done it, maybe. Closed the case. That I could still do it, even after everything.

"We'll talk later," I said, and hung up.

I finished braiding my hair and sat in the chair, staring at the television. I must've dozed off, because suddenly I woke. I heard the scuffling, the faint *shit,* and in a single seamless instant—I knew. I should have realized earlier that it was a lie—*a guest, an appointment*—but I'd been in bad shape.

Nile wasn't Ski Mask. She hadn't been on the island to kill me and Aaron, but to stop TJ.

The next disjointed moment I was standing in the hallway, Aaron's spare key card in my hand, wearing the T-shirt I'd borrowed to replace my nightgown. I had no gun. No stun baton. And I was half-asleep and more than half-depleted.

No choice. I opened the door.

She was standing above Aaron, the terrible slits in her eyes glazed over. She was whispering, a stream of words. Aaron was dazed, his mind slipping gears, but he heard a soft intake of breath from the doorway. And Brigid was there.

Leanne swung swiftly away from him. Handcuffed to the antique dresser, he was no threat. He wouldn't have been a threat even without handcuffs. His body was a lump of meat. He only distantly felt his knee throb, his wrist ache, his ribs burn from some jagged edge spearing into him.

Brigid slipped into the dark room, followed the wall from the door to the dresser. The two women stood motionless for what was probably only a fraction of a second.

"Something you want to say?" Leanne whispered.

"Yeah." Brigid said. "Fucking speak up."

Leanne's hand moved, the stun stick gleaming in her hand. Before Aaron could shout a warning, Brigid—ten feet away—kicked at the darkness. The garish lobster trap flew through the air and caught Leanne on the chest. She batted it away and Brigid leaped at her.

Caught her on the shoulder, knocked the baton away and shoved her off balance—but Leanne was quick. She fell backward onto the bed, rolled, and came up standing on the other side. Brigid was after her before she was fully upright, and relief washed over Aaron. Then he caught a flash of Brigid's face—haggard, fatigued, she had nothing left.

Still, it was almost enough. For ten seconds, there was a silent, deadly contest in the dark. Then Brigid took an elbow in the stomach, and folded. Leanne threw her against the wall and kicked her savagely in the back. Brigid grunted in pain, and Leanne grabbed the stun stick from where it had fallen and clubbed her twice.

"You had to," Leanne said. "Didn't you?"

No longer whispering. Aaron thought she'd forgotten he was in the room. Lying still, handcuffed to the dresser.

"You couldn't leave us alone. All I wanted was—" Leanne was weeping. She shook her head and prodded Brigid a third time. "How did *you* like it? The barrel? The cars?"

Aaron strained against the cuffs and felt the crowbar beneath him. He could almost reach it.

"The traffic? Let's go for a ride. Have you ridden in a trunk? Have you— I know where you live. I know all about you. Go to sleep one night in Santa Barbara and wake up in a barrel, middle of the highway, the road shaking, the engines—"

He'd thought Brigid was unconscious until he heard her soft wordless plea. The sound enraged Leanne. She kicked Brigid and leaned in close, her voice flat as she described how Brigid would die.

Aaron's stomach went cold, turned to a block of ice. A distantly familiar feeling.

He had no memory of snapping the dresser leg he'd been cuffed to. He was suddenly standing behind Leanne, the weight of the crowbar in his hand.

Leanne turned. Her eyes behind the mask shone with tears.

He didn't threaten, he didn't warn, he didn't say a word.

He swung the crowbar.

The cool morning air smelled of desert and ocean. I didn't mind the mornings, anymore. Because I didn't hike down to the road, anymore. I wasn't going to uproot the fear that way. I knew how I'd do it—and a morning stroll to the mailbox wasn't the way.

I was sitting on the steps of my cabin—okay, yeah, it was still a trailer—feeding the dark-eyed juncos, the sparrows and finches. Teeter was three feet from me. Close as he ever came, these days.

I grabbed more seed off the unopened FedEx package propped next to me. Only three weeks, and they wanted me back. Return address said Bureau, this time, not NTSB, but it made no difference. Three weeks wasn't enough time to patch myself together.

The calls had finally tapered off, though. Not my mother's calls. They were a constant, like death or taxes. But from Ralph, from Theresa, from Van Huut. From Aaron.

I scattered the seed and watched the birds hop after it. A shadow cut across the yard. Footsteps. Someone coming. I didn't have to look up. I could feel him without seeing him.

"What are you doing here?" I said, watching Teeter hop back as Aaron approached.

"I rented a house in Santa Barbara. Lower Riviera. It has a little garden. I think you'll like it."

"What are you doing *here?*"

"Ralph told me you weren't answering the phone," he said.

"You and Ralph are what? Buddies?"

"Didn't need Ralph to tell me. I figured it out myself, the fifteenth time I called and got the voice mail. Your message needs work. You sound depressed."

I almost laughed. "What do you want?"

"You know what I'm doing here." He sat next to me on the step, reaching behind me for a handful of birdseed. "You know what I want."

I felt the warmth and closeness of his arm. "What does Ralph want?"

"To pass on a message. From Walter."

"The Van Huut?"

"Et-Special Agent-cetera."

I tapped the FedEx package. "I got it."

"That's the package, not the message." He leaned forward, showing Teeter his handful of seed. As if the bird would eat out of his hand. "You remember the senator? The one with the missing niece?"

"Morrisey."

"There's been an accident. They found her body."

"You think I want to go through that again?"

He was silent. I thought he might try to hold me. I wasn't sure yet if I'd let him. "No," he finally said. "I just think you have to."

He was right.

"When?" I asked. When did they want me?

"Yesterday."

I couldn't think what to say. "Same rates?"

"Does it matter?"

"What about transportation?"

I still hadn't looked at him, but I could feel the smile.

"You're talking to him," he said. "Community service, baby."

Meaning, I supposed, in return for the cursory investigation of Leanne Laclaire's death. It had been called self-defense—and treated far more open-and-shut than it might have been. How did it make him feel, killing Laclaire? Did he lie awake nights, hearing the thunk of the crowbar hitting her skull? Did he need help patching himself together, as I had? Maybe that's why he was here; maybe he was asking for something, not offering it. That would change everything, that would— But, no. He didn't need my help. He was the unflappable Aaron White.

"Wonderful," I said, but without the tinge of my usual sarcasm.

"And listen, Brigid." His deep, smooth voice became deeper and smoother. The ever-present amusement resonated against something with such gravity it alarmed me. "I want to tell you— The thing is, I think we should, you and I—"

"No."

"Listen—"

"No."

"Brigid—"

"No."

There was silence. Shadows moved across the trees. The clouds lost their shapes and found new ones. Teeter hopped into Aaron's hand, took a beakful of seed and scattered them with a toss of his head. Traitor.

"No," I said again, and turned to face him for the first time. He held me with his velvet eyes. Something caught in my throat.

Teeter took flight. Aaron tossed the seed to the ground and stood.

"But, Aaron?" My voice too soft. "Thanks."

"No, Brigid," he said. "Not this time."

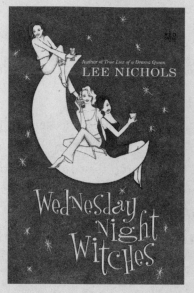

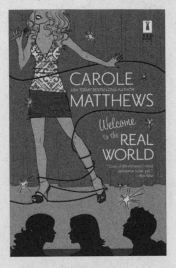

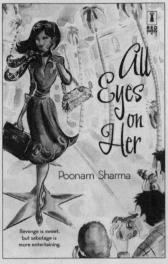

Keep your friends close…
and the blondes closer.

Jodi Gehrman

When her boyfriend, Coop, invites her on a romantic road trip
from L.A. to Mendocino where his college chums are getting
married, Gwen regards it as good news. After all, she typically
enforces a three-month expiration date in her relationships;
the open road and some QT just may be the antidote to break
her of the cut-and-run cycle this time around.

Enter the bad news: not only will Coop's best friend, stunning yoga
celebrity Dannika Winters, be joining them as the blond Satan behind
the wheel, but Gwen's about to feel like the third one, so to speak.
Hello, jealousy. So in an effort to avoid committing blondeicide, she
decides to record her every thought…from the backseat.

Notes from the Backseat